TASTING EVIL

◇◇

◇
◇

◇   ◇   ◇

◇

The Complete Collection

WRITERS COOPERATIVE
OF
THE PACIFIC NORTHWEST

Writers Cooperative of the Pacific Northwest
PRESENTS

TASTING EVIL

The Complete Collection

2019

First Printing, 2019
ISBN: 9781687330437
Permissions:
Town Brochure ©2019 Joel Swetin; The Old Man in the House on Maple
Grove Drive ©2019 E. G. Sergoyan; Cutting Edge Sales ©2019 Sonya Rhen; The
Novelist ©2019 Stephen Christiansen; Best Selling Author Joshua Cain Book
Signing ©2019 Stephen Christiansen; Reunion ©2019 Kai Bertrand; The Grey
Bride © 2019 Deron Sedy; Estate Auction ©2019 Chloe Holiday; Modern-Day
Nostradamus ©2019 Chloe Holiday; Spirit Lake © 2019 Celena Davis; The
Honeymooners ©2019 Toni Kief; Lola's Cottage © 2019 Yazz Ustaris; Special -
Centennial Weekend ©2019 Toni Kief; Dark Art ©2019 Sonya Rhen; Venus Fly-
trap ©2019 Susan Old; The Costume ©2019 Hugh Mannfield; Hunter Falls to
Death; MPHS Track Star Shot ©2019 Hugh Mannfield; A Good Family ©2019
Christine Gustavson-Udd; Overturned © 2019 Matthew Buza; Sometimes Nice
Girls Do ©2019 Sonya Rhen; The Hitchhiker © 2019 Robin Ridenour; The
Omen ©2019 Stephen Christiansen; Deadman's Curve Claims Teen Victim
©2019 Sonya Rhen; Exchange Werewolf ©2019 Hugh Mannfield; Beware
Animal Attack! © 2019 Kristi Radford; Deadly Drowning by DUI ©2019
Sonya Rhen; The Wedding Guest ©2019 Sonya Rhen; Knotty Kitty © 2019
Roland Trenary; The Boys © 2019 Toni Kief; First Do No Harm © 2019 Robin
Ridenour; Sausage Fest © 2019 Robin Ridenour; Jojerry © 2019 Susan Brown;
The Fight © 2019 Deron Sedy; I Am the Lake © 2019 Celena Davis; The Mirror
Clock © 2019 Linda Jordan.

Managing Editors: Matthew Buza & Sonya Rhen
Editor: Sonya Rhen
Contributing Editors: Matthew Buza, Diana Willadsen, Roland Trenary
Production Team: Matthew Buza, Sonya Rhen,
    Diana Willadsen & Joel Swetin
Illustrations: ©2019 Roland Trenary
Paperback Book Interior Design: Roland Trenary
Cover Design by James, GoOnWrite.com
Town Conception: Matthew Buza
Locale and Locals created by participating authors from
    the Writers Cooperative of the Pacific Northwest.

Published by the Writers Cooperative of the Pacific Northwest.
For full-size maps and illustrations, please visit our website.
http://writers-coop.com/TastingEvil

For more works by these and other members of the
Writers Cooperative of the Pacific Northwest , visit http://writers-coop.com/

This book is dedicated
to aspiring writers,
and to you,
our
fabulous
readers.

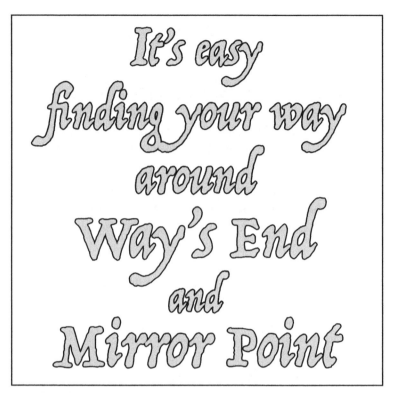

It's easy finding your way around Way's End and Mirror Point

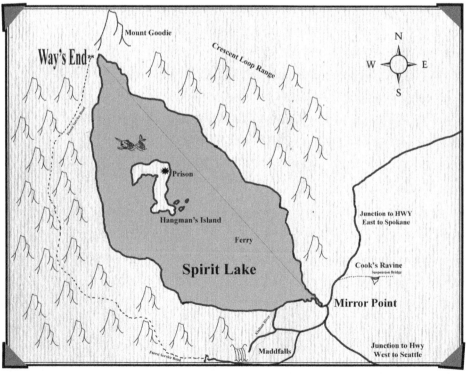

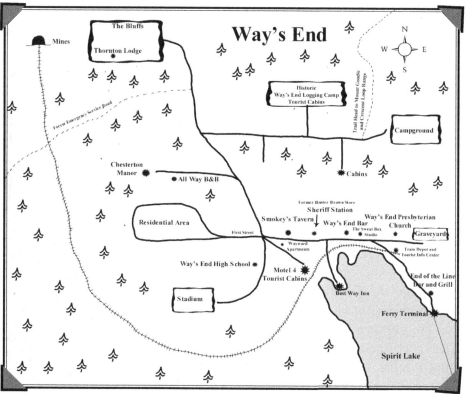

Way's End

Mines

The Bluffs

Thornton Lodge

Historic
Way's End Logging Camp
Tourist Cabins

Campground

Chesterton Manor

All Way B&B

Cabins

Former Buster Brown Store

Sheriff Station

Smokey's Tavern   Way's End Bar

Way's End Presbyterian Church

The Sweat Box Studio

Graveyard

Residential Area

First Street

Wayward Apartments

Train Depot and Tourist Info Center

Way's End High School

Motel 4
Tourist Cabins

Best Way Inn

End of the Line
Bar and Grill

Stadium

Ferry Terminal

Spirit Lake

Trail Head to Mount Goodie and Crescent Loop Range

Forest Emergency Service Road

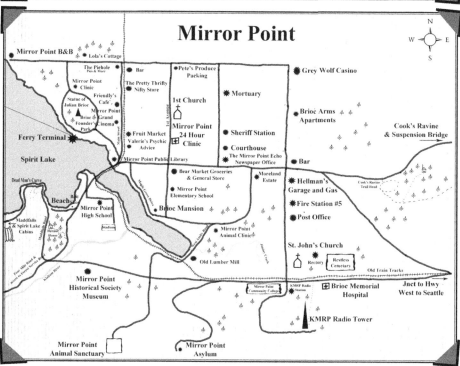

Mirror Point

Mirror Point B&B

Lola's Cottage

The Piehole
Pies & More

Bar

Pete's Produce Packing

Grey Wolf Casino

Mirror Point Clinic

The Pretty Thrifty
Nifty Store

Mortuary

Statue of Julian Brioc

Friendly's Cafe

1st Church

Brioc Arms Apartments

Cook's Ravine
& Suspension Bridge

Brioc Grand Cinema

Mirror Point Founder's Park

Mirror Point
24 Hour
Clinic

Ferry Terminal

Fruit Market

Valerie's Psychic Advice

Sheriff Station

Spirit Lake

Mirror Point Public Library

Courthouse

The Mirror Point Echo Newspaper Office

Bar

Cook's Ravine Trail Head

Dead Man's Curve

Bear Market Groceries & General Store

Moreland Estate

Hellman's Garage and Gas

Best Beach

Mirror Point Elementary School

Fire Station #5

Mirror Point High School

Brioc Mansion

Post Office

Maddfalls & Spirit Lake Cabins

Mirror Point Animal Clinic

Hermit's House

St. John's Church

Old Lumber Mill

Rectory

Restless Cemetery

Old Train Tracks

Five Mile Road & Access to Forest Service Road

Mirror Point Historical Society Museum

Mirror Point Community College

KMRP Radio Station

Brioc Memorial Hospital

Jnct to Hwy West to Seattle

Mirror Point Animal Sanctuary

Mirror Point Asylum

KMRP Radio Tower

LIST OF ILLUSTRATIONS

TABLE OF CONTENTS

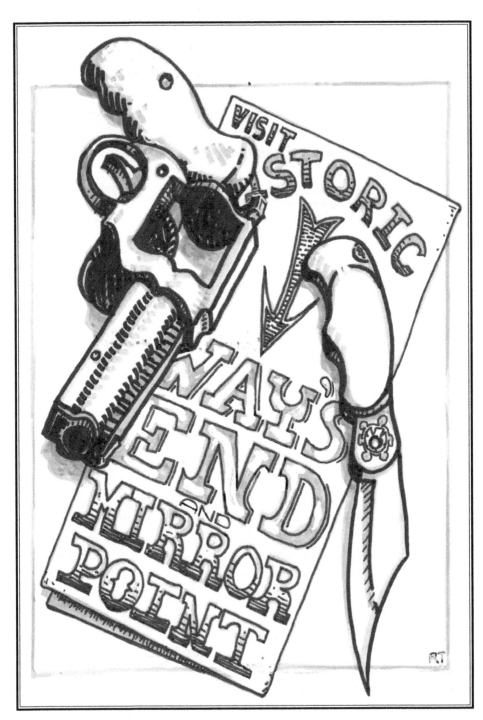

"But wait, that's not all!"

Town Brochure
by Joel Swetin

The sister towns of Mirror Point and Way's End are celebrating our 100th anniversary. If you have been looking for a weekend get-away, a long vacation or possibly someplace to call home, come for a visit. Virtually any type of activity that piques your interest is available in our lovely scenic area. From hiking and camping to boating and river rafting, you will find it here, and more.

For the history buff a short walk from downtown brings you to the Mirror Point History Museum, with hands-on exhibits where the kids can learn about mining and logging. It may be small, but the volunteers know all about the history of the area and can tell you some wonderful stories about the town legends and lore.

At a local business, pick up a walking tour map of Mirror Point. It will guide you to the Brioc Mansion, the Moreland Estate, the Mirror Point Grand Cinema, and all our wonderful historic buildings. Don't miss the stunningly beautiful Mirror Point Library built in the Art Deco style, which holds a wonderful mirror clock crafted in France. The old sawmill at the south end of the lake has been restored so you can actually see how lumber was milled 100 years ago. As a special bonus, during our Centennial Celebration tours will be available at all these locations free of charge.

Head over to Brioc Founders Park to see the beautiful bronze statue of our founding father, John Brioc. Just across from the park have a good old-fashioned lunch at Friendly's Café or maybe one of the ten varieties of apple pie available at the Piehole. Then perhaps find some wonderful treasures at the Pretty Thrifty Nifty Store or take in a movie at the Grand Cinema.

Our hiking trails are rated from easy to difficult, day hikes to overnight backpacking. The views are spectacular, crystal clear streams and, of course, lots of waterfalls. Our favorite is the breathtaking Madd Falls just past Dead Man's Curve on Madd Falls road. The view is beautiful but keep your eyes on the road. The Pacific Northwest is known for suspension bridges so make sure you visit our own suspension bridge over Cook's Ravine. While it may not be the highest or longest, it is almost 100 feet above Hidden Creek. As you walk across you can actually feel it sway. But don't worry. We haven't lost anyone yet!

Like many Pacific Northwest towns, it all began in the 1880s when the railroad opened the territory to settlers seeking a new start. A Welsh immigrant, Julien Brioc (trained by his father to be a surveyor), moved with his family to the new territory and was commissioned by the Territorial Governor to survey the area. His real dream was to raise sheep. With his connections to the Governor he gained mineral and access rights. By selling land and right-of-way to newcomers he became very prosperous. In 1919 he sold access to lumber and mining companies and become even wealthier.

The mining company wasted no time in building roads, a narrow-gauge rail line to the mine, and a mining camp that became the town of Way's End. Once the mines were no longer producing profitable amounts of ore, the growing population of not only the Pacific Northwest but the country as a whole was hungry for lumber to build homes and businesses, and the area was rich in that resource. Logging became the new "mother-lode." A lumber mill was built on the southern tip of Spirit Lake and the town of Mirror Point sprang up to supply the lumber camps with anything and everything they needed.

Unfortunately for Julien Brioc, some of his sheep began to mysteriously disappear. A few were found, appearing to have been killed by bears (although there were only small black bears in the area). Then his flock came down with an untreatable illness and he was forced to harvest the wool and mercifully end their suffering. He sold the remaining wool, his land and mineral rights, then moved to Mirror Point and built Brioc Mansion, which stands to this day and is open for tours.

Of course, the mysterious sheep disappearances and illness led to all kinds of rumors. Some blamed Big Foot or UFOs, and even the local tribes got in on it saying there was a curse on the town of Mirror Point. For poor John Brioc things got worse. He lost his fortune during the Great Depression and was abandoned by his family. Make sure to keep your camera close by in case you catch a sighting of the Pacific Northwest's most famous resident, Sasquatch, or even spot some UFOs in the night sky. It certainly makes for great "ghost" stories around the campfire.

As they say on TV, "But wait, that's not all!" In the middle of Spirit Lake is Hangman's Island. You may wonder how it got its name. About the time of the sheep disappearances a couple loggers went missing. When their bodies were found, a massive search was conducted to find who was responsible. Someone thought that a deserted island would be a good place to hide out; there they found a hermit living in a tent, decided he was the killer, and the mob lynched him. The island is still called Hangman's Island and is now the site of a state prison. Only the special prison ferry is allowed to dock at the island.

Perhaps you are an animal lover. Just outside of town you will find the Mirror Point Animal Sanctuary that does an amazing job of rehabilitating rescued wild animals (only the four-legged and winged kind). Maybe you are more of a night owl. At the Grey Wolf Casino, you can gamble to your heart's content 24 hours a day. You can enjoy world class entertainment at the indoor Orca Auditorium or the outdoor Cascadia Amphitheater at the casino.

For accommodations, your choices are many. We have B&Bs, great for a quiet romantic get-away. For a once-in-a-lifetime family adventure you can rent a yurt at the Way's End campground. Of course, we have great sites for your RV. If roughing-it isn't your style, the Grey Wolf Casino Hotel is rated four stars! You can check with our Chamber of Commerce for a full list of hotels and motels nearby.

As we celebrate our Centennial throughout the year, there will be events almost every day. The Mirror Point Chamber of Commerce, representing many of our local businesses, is sponsoring street fairs throughout the summer, where you can find one of a kind glass sculptures, paintings, jewelry and many other works of art produced by local artists. You can rock out at outdoor concerts at Brioc Founders Park or at the Grey Wolf Casino Orca Auditorium. We have booked some great local bands as well as nationally famous headliner groups with music ranging from rock to country to folk.

No celebration or fest would be complete without face-painting, balloon sculpting, and plenty of games and activities for the kids. Plan your trip around our huge Fourth of July Celebration ending with a massive fireworks display over the lake. For all you foodies, check out Sausage Fest with award winning sausages, an outstanding variety of jerky, pies, and wonderful local cold beer and wine.

Way's End is a short 10-minute ferry ride across Spirit Lake, cruising past Hang Man's Island. On the north end of the lake you can explore the old mines, take a train ride in an old mining car, or see what life was like a hundred years ago working and living in a lumber camp. Every weekend there will be demonstrations of lumberjack skills and chainsaw carving in Way's End.

We can truly say there is something for everyone. Fly across the lake on a jet boat or just have a lazy day at the beach on Spirit Lake. And of course, no visit would be complete without taking a spooky ghost tour of the many haunted houses, mansions, and other places the lost and lingering spirits visit nightly.

We are less than two hours from Seattle but a world away from the city chaos. You could say Mirror Point and Way's End are real-life versions of the TV town of Mayberry. An idyllic peaceful place where people leave their doors unlocked and strangers will smile and greet you. Pack your bags and leave your worries behind. We can't wait to see you!

A word of warning, you might plan on just coming for a weekend, but you might never leave!

... he was turning to the oversized carved wooden doors when ...

The Old Man in The House on Maple Grove Drive

by E.G. Sergoyan

The Reporter

Danny Philips was sitting in his car across the street from the old Brioc mansion, a dilapidated large house on Maple Grove Drive not far from the town center. He had been sitting in his car for almost an hour trying to work up the courage to approach the front gate. Danny had not been on this street or near that creepy, overgrown mansion for years. It all started on Halloween …

He remembered that Halloween fifteen years ago, when he and his pals dared Bobby Morrison to go through the gate, knock on the large double doors, and face old man Headley. Headley had lived on Maple Grove for decades, yet people rarely saw him. He was the town recluse who chased off anyone who came onto his porch.

When the Morrison boy finally gathered his courage and accepted the double dares from his friends, he approached the rusted gate attached to the broken picket fence and slowly walked up splintered front steps with a trick-or-treat bag in hand. At the front doors, he turned to see his friends gesturing him on. Offering a smile to steel his courage, he was turning to the oversized carved wooden doors when suddenly the doors flew open and old man Headley appeared, screaming at the boy.

He scared Bobby so severely, the boy fell backward off the porch, his bag of candy flying in all directions. Bobby hit his head hard; even across the street, the sound was like a coconut struck with a hammer. He lay there moaning, and no one dared to approach him to help.

When the police and ambulance finally arrived, Headley met them outside his doors and pointed to the 'NO TRESPASSING, NO SOLICITATION' sign on the front fence. "It was the damned fool kid's fault," the old man growled loudly. "Nobody invited him here."

Now Danny Philips was a grown man but was still nervous about that old house and that crazy old man. People walking past the house were always reporting strange noises and howls coming from inside the dilapidated house. Everyone avoided the house and the recluse living there.

Danny was a reporter for the local area newspaper, The Mirror Point Echo. He had a weekly column. The paper was published in Mirror Point, and Danny's human interest articles were popular in the three counties that bordered Spirit Lake, the nearby Klaliam River, and the surrounding valley. Danny, who was born in the town, started in the news business by delivering the paper when he was a boy. Then after graduating college in journalism, he came back to his hometown to hone his writing skills and maybe someday become the next managing editor.

His latest assignment was to interview the oldest citizens of Mirror Point and get some interesting stories about the town's past. The town of Mirror Point, on the shores of Spirit Lake, was celebrating its hundred and fiftieth anniversary of the first settlers who came down to the lake and the surrounding valley. This also coincided with the Centennial of the town's incorporation.

Danny had combed the archives for stories about the settlers, the founding of the town, and the origin of Way's End, the sister town on the other side of the lake. But all he had were dry facts with few details of interest.

His first installment on the town's history read like a short Wikipedia page:

> After the railroad opened the territory, settlers came to homestead and farm the local valley. Wagon loads of people started to move into the area in 1880. The first among them was Julian Brioc, a Welsh immigrant. Julian's father was a surveyor back in Wales and taught his son the craft when the family immigrated to America. But Julian wanted to raise sheep. He moved his family to the Northwest to start a farm in the new territory. Later, around 1889,

he used what his father had taught him to survey and plat the area for the territorial governor. It was his connection to the territorial capital in those early days that prompted many rumors about corruption, bribery, even thievery and violence.

Julian became a successful sheep farmer with a lot of political influence at the territorial capital. He used his connection with the governor to slowly acquire mineral rights and access rights-of-way to vast sections of the wilderness around Spirit Lake all the way up from the shore to the tree line. Since he had surveyed the original plat, the territorial governor appointed him to manage access in and out of the valley and who had access to the wilderness above the lake. When wagon loads of people started to move into the valley, Brioc was able to sell right-of-way and property to the newcomers and became prosperous.

The valley quickly became a thriving farming community and when the territory became a State, people began extending the town and central market where the river exits the lake. The village of Mirror Point grew from that market. Then in 1919 a timber and mining company approached Julian Brioc about building a sawmill and harvesting the timber up in the hills.

Using the land for grazing sheep or cattle was not possible, and it was too steep for farming. So Brioc sold access to the property. The timber company harvested timber to make lumber, and they began mining for gold, silver, and copper in the foothills above the lake. But the agreement was that the loggers were only allowed to harvest timber on the western side of the lake.

The opposite side of the lake led up to the Crescent Loop Mountains, and the cliffs made it impossible to log timber efficiently. There were no trails along the cliffs.

When the town was incorporated, many people were already working for the lumber company. In the town square, produce was sold and shipped by local merchants. Later, with the new church, people started feeling like a community. The town prospered as the mill turned local timber into lumber that built homes as far south as San Francisco. Brioc became the wealthiest man in the valley. But he refused to sell access to the opposite side of the lake.

The official archives were incomplete and lacked impact. The reporter wanted to know more. He also needed a personal perspective for his story. So he interviewed Mrs. Caroline Graham.

The Widow Graham

The widow Graham was nearly 100 years old and had lived in Mirror Point her whole life. She lived with her daughter at the edge of town near the old church. When Danny explained himself, she was thrilled to provide background and details for his next newspaper installment about the early days. Danny always carried a mini-recorder with him on interviews. It gave him a permanent record and protected against quoting out of context during an interview. He sat comfortably and sipped the widow's tea, occasionally asking a question or two. Mrs. Graham gave Danny all kinds of anecdotes about the first settlers, life on a lake, how the town was laid out, and how the sheep farmer, Brioc, financed many of the first businesses, even the early church. She was eleven when the sheep farmer built that giant house on Maple Grove Drive.

Now she was a frail old lady who could not walk and spent her days reading and doing needlepoint. Her wrinkled mouth nervously puckered, even when she was not talking. There were numerous pauses of awkward silence as she tried to form stunted words to her thoughts. But she regarded the young reporter as a beautiful distraction, was not intimidated by the recorder, and often chuckled at the young man. She was particularly animated about the feud between the farmer Brioc and the timber and mining company that set up a mill in 1920.

Based on the widow's recollections, Danny's second installment focused on the life of sheep farmer Julian Brioc, his feud with the timber company, and his tragic death in Mirror Point.

Julian Brioc was the wealthiest man in the valley. As surveyor for the county, he controlled the right-of-way and shared access to the undeveloped land around Spirit Lake. That control had provided him with influence and income. The logging company put pressure on him for access to the timber east of the lake, but he would not allow any trails or skids cut into the steep slopes. That led to trouble between the local government (who supported Brioc) and the loggers.

The logging company began to spread the rumor that Brioc's sheep were destroying the grazing land in the valley. He had expanded his herd to a point nothing could grow where the sheep were grazing. Meanwhile, the locals wanted the logging operation moved away from the town because of the smell. People were taking sides in the feud. The quip of the day was: What's worse? The sweet smell of sheep manure, or the sweet smell of rotting sawdust and wood chips?

Then terrible, grisly things began to happen in the valley. Sheep began to disappear; some were found mutilated and torn to pieces as if killed by a huge bear. But there were only small black bears in these woods. Julian had large dogs that he used to protect the sheep from wolves, coyotes, and bear. One night the dogs caught a scent and ran into the darkness … and never came back. Hunters found their carcasses hanging in the trees. The local tribes began to circulate a rumor that a curse had descended on the town. Somehow, the dispute between the farmers, the townspeople, and the loggers had enraged some ancient evil spirit up in the mountains, a vengeful spirit. After that, people were afraid to venture into the woods for fear of encountering 'the curse of Mirror Point.'

The company doubled down on expanding its operation. They quietly established a logger's camp on the east shore. That was the origin of Way's End. But Way's End could only be accessed by ferry. There were no roads or trails. The lumberjacks would travel across the lake and up into the hills to harvest timber. But they couldn't get the timber to the sawmill. The locals blocked all attempts to move logs across the lake.

After the killing of the sheep and the dogs, Julian Brioc moved his herds further away from the town. But the sheep began to show signs of a strange illness. The illness took control of the animals and spread rapidly. Their bellies would inflate and create great pain for the sheep. The animals were found lying in the grass unable to move, screaming. The only way to relieve their suffering was to puncture the belly so the gases could seep out of the opening. The valley became a nightmare of sheep walking wounded and continuously bleeding. Brioc couldn't stand to see his animals suffer. In the end, killing them was a mercy.

Julian Brioc was convinced that the timber company had hired thugs to damage his farm. He suspected they poisoned his sheep, but he couldn't prove anything. Finally, he was forced to kill off his entire herd, harvest the wool and sell the remainder of his land on the western slopes to the timber company. He built the mansion on Maple Grove Drive and moved his family into town. When Brioc abandoned his farm, the company was able to expand its holdings, and things quieted for a few years. Way's End grew into a self-sufficient community. The valley prospered. It prospered until the Great Depression.

The Great Depression affected Mirror Point with many hardships. Way's End became a virtual ghost town. Many could barely manage to hold on to their homes or farms. The sawmill came almost to a standstill. Everyone suffered.

But for Julian Brioc it was worse. Brioc lost his fortune during the Depression, and his family abandoned him after a fierce argument. The family believed in the curse and felt that the old farmer had brought misery to the town. They moved to the city and wanted nothing more to do with Brioc or the town. The old farmer who had helped to create the town could not bear to leave it and was devastated when his family abandoned him. He died alone in his large home. When the authorities found the body, people said he had been half eaten by his favorite house dog. The house stood vacant for years and fell into disrepair.

The widow Graham had been a well of information. But it was what she said at the end of the interview that gave Danny an opportunity for a third installment on the history of Mirror Point.

After an hour of talking, the widow had grown visibly tired. She slumped in her wheelchair, and her daughter signaled to Danny that they should stop. Graham's daughter brought out some photographs of the family and the town. The widow brightened when she saw them.

In 1940, Caroline was a young girl of twenty with delicate features and a broad smile. That year, she married a logger named Graham who worked for the company. "I've always had a soft spot for muscular loggers," she whispered to Danny with a grin. "Mr. Graham and I had nearly thirty good years together. Then he died at the mill in some industrial accident. That was how I met Headley, by the way."

In 1970, Headley was working at the sawmill as a bookkeeper. He and his friend, Jimmy Mathis, had bought the old Brioc house for a song, and they were going to repair it. Graham, Caroline's husband, was one of the sawyers in the mill, but Headley barely knew him. Headley took care of day-to-day operations whenever the bosses were away on business. That was how he came to meet Caroline. It was his unpleasant duty to knock on her door with the sheriff and tell her that Graham was killed in an industrial accident at the sawmill. He was kind, respectful and patient. Headley explained that the timber industry was one of the most dangerous occupations. The company was offering compensation for her loss, and he was available to answer any questions.

After a reasonable period for grieving, Headley showed up again at Caroline's home and began to see the widow regularly. Caroline and Headley were both middle-aged and enjoyed each other's company. The widow bragged to her friends that she had snagged another logger.

But when his friend Jimmy Mathis disappeared, Headley could not get anyone to do anything. He was never the same after Jimmy disappeared. Headley tried to get the company to conduct a search. He became so belligerent and erratic his bosses fired him. After that, Headley locked himself in that huge dilapidated house and became a recluse. He chased away everyone including Caroline. The widow believed that something had happened when Headley and his friend climbed up Mount Goodie. That was fifty years ago.

Old Man Headley

Phillips sat in his car looking at the broken old mansion that Julian Brioc had built nearly 100 years ago. He played his mini-recorder and tried to review some of the details provided by the widow. The story was incomplete. Only one person knew what happened on that mountain fifty years ago. But Phillips' irrational fear paralyzed him. He could see Bobby falling off those steps and Headley screaming.

The next year, Danny wanted to face his irrational fears and tried to approach the house again. An evil sense of boding filled him as he went around to the side where several half windows covered in cloth led to a basement. He was sorely tempted to break in and see what the old man was hiding. As he bent down to see if the windows might swing open, discordant noise and deep growls seemed to shake the house. Danny jumped back and ran away terrified. He was certain the old man had somehow created the din to drive off the curious.

Now as a young man he still couldn't work up the courage to walk up there, knock on the door and face the old man that had terrified everyone, particularly children, for years. It was not rational to be scared of a growling old man, but he couldn't shake the terror.

As Phillips sat and watched the old house, a van pulled up. The sign on the side of the van indicated that it was from the Bear Market in town, the grocery and general store that supplied the community. A young man wearing an apron exited the van, took a large cardboard box filled with goods and made his way up the wooden stairs to the double doors of the dilapidated mansion. The man put the box on the porch, rang the doorbell but didn't wait for anyone to respond. He just turned, walked down the stairs, got in the van, and drove off.

"So that's how come that old man doesn't starve in that house," Danny said to himself. He apparently had an arrangement with the local grocer to provide him with regular supplies.

Danny realized this was possibly an opportunity (or at least an excuse) for approaching the house. He finally got out of the car and walked across the street. The reporter opened the rusty gate and approached the old man's door. Just as he reached the door to work the knocker, one of the double doors swung open and old man Headley growled at Danny.

"I seen you staring at my house from your car. What do you want here?"

When the reporter did not respond, the old man bent over and grabbed the cardboard box on the porch and turned to close the double doors. Danny finally found his voice and asked, "What did you see on the mountain, Mr. Headley? What happened to your friend Jimmy Mathis? Why didn't anyone believe you when you reported what you saw?"

The double doors slowly opened again, and Headley stared at the young reporter. "Who the hell are you? What do you want with me?"

"I'm a reporter for the Mirror Point Echo. My name is Daniel Phillips. I'm doing an article on the town, its history and some of the things that have happened here over the past hundred years. I just finished interviewing the widow Graham. She told me about what happened to you and your friend. How you saw something up in the mountains that changed you."

Danny's voice cracked as he quickly added, "I want to share my notes and see if you could provide some details. People want to hear your story."

Danny remembered Headley as much larger and broader, but age was shrinking him. The old man before him was bent and small. The fierce scowl that scared the neighborhood children was still there, but not much more. Danny was no longer a boy; he began to stiffen with resolve.

Headley again turned to go back in. So, Danny tried one last play. "You're very old, Mr. Headley. I may be the last opportunity you have to tell your story, tell what happened."

Unexpectedly, Headley opened the door wide. As they walked into the house, Danny adjusted to the gloom and shadows. An unidentified smell assaulted his nostrils. The house was clearly falling apart. Massive, musty, heavy furniture was visible in each room, and there were stuffed animals in the hall and on the walls. The drawing room where the old man headed had skins on the floor. The foul smell mixed with mold from the furniture was everywhere, and Danny suspected that much of the odor was the skins and hunter trophies scattered about the house.

He didn't know how to start the conversation with the old man, so he began by asking an obvious question. "It looks like you have an enthusiasm for taxidermy."

Headley ignored the question as he sat down. The two stared at each other for an uncomfortable length of time and finally, Headley said, "I learned taxidermy when I was a teen. But I was never good at it. I collect carcasses and skins from a guy who runs the bait shop down the lake. He gives me stuff that the hunters turn in and don't want. I get to practice on them."

The room got quiet. At last, the old man broke the silence, "Now that we're finished with socializing, what is it that you think you know?"

The reporter turned on his mini-recorder and quickly reviewed what he learned from the widow Graham. He spoke about Brioc and his sheep, the logging camps, and the dispute with the timber company. But before he could ask about the day he and Mathis climbed Mount Goodie or his friend's disappearance, Headley grunted loudly and interrupted.

"Mathis and I were pals in those logging camps when we were young. We started as loggers and worked our way up the food chain. Mathis became a sawyer at the mill. I took some business classes and became the bookkeeper when the old bookkeeper retired. We hung out together for years. We had this crazy idea to buy this old house and repair it so we could rent out rooms for travelers - maybe make some extra cash. But it didn't work out. Turns out nobody wanted to sleep in this broken-down old house, and the mess the company made of the lake didn't help."

"Wait a minute," said Danny putting down his notepad. "What mess on the lake?"

"I'm not surprised you don't know much about that. The company tried hard to keep it quiet. After World War II, the camp at West Mirror Point became the small town of Way's End. But that little town couldn't survive without the timber company. So a lot of accommodations were made. The company had decided that the only effective way to move timber from Way's End to the mill was by running skids down from the hills and dumping the timber into the lake. They wanted to use the cold water to preserve the logs until we could use a barge to pull the logs across the lake to the mill. But the skids and the logs also dumped mud and debris into the lake. Within a year, the lake began changing color. Hardwood which was also harvested didn't float well. A lot of timber sank. In fact, to this day the bottom of that lake is littered with hardwood timber that got loose and sank. Hell, there's a whole underwater forest at Way's End.

"The townspeople complained about the mess that the skids and the timber were creating, but the company wouldn't listen. Everyone was getting upset and fights started breaking out each weekend between the loggers and the locals. Things got so bad in town, the new sheriff, Jack Hammer, started arresting anyone found drunk on the streets after dark. When I got promoted to bookkeeper in 1960, they were dumping and moving timber from Way's End to town every week. The lake had turned brown, and the waste stunk up the whole area. Mathis and I often went climbing to get away from all the fighting, the noise, and the foul water. After one particularly rough weekend, we decided to escape by climbing Mt. Goodie. Turns out that was not a good idea."

"What happened on the mountain, Mr. Headley? What happened to Jimmy Mathis?"

The old man stared at the worn carpet long and hard. All this talk was bringing back bad memories, but it was apparent he needed to tell someone. Headley was approaching 100 years, and he could feel that the end was near. He knew the story needed to be told. This interview could be his last chance.

"In 1970, Jimmy Mathis and I climbed up Mount Goodie in the Crescent Loop Range. The trailhead starts just outside Way's End above the lake. The trail goes up to the range that divides the State. Goodie is the tallest in the range. It's an extinct volcano that blew its top long ago. The challenge is avoiding several large glaciers with bottomless crevasses and a long snowfield that ends at a flat summit. It's not a technical climb but a good workout for two fifty-year-old ex-loggers. We were going to do the climb in one day and glissade down to the tree line before dark. We were within 500 feet of the summit and stopped to rest before making the final push to the top. It was late in the day, and we were on the snowfield among some boulders. That's when we began to see the lights above us."

"The lights?" asked Danny.

"It was above us over the ridge, flashing green lights coming from the summit."

"You mean like the aurora borealis, the northern lights?"

"I know northern lights, young fella," Headley said with some irritation. "We live far enough north that you see the lights at dusk if you go camping high up in the mountains. I've seen northern lights. This was different. It was something unique, like advanced landing lights."

"Then a strange fog rolled in. It wasn't heavy enough to obscure the snowfield, more like a mist had fallen on us. That was when we saw him, out on the snowfield, in the mist. He was coming down from the summit in a long gait, his long thick arms swinging back and forth as he hurried down the mountain. He was focused on getting down quickly."

"I don't understand. What was it?" asked Danny. "What did you think you saw?"

"I know exactly what I saw," grunted the old man. "He was at least eight foot tall with a huge pointed head. He walked upright and had arms that nearly reached the ground as he swung them back and forth. We only saw him briefly, but we both saw the same thing. A huge upright beast covered in fur coming down from the summit. Luckily he didn't turn and never saw us standing off to the side of the snowfield.

"Once he passed out of sight, we walked over to where he had been walking. We could see his huge footprints in the snow leading down to the tree line several thousand feet below. But no tracks were leading up to the summit, nowhere in the area. He was coming down, but there were no tracks going up. Nothing to explain how he got up on the summit either. Unless you wanted to do some tough cliff climbing on ice, the snowfield we were on was the only way up or down from the top.

"When Jimmy and I got to the summit we found the creature's tracks coming from a large circular burnt area in the fresh snow. There was nothing else. When the mist lifted, we decided to get off the mountain. We glissaded as fast as possible down the snowfield and got out of there. We purposely avoided the trail where the creature had disappeared into the trees."

Danny did his best not to laugh out loud. He lowered his head and pretended to take careful notes on his pad. But the reporter could feel Headley watching him and getting more and more agitated. The old man was standing now with arms folded in front of him as he hissed, "I'm telling you that something landed on that summit, young fella. Either that creature had been waiting there a long time and was greeting someone, or something landed and dropped that monstrosity on the summit and then flew off."

Danny bit his tongue to suppress a smile and asked, "Did you report what you saw?"

"And what exactly could we report?" Headley growled. "That we saw the shadow of Sasquatch in a fog lopping down a mountain? That we saw flashing lights and a burn mark on the summit? Who would believe us? What evidence did we have?"

Headley wrung his hands and sat down again. "We decided to keep quiet. We didn't want people looking at us the way you're looking at me right now."

Danny turned away and tried hard to regain his composure. He was thinking about his editor's reaction, when suddenly Headley said something that made the reporter sit up and take notice.

"It was a week later that things started to go wrong down at Way's End."

"What things started to go wrong?" Danny asked tentatively.

"Like I said, people were upset. The townspeople and the loggers were creating trouble in town. But then lumberjacks working above Way's End reported strange howls and noises from the tree line. It was all just like before, just like with the sheep. Cattle was mutilated. Other animals found torn to pieces: deer, mountain goat, even bear and wolf. Then the ferry that moved people across the lake was attacked. Its side was stove in by something in the lake. The sheriff claimed it was some debris that broke loose from the logging operation. But people said they saw a large creature swimming in the dark. It wasn't some loose log. This thing punched holes in the side of the ferry. And after that, the weekly barge that moved the logs to the mill was torn apart in the middle of the night. Finally, two loggers didn't return from a clear cut; they went missing.

"The company tried to dismiss the whole thing as men getting drunk, creating mischief and wandering off. But when the sheriff couldn't find any trace of them, people began to talk of the Mirror Point curse, about what happened before, to the sheep farmer and the animals.

"Jimmy was sure it was something more than a couple of drunks breaking equipment. He and I finally decided to report what we saw near the summit of Mount Goodie. But Sheriff Hammer looked at us like we were crazy or drunk. He said as much. He laughed at us and didn't even bother to send anyone to look around the mountain.

"Everyone was nervous and jumpy. Nobody wanted to be out alone. The whole thing came to a head when the loggers' bodies were found: torn, gutted open, hanging in the trees near Way's End. The locals and the loggers didn't wait for the sheriff. They began searching the area for answers. They wanted to find something to blame for what had happened to the men."

Headley bowed his head and studied his hands. He was sharing some painful memories as he murmured, "You know that small island in the middle of the lake? Well, they found someone living there, a tramp living in a tent. He claimed to know nothing, but the loggers and the townsfolk decided that he'd done the killing. A lynch mob took the tramp to the center of the island and hanged him. That's why the island is called Hangman's Island to this day.

"Because of that lynching, Jimmy was concerned that the curse was driving people crazy. He said he knew what was really causing all the trouble. Jimmy was sure it wasn't some tramp. It was the creature that we'd seen. He picked up his Winchester and decided to climb Mount Goodie and track down that beast. He went up that mountain and was never seen again."

Headley paused for what seemed like an interminable silence and then sighed. "Sheriff Hammer and the rangers thought that Jimmy Mathis fell into a crevasse up on the glacier. They didn't hold out any hope that he'd be found. But I know that Jimmy was too skilled a climber to fall into any hole. He found something up there, confronted it and paid with his life.

"Later, I tried to convince the logging company that a creature was causing all the damage. I got into a fight with my bosses, and they fired me. I had no luck trying to find Jimmy on my own. In the end, I just locked myself in this house. And I've been here for the last fifty years."

The old man was so morbid he was shivering by the time he finished his story. He looked tired. Telling the tale had somehow aged him. Headley sat in silence as Danny turned off his recorder and prepared to leave. Finally, he looked at Danny and whispered, "So, that's it. That's what happened out there on that mountain. There's your human interest story about the town and the curse. Now let's see if you've got the guts to publish it."

The Curse?

Several days came and went. Danny couldn't get any work done on the third installment to his article. He sat at his desk at the Mirror Point Echo office and tried to make sense of his recordings and his varied research notes.

Growing up in Mirror Point everyone had heard rumors. Some people joked about the curse. The locals told the breathless wide-eyed tourists that monsters were living at the bottom of the lake, ready to gobble up anyone who swam out too far. There was talk of giant beasts wandering the forest and the foothills, particularly when a hiker happened to find animal bones or weird footprints. Each season had Big Foot and UFO sightings somewhere on the lake.

The children grew up believing that the rumors were designed to keep them from wandering off on their own. 'Stay close to home. Stay together. Don't swim too far when you go into the lake. Do as I say, or the boogeyman will get you.' It was that sort of thing.

But the tale that Headley told was different. Something about his story had a continuity. It was a curse with a purpose. But how could Danny submit any of his notes as an article? Even the story of Brioc and his sick sheep had alternative explanations. Animals get sick; people disappear. You don't need answers that involve crazed monsters coming to exact vengeance on polluters, loggers, and greedy capitalists.

Danny sat contemplating his notes when the phone rang. It was the town clinic. One of the doctors was calling to tell him they found old man Headley on his front porch unconscious. He had suffered a massive heart attack and was calling for Danny Phillips.

When the reporter arrived at the Mirror Point Clinic in the center of town, the desk nurse said that the old man was only just barely hanging on and was begging to see him.

Danny walked into the trauma room and found Headley laying in an elevated bed with tubes in his nose and sensors strapped to each arm. A large monitor on the wall was indicating a faint, steady reading. Headley opened his eyes and motioned for Danny to come close.

"I'm glad you came in time. I want you to know I'm leaving the house to you. I got nobody else. The key to the doors is under the mat. It's all yours. Be vigilant and take care of it."

As the reporter began to form a question, Headley groaned and raised a finger. "Be vigilant. You need to be on guard. They're coming. They drop off one every fifty years, every fifty years."

With that, the old man sunk back into the bed and the monitor issued an alarm. A moment later the room was filled with doctors, nurses and staff trying to revive the dead man. Danny slipped out unnoticed and decided to drive straight to the old mansion to look for answers.

He found the key and entered the house. The foul smell was still in the air combined with the smell of musty old carpeting and decaying wood. "I guess the first thing I'm going to do is get rid of all these stuffed animals and skins," he said out loud as he looked around.

He proceeded down the hall to the drawing room. He wondered why the old man had left this broken down old house to a virtual stranger. Was he really now responsible for this place?

Danny was nervous just being in the old house alone. The house was the source of his childhood Halloween fears. He spoke to himself to relieve the anxiety he was feeling. "He said he had no one else. I was the only one he had spoken to or seen in years. Who could he trust to take care of his old house? And what did the old man mean with his last words? Perhaps, the old guy lost it in the end or he wanted to leave me with a mystery."

The floor creaked as he exited the drawing room. He walked back down the hall to the stairs that led to the upper floors of the mansion. He noticed that the rancid smell lingered near a door under the stairs. Danny tried the door and found it locked. He didn't have the patience to search the house for any other keys, and the lock wasn't very sturdy. He put his shoulder to the door and managed to force it open. There were stairs leading down and he peered into the darkness.

The stairs were leading to a full basement barely visible in the dim light. The basement had a nine-foot ceiling and must've been used for storage of wine and canned goods. But now it was full of excess broken furniture, rotten wooden shelves, and rat-infested debris. The smell was definitely worse here. At the bottom, Danny looked for some light.

He flipped a wall switch, but the only illumination was a naked light-bulb in the center of the room hanging over a folding chair. The quiet was broken when the old furnace came on and made strange noises as it rocked on its foundation. There were heavy shadows along the far walls. The basement had several half windows, but they were all covered with dirty cloth and provided little light. The whole place smelled like wet fur and rotten meat.

As Danny walked about, he finally noticed on one shadowed wall something substantial. When he approached it, he recoiled and realized that it was the skin of some kind of furred animal. The oversized fur was somehow strung up on the wall. The animal must've been over eight feet tall with long, heavy arms, large thighs, and long legs. The elongated head was the size of a grizzly bear. It might have been mistaken for a bear, but the fur that covered the skin was somehow the wrong color. It was coarse, matted, long, dirty, yellow hair. The top of the pointed head touched the ceiling, and the massive skull leaned forward. The head seemed to stare at the floor in front of the folding chair in the middle of the room. The oversized feet reached the floor.

Danny pulled the folding chair a bit closer to the monstrosity. He looked at it and tried to contemplate what this could be. He sat down and took his mini-recorder out of his pocket. He decided to record his observations while his thoughts were still fresh.

He spoke softly, "I don't understand why the old man would make such a thing out of bits and pieces of fur? Is it possible, he was using this weird Halloween costume to scare the townspeople? He must have been doing this for years. He put this thing on and hid in the woods terrifying people. Maybe this was his revenge against those who refused to search for his lost friend. Or maybe he was upset with everyone who laughed at his ridiculous story. He probably practiced his howls and growls on anyone who ventured close to his house. He must have been the one who mutilated the animals and destroyed property to keep the myth alive. That poor old fool must have spent his days walking around this broken house with the fur suit, slowly going mad while he plotted against the town and everyone in it."

The reporter stood and walked forward at what he was witnessing. He raised the recorder and finished his comments, "Everything fits. It all makes perfect sense. Old man Headley was the curse of Mirror Point. He did it all with this crazy suit."

At that moment, the creature's eyes opened, and it lunged forward with outstretched arms that almost reached Danny's throat. There was a heavy growl as the reporter screamed and fell backward into the chair. He was still screaming as he crab-walked back as fast as he could to the opposite wall. He stared as the creature stretched and pulled on a thick heavy chain that was wrapped around its waist, a chain attached to a thick steel pipe embedded in the concrete of the basement floor. The beast strained against the restraint. The metal of the chain rubbing on the metal pipe made an abysmal screech that added terror to the creature's loud growl. Danny was petrified as he lay on the floor. He prayed that the restraints would hold.

Finally, the monster eased on the chain and backed into the shadows, quiescent. Danny swallowed hard and tried to return the folding chair upright. He sat shaking, and studied the unbelievable sight before him. The fur was matted and discolored with bare spots rubbed raw. Yellow teeth, a heavy brow, and cold eyes showed past a swollen face filled with murderous intent. But with all the horror, as Danny observed the creature, he realized that it was old – ancient, bent and starved. It was sick and feeble.

Danny sat and stared. What will the locals do if they see this monstrosity? What will the authorities do? If this is revealed, there will be panic and even a quarantine will descend on the town and the valley. No wonder Headley was driven mad. The old man spent years sitting in that chair, staring at that creature, and trying to decide what to do.

Then suddenly a new panic gripped Danny Phillips. The reporter remembered the old man's last words:

"Every fifty years they drop off another one, every fifty years, every fifty years..."

Cutting Edge Sales

by Sonya Rhen

"Can I interest you in a set of knives?" Len Lester had his foot in the door of apartment 205. He held up his briefcase, flipped the latch and revealed a shiny row of knives in various sizes.

The man holding the door against Len's shoe shrank back at the sight. The door yielded and Len took the opportunity to elbow it open.

"I know what you're thinking," Len said, "you already have a good knife, but can your knife do what the amazing Cutsall knife can do?"

The occupant of apartment 205 was starting to sweat. His hands trembled and he took another step back. His nightmares were starting to flood back to him. Waves of images made his heart race. His hands trembled.

Len took that as a welcoming sign and he crossed the threshold. "Let's just compare," he said. "I have in my bag a tomato."

He reached into the messenger bag slung across his chest and pulled out an apple. He walked through the living room to the kitchen area.

The slump shouldered occupant of 205 watched him with hooded eyes but seemed unable to speak.

"No, that's not it." Len replaced the apple and pulled out a tomato. "If you would like to get out your best knife…" He paused and looked up.

The occupant still did not speak. Sweat had broken out on his forehead and he took a hesitant step toward the kitchen. He wanted this Len-person gone, but his brain seemed incapable of finding a way to make it happen.

"Don't worry," Len continued, "I'll get it." He began opening drawers. Utensils clattered as he rummaged through them. He finally pulled out a tarnished butter knife. A quick glance at the sparse countertop did not reveal anything sharper.

"You're makin' my job easy," Len laughed. "I think you'll find the Cutsall knives can do a lot better than this here butter knife." He unlatched his briefcase again, the glow of the ceiling light gleaming off the blades. "Let's see, for tomatoes you want a really sharp blade."

Len looked around, but finding no cutting board, he grabbed a plate from the cabinet. All the while he continued his spiel. "Every Cutsall knife comes with a one year guarantee. If the blade goes dull or the handle breaks, we'll replace it for free."

The occupant of 205 grunted.

The bright red tomato sat in the middle of the white plate.

The occupant stared at it, transfixed.

Len took the butter knife and cut off a chunk of tomato. He held up the smashed slice. "See how poorly your knife cuts this tomato."

The occupant nodded. He knew from experience that the butter knife was not the tool for this job.

Len chose a long sharp knife.

The occupant closed his eyes, but he couldn't erase the image of the blade from his mind.

"See how the Cutsall knife slices through the skin." Len cut from the other side of the tomato. "Perfect paper-thin slices for the best BLT you'll ever have."

The occupant of apartment 205 had gone ashen. With each slice a picture flashed in his brain. His mouth was dry as he stared at the translucent tomato slices lying in the pool of red on the white plate.

Len took the apple from his bag and placed it next to the plate. "Here, you try. See for yourself how well these knives cut." He pushed the knife into the other man's hand. The fingers trembled and did not close.

"Um, let me, um," Len faltered, "um, help you. Here." He squeezed the trembling fingers over the handle.

The fingers curled.

The tentative grip grew stronger.

Len picked up the plate. "Your garbage?" he asked as he turned and opened the cabinet under the sink.

The knife was sharp and cut a smooth straight line.

The plate shattered on the floor.

Red dripped off the broken white shards.

The occupant of 205 stepped over Len's body. He rinsed the blade in the sink. It was the right tool for the job.

He looked out the window across the lot to the Brioc Arms Apartment sign. He held up a steady hand and a smile began to play on his face.

"Look out Mirror Point, ol' Bernie the Knife is back in town."

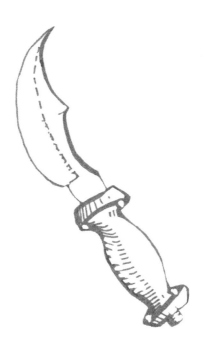

The Novelist
by Stephen Christiansen

Sally Fox moved through The Piehole: Pies and More Café with wide eyes, her book clutched tight up against her chest as if it were the most precious thing in life. Her heart was beating hard and fast. Her body was shaking with anxiety and excitement.

It was him, Joshua Cain, her favorite author. He was here; he was really here in Mirror Point. She couldn't believe it.

She had been a fan of his for what seemed forever. The stories always seemed so alive to her and she could never put them down. She had always dreamt of meeting him, of telling him just how much she appreciated his novels. She had dreamt of this moment. Now she didn't know what to do.

Sally watched from a distance at first, trying to figure out how to engage in a conversation with him. He was currently having pie with another guy and it was hard to tell at first just how important the conversation was or if she could interrupt. She listened.

"Look, Joshua, the story is great and all, but it just doesn't have the feel of your other novels. You need another big hit, and in a bad way, sorry to say. I'm not just telling you this as your agent, but as a friend. You've got to ..."

"Hi."

Sally had found the courage to advance toward her hero. She had found the courage to interrupt their conversation. Now she wished she hadn't. She had just realized how foolish and desperate she must look. Yet, she had gotten his attention. If she ran now, it would look even worse. It was now or never.

"I really like your books. I'm Sally, by the way, and I don't think you need a big hit. Really. They're all great. I even brought one to ..."

She stopped. The words just weren't coming out the way she had imagined. She was stumbling over her own thoughts. This wasn't going as she had hoped that it would.

"You were hoping for an autograph?" Joshua asked with a smile on his face.

Sally gave a deep sigh and nodded as she handed her book over. She worried he might say "no," or that he would have shown some form of disdain in her blundering attempt to even ask. Yet, here he was with a smile on his face, reaching for her book.

"Who do you want me to make it out to?" Joshua asked as he brought forth a pen from his jacket pocket.

"To me ... I mean to Sally, Sally Fox ... please."

Sally watched as Joshua scribbled down her name and a few words before handing the book back to her. Her trembling hands took it from him. She couldn't believe it. She couldn't believe that anything could be more exciting than this, until he spoke again.

"How would you like to get together later tonight?"

Sally's blood nearly froze. Was he really asking her out on a date? She nodded before she realized what she was doing.

"I'm a little busy right now, but how about, let's say six o'clock tonight, down by the lake, at the dock?"

She nodded her head again and before she knew it she was heading home to get ready.

"No, no, no," Sally stated as she tossed one dress after another on top of the ever-growing pile on her bed. She wanted to look her best without looking too desperate. She didn't want something too revealing or too prudish. Eventually, she chose something that held a middle ground, yet still wasn't what she had hoped she would have in her closet.

"Oh my gosh, the time ..." If she hurried she might be able to meet him on time. Without a second thought she grabbed her purse and rushed out the door.

The walk through town took longer than expected. She wanted to rush as quickly as she could yet she didn't want to break her heels and then cursed herself for even wearing them. Her anxiety almost turned to panic.

What if I'm late? What if he doesn't wait? What if he wasn't there at all? What will he think of me? Am I ...

Her negative thoughts stopped when she turned the corner and saw him waiting by the dock. She slowed her pace to not give away her anxiety. Sally mustered a smile and quieted her beating heart as she approached.

"Come, let's walk," Joshua stated as he gently took her by the hand and started their journey around the lake.

They walked in silence for a while and Sally couldn't help but feel giddy. She didn't know where he was taking her, but she would follow him forever. He only stopped when they had found an old bench away from the rest of the town overlooking the lake. He beckoned to have her sit beside him.

Sally blushed. She didn't know what to say. The silence was killing her. She had to break it somehow. With a deep breath she asked the very question that she was dying to have an answer for.

"How do you do it?"

"Do what?"

"Write such good stories?"

"It's easy, really, with inspiration and the right motivation. Sometimes I just feel possessed, like a story won't let me go and I just have to tell it. When it screams at me long enough, I start my process by laying out the characters. This I do by going out and meeting new people and finding out about them, I get to know them, and then put them in my novels. They are the core of my books; they help make my stories come alive."

"Getting to know people? You mean like what you're doing now?"

Joshua turned to her and smiled. "Would you like to be in one of my books?"

Her eyes went wide again. She was going to be immortalized in one of her favorite author's books. "Oh, yes, please, I would love it. Would you ...?"

Sally's sentence stopped short. Pain shot through her gut where Joshua had thrust his pen deep into her. Panic overcame her. This wasn't a dream come true; this was a nightmare. She needed to run. She needed to find the police, to find the hospital.

Sally's mind swam as the world around her spun. The light of the world grew dark. She tried to scream, but all that came out was barely a whisper.

Joshua watched as his pen continued to do its job. Sally's form began to wither. Her eyes became sunken. Her hair turned ashen. Age came upon her swiftly until she was too old, too frail. Her heart gave way before her body did. As her dead form fell towards the ground, it turned to dust and by the time it was over there was nothing left.

Joshua clicked his pen again. He could almost hear Sally's voice trapped deep inside. Her soul had been captured, her essence preserved.

He had to smile at this. His agent was right, his novels weren't as strong as they used to be. Now, with Sally's soul, he would bring life to his stories once again.

BESTSELLING AUTHOR
JOSHUA CAIN
BOOK SIGNING

Mirror Point Echo – Saturday, February 16, 2019

Joshua Cain, bestselling author of numerous thriller books, will make a special visit to Mirror Point at the Public Library on Feb. 24th at 2:00pm to help celebrate our town's Centennial celebration.

Fans are invited to hear Mr. Cain read from his newest book, *Monsters,* a thriller about a man haunted by a beast wherever he goes. A book signing will follow this public reading.

Joshua Cain is the author of more than twenty thrillers, including the New York Times best selling *Lost Souls.* There is no charge for this public reading and book signing, but seating is limited and reservations are recommended. Please call the Mirror Point Public Library for reservations and information.

The path had become overgrown ...

Reunion
by Kai Bertrand

Blood dripped from the end of his finger onto the ground at his feet. The old dock at the lake was strewn with broken beer bottles. Father Foxland had been careful not to step on any of it but didn't see the brown shards on a pylon before he put his hand there. Sharpness made him draw his hand back to see the miniature stab wound welling at his fingertip. Unable to do anything about it, he shook his finger, allowing the blood to fall to the ground, and went back to his car. He'd clean himself up when he arrived at the rectory. It would be his first task as the new priest at St. John's in Mirror Point. That was a month ago. The excitement he felt at the time had left him soon after Joshua Darnell's body had been discovered.

With each gust of wind that blew, the windows of the rectory rattled. A storm system thundered overhead. Buckets full of rain fell on the roof and blurred the panes. High winds shook even the sturdiest of pine trees nearby. Father heard scratching on the side of the house, assuming it was the bending branches scraping the building. The lights flickered threatening to plunge the small building into the deepest of darkness. Father Foxland sent a silent prayer to the man upstairs to keep the lights on until the sun saw fit to cast its light again. In case his request wasn't to be granted, he rushed to find the spare candles. He would probably be up all night.

The nervous priest had locked himself in the rectory before sunset as he'd done every night for the past two days, making sure the door and windows were bolted tight. The town had been strange lately, and he hadn't been able to ignore it, but he chalked up the feeling of unease he carried due to the accident that had happened last week. A well-liked man named Joshua Darnell who worked for the local logging company had been killed.

Many of the townspeople had come to the church to seek comfort and Father Foxland had welcomed them all. There were a few who would not be seeking support from him such as Valerie Callahan, the town psychic, but as long as she didn't bother him, he'd let her be.

The Mirror Point Echo, the newspaper in town, had reported the findings of the police saying that Joshua Darnell had not died in a logging incident as everyone had believed. He'd been killed by a wild animal. Father Foxland had been given information not divulged to the public and wished that he'd been spared the grisly details.

Joshua had been found hanging upside down by his feet in the woods, his body clawed almost beyond recognition. The local hunters didn't believe it was the work of a wild animal despite the paper reporting that it must have been a bear. No, Father Foxland thought it was something else, something larger and much more dangerous than one of God's creatures. It was the reason he'd locked the church before sunset and made sure he was safely inside with the curtains closed and the lights on.

Sitting in his favorite chair, he began to pray in earnest. While focusing on his recitation, images of the townspeople flashed through his head. The one person who had been coming back to him was Martin Wilson, a reporter for the newspaper. Martin had come to see him a few days after Joshua was found. The logging company stated there was a vicious animal on the loose. Martin believed something else was stalking the town.

The day he came to visit, the expired votive candles had been replaced with new ones in preparation for those who wanted to light a candle for the soul and family of Joshua. Father prayed over the candles that those who came to light them would find comfort in their flames. The front door opened, and Martin walked in, dipping his finger in the holy water and crossing himself while genuflecting at the first set of pews. He hurriedly rushed up the center aisle. His balding pate gleamed with perspiration surrounded by a rim of dark hair like Caesar's crown. Middle age had firmly taken hold of Martin's body with his spare tire waistline, but the fire of youth still played in his hazel eyes.

"Martin, I don't often see you on Sunday, and here you are on another day of the week," Father said.

Martin's wry expression showed the priest had made his point. "I'm sorry, Father. You know I'm always tracking a story. The news doesn't stop for Mass."

Father nodded. It was an excuse he heard repeatedly. Most of the people who lived here were good, and he wasn't arrogant enough to believe that those who chose to grace the church with their presence on Sunday proved to be any better than the rest. There were a few who came regardless of the weather and it had nothing to do with grace or being good.

"I'm glad to see you whatever the reason, but you seem anxious about something."

"Father, I," Martin looked down at the floor seeming to gather his thoughts. Father Foxland waited patiently for him to speak. Part of being a keeper of the flock is to let patience encourage the sheep to express their discomfort and then help them to alleviate it.

Martin shuffled his feet in his well-worn shoes and clenched his hands before sighing. "Father, I think there's something wrong. I'm suspicious of the circumstances surrounding Joshua's death."

The priest smiled and stepped toward the nearest pew and invited Martin to sit. "Why don't you tell me what you found?" Martin sat next to him with a concerned look on his face. Father Foxland was glad to note that Martin hadn't asked for their discussion to be conducted in the confessional. It couldn't be that serious.

"I'm sure you've heard that the company said it was a bear attack?"

Father nodded. "I was called to perform the last rites, but I only saw his face after he'd been cleaned up. It wasn't necessary for me to see the rest of him and I chose not to out of respect. As soon as the case is closed, I'm to perform the funeral."

"In that case, Father, I don't know when Joshua will be buried, because I doubt the case will ever be closed."

"What do you mean?"

Martin turned towards him, draping an arm over the back of the pew. "Father, I've seen him." Martin looked down at the dark wood between them. "It was bad."

Father folded his hands together. "I can't even imagine, but why would you have seen him?"

"I happened to be at the coroner's office when they brought him in. I'm telling you, Father, those marks are not from a bear. I've seen pictures of grizzly attacks, it isn't the same. This is something else." Martin spoke with such conviction that the priest considered his words. The reporter loved a good story and would often annoy the townspeople to get it, but he was an honest man. Not a word he printed in the paper was ever found to be untrue.

"Then you think it was a large wolf or a mountain lion?"

"None of the above," Martin said. "I think it's something else, Father, something that falls into your line of work."

Father Foxland leaned forward. "What do you mean?"

Martin leaned closer and lowered his voice. "I think that the thing that attacked Joshua wasn't anything created by God."

The priest leaned back shocked by what he heard. "What are you saying, that you think the thing that attacked him was supernatural? You can't be serious."

"Oh, I'm deadly serious, Father. I've heard rumors in town that Joshua was dating Valerie Callahan."

The priest chuckled. Father had greeted her warmly when she first arrived, but there seemed to be enmity between them regardless of his efforts. He assumed that her experiences with the deeply religious in the past had not been pleasant and, while she'd been rude to him on many occasions, he chose not to hold it against her. "There's no accounting for taste, but what does that have to do with Joshua's death?"

Martin looked around the room furtively as if searching for spies. "Rumors say that Valerie is part of a coven of witches and that she and Joshua were having problems. She suspected him of fooling around. Some think Valerie might have conjured something."

Father got to his feet. "Conjured something? Martin! I don't particularly care for the woman, but I have never heard of her being involved in such things. It's preposterous."

The reporter stood and looked squarely into the eyes of the priest. "I followed her one day, Father. She has a cabin in the woods, not far from Cook's Ravine. After she left, I went in. There are symbols drawn on the walls and a circle on the floor surrounded by candles. There was blood in the center of the circle. I'm telling you, Father, this was more than a simple place of Wiccan ceremony. It made my skin crawl."

"Are you certain?" The priest couldn't believe something like this would happen in the peaceful area they called home.

Martin dug in his pocket and took out his phone to display pictures of the dark inside of a cabin showing the symbols in white scrawled on the walls. The priest noticed the blood on the floor.

"I've researched some of the symbols. They're demonic, used in ritual sacrifice for summoning. It's all here, Father. I don't know if Valerie was directly involved in Joshua's death, but she knows something, I'm convinced of it."

He asked Martin to take him to the cabin. To see it with his own eyes would make it real. Once he could acknowledge that it was, he would do what needed to be done. His soul was safe, but he couldn't let his congregation be cast down. If what Martin thought turned out to be true, Father would battle the forces of Hell until the bitter end.

A day later, Father Foxland walked out of the rectory and told his housekeeper Mrs. Carson that he would be out for most of the day. He drove to the nearby state park where he was to meet Martin a half-mile along the main trail and follow him to the cabin. The path had become overgrown during the months it was too cold to be outside. The bushes that caught at his sleeves and pant legs were annoying. The cloudy sky added to the burden he felt about the situation, and he'd slept very little thinking about it. The air felt thick and heavy, the scent of grass and moss clogged his sense of smell, the spongy earth beneath his shoes made him uneasy and off balance. The birds overhead cried to one another as he walked.

The priest took his time to avoid being the one to wait should Martin be late for their appointment. It would look odd should someone see him and wonder what he was doing there. Father wasn't known for taking walks in the woods. It would be the subject of town gossip should someone discover him standing there. As he neared the half-mile marker, the priest glanced through the trees ahead to see if Martin was already there. He sighed relieved that he didn't have to wait.

"Father?" Dressed for hiking with neutral colored clothing, Martin seemed tired, the bags under his eyes confirmed it.

"Good morning. How far is it from here?" Father asked silently chiding himself for not exercising more. He hadn't walked very far, but his legs were already aching.

"It's not far, another half-mile from here." Martin gestured toward the northeast.

The priest nodded and gestured for Martin to lead the way. Leaving the trail, they moved into the thickening underbrush. Father was conscious of staying close to Martin's footprints as he would be watching for snakes and other fatal creatures of nature they might inadvertently disturb.

The slightly rising grade of the land caused the out-of-shape priest to begin panting. The exertion made his heart pound, and sweat ran down his back. His nose ached from the coldness of the air around him. It would be several hours before the heat of the sun penetrated this part of the forest through the canopy overhead.

They didn't speak at all for which Father was grateful. He could barely catch his breath with the pace that Martin had set for them, but he didn't complain. They were on an important mission. Determination needed to be their guiding principle if they were to accomplish what they hoped to do. Gritting his teeth, Father Foxland put more energy into his step.

After what seemed like forever, Martin stopped walking and placed a finger over his lips indicating the need for quiet. From there, the priest was careful where he stepped to avoid snapping twigs or crunching leaves. Up ahead, he could see the cabin through the trees. It was about a hundred yards from where they stood. Father glanced up into the trees noticing the lack of bird sounds. The stillness felt unnatural.

Martin took a step forward, and the priest shivered at the chill that ran up his spine. Broad daylight felt like midnight. Every moment they moved closer to the cabin, Father felt as if he was pressing *into* something. It was an energy that was soft and comforting, strangely familiar, yet dark, sinister, and suffocating. The cabin lay ahead and the two men crouched waiting to see if anyone else was nearby. Father spied the dirty window of the cabin half expecting to see a light from inside, but it remained dark the entire time they waited. Moss grew at the edges of it.

Martin looked at him, straightened, and walked toward the front door. Taking the two steps up to the small porch, Father Foxland was careful to step lightly to avoid the creaking of old wood. He watched Martin wipe his forehead with the back of his hand. It was cool here but Martin was sweating. Father knew it had nothing to do with the effort of getting here.

Looking carefully around the door before grasping the doorknob, Martin hesitated. Once satisfied there was no threat, he turned the handle and pushed in. Only a whisper of sound came from the hinges as the door swung open. Unsettled dust wafted in the dim light coming through the windows and tickled the priest's nose. Stepping onto the wood floor, he felt it bend slightly and wondered at the soundness of the structure.

"Father?"

Martin's whisper startled him in the quiet. They had entered a one-room cabin that would have been a welcome retreat for someone. A large fireplace stood along one wall, ready for a fire on a cold night. Modern plumbing had not been installed, but an area off to his left had been fitted with cabinets and counter space. The rest of the room was empty except for a small round table with two chairs along a far wall next to a tightly rolled mattress and bedding.

The ordinary soon gave way to the strange. White chalk marks marred the walls with serpentine figures winding around glyphs he'd never seen before except in nightmares. The smudged remnants of a large circle and pentagram were on the floor. Hollow spheres of hardened candle wax lay at the points of the star.

Martin moved to the right near the bedroll and pointed to a squiggle on the wall. "Father, this symbol here is used to gather energy for rituals."

The priest nodded absently as Martin continued to rattle off the information he'd uncovered in his research, not paying attention to the details. Father was more interested in the reason these symbols were needed. From the wax on the floor, he could tell that this space had been used frequently, but for what purpose? If it were what Martin suspected, it would be a terrible thing.

A cold breeze chilled the back of his neck and Father moved from the spot where he stood to step inside and close the door. Out of the corner of his eye, one of the figures on the wall caught his attention as it seemed to move. On closer inspection, it was nothing more than a line drawn in such a way as to be undulating as he turned his head. Laughing at himself he let Martin continue to talk.

Raising his hand, Father was tempted to touch the figure but hesitated as the tip of his finger started to prickle the closer he moved toward it. Feeling his courage fail him, Father Foxland turned to carefully view the wall where Martin stood with his nose practically pressed to another glyph.

"Now that you've seen it, Father, what do you think?"

"I think we have some very disturbed individuals in our town and we need to be extra vigilant." It was the only thing the priest could think of to say. Once he took in the magnitude of what was there, he was astounded. Someone had even taken the time to draw on the ceiling. "Martin we should go."

The journalist nodded while making a few notes in a small book he'd pulled from one of his pockets. Tucking those things away, he went to the window to look out. "Something feels funny now, don't you think?"

The priest agreed. It was definitely time to leave. Father stepped out onto the porch and took in a breath of fresh air then coughed. The sound of it echoed in the trees. Martin closed the door with a quiet snick as the lock engaged.

"I feel like we're being watched," Martin said. Father quickened his step to leave the haunted place.

He'd left the cabin three days ago and had very little rest since. Nightmares had assailed him every time he closed his eyes. They were always similar, but never the same. Images of him and Valerie sitting in the cabin having a conversation while monsters of all shapes and sizes stood around them: watching, waiting. As Father sipped his third cup of coffee this morning to prevent him from falling asleep again, he prayed silently for God to take away the images in his head. He remembered so vividly sitting across the table from Valerie, her pretty face smiling, her manner gentle, and her words, destructive.

"It wasn't a coincidence that you were brought here, Father, you were called here," she said.

"What are you talking about? I moved here before you did," he replied in the dream.

Valerie shook her head giving him a sly smile. "Weren't you raised not far from here?"

The priest nodded. "So? I wanted to come back to the area where I grew up. The bishop was happy to allow that to happen."

Tilting her head, she smiled again. "I'm not sure you're aware of the history of the area, Father. When the white settlers arrived, the natives warned them that this area was sacred, but the warnings were dismissed. It's due to the creature that lives here."

"Creature?" Father scoffed. "If there were one, Harold Whitmore would have killed it by now. He's got the head of at least one of everything in this area on the wall in his game room."

Valerie drummed her fingers on the table where they sat. "Why would he kill someone he knows?"

Startled awake by what she said, Father had bolted upright, beads of cold sweat prickling his skin.

As time had gone on, the dream continued night after night as if their conversation had only paused for a time. Valerie told him that he was indirectly involved with the death of Joshua, but refused to tell him how.

He woke exhausted on the third day. Fog formed from exhaling his shaky breath. He held still listening for the sound of the heater, hearing it running. Why was it so cold? Pushing away the primal desire to stay in bed and pull the covers over his head, he forced himself to get up. Ignoring the aches in his body, the priest went to check on the thermostat and found it set to the normal temperature. Shivering again from the cold, he shook his head. Despite it being the middle of the night, he went to begin his day.

Sitting at the table sipping coffee, Father wrapped his fingers around the warm mug and inhaled the steam drifting from the center of the dark brew. He took the time before dawn to contemplate what his next step should be. From the silence, the priest could tell the wind had died down, but the rain still came down in sheets. The path from here to the church would be little more than a stream of mud with dirty stepping stones. He would wait until the sun rose before going over there to check on the church. It was a sturdy building, not likely to be disturbed by the elements but it would reassure him to know that the old structure could still weather any storm.

The cup cooled in his hands. Sighing, he put it down. The dreams were disturbing and still had no meaning. Valerie kept repeating something about darkness, but he couldn't remember what she meant by it. Rubbing his eyes to drive away the tiredness, he stood and went to find where he put his umbrella.

The church was already open when he arrived. Father could hear Mrs. Carson's voice echoing inside as she spoke to someone. He stood to the side waiting, reluctant to interrupt and eavesdrop on the conversation. He was close enough to hear their voices, but not what they were saying. He would be polite and wait.

"I wasn't aware it was Father's habit to lurk in the shadows."

The priest felt his face heat up. He stepped out from where he stood. "I didn't want to interrupt." He was surprised to find who was there. "What brings you to church, Ms. Callahan?" The priest caught himself before he called her Valerie as he'd done in the dreams.

"I need to speak to you urgently about something, Father," Valerie replied.

Mrs. Carson quickly excused herself, showing how uncomfortable she was with Ms. Callahan. Father wished he could have disappeared as fast, but Valerie settled onto a pew with an expression that said she intended to stay until he heard what she needed to say.

Sighing, Father sat near her and waited for her to speak. The church was eerily quiet at this hour, and despite the bright light of day streaming through the windows, the priest felt the prickle of nervousness at the center of his back and the pit of his stomach.

"What is it that you wanted to talk to me about?" He couldn't prevent the impatience in his voice.

A smirk crossed Valerie's face. "I know you've been to the cabin, Father."

He scoffed, but said nothing.

Valerie smiled. "I don't mind. It makes things easier. When trapping an animal, it's always best to have bait."

"What are you talking about?" He rubbed the back of his neck trying to soothe the headache he felt forming.

Valerie turned and looked at the crucifix on the wall. The icon was beautifully hand-carved by artists who loved their work. It was evident in every line and curve of the sculpture. Those who were hired to light it had done so to show Jesus in the best way. It gave one a sense of strength, courage, and hope. Father looked to the figure knowing that his life was in God's hands and nothing and no one could break that bond. To see Valerie look at it with such reverence surprised him.

"How well do you know your family history, Father?"

The priest stared at her wondering what that had to do with anything, then remembered them having a similar conversation in one of his nightmares.

"If I've given you the impression that I like puzzles and riddles," Father said, "I apologize. My family and I have always been plain-speaking people."

The psychic laughed. "I'll get to the point. You think you have no living relatives, but it's not true. There is still one left, and you're going to help me catch him."

Father Foxland shook his head. "I'm sorry, but you're mistaken. The reason I was sent to a Catholic orphanage was that I had no living relatives."

Valerie huffed out a breath as if losing patience with him, but the priest couldn't understand this absurd conversation.

"Perhaps we should choose another time and place to continue this," Father said. "I have things to do, and I'm sure you do too." He stood, but Valerie reached out and grabbed his wrist encouraging him to sit down.

"This is too important to discuss anywhere else, Father, and this is the safest place. Speaking to you in the dream state takes too long. I need your help, and I need it now before someone else is killed."

The priest got to his feet then and looked at her, exasperation coloring his words. "This is nonsense. If you don't have anything important to talk about, I must insist on returning to my duties."

Valerie stood and brushed imaginary dust from the front of her dress. "If you don't listen to me, you'll be responsible for the deaths of everyone in Mirror Point. The spirits are telling me that something is about to be unleashed and unless you help me, people will die."

"The spirits?" Father crossed his arms over his chest. "Do you expect me to take advice from someone who claims to talk to ghosts?"

"What is so different from you and I, Father?" Valerie raised an arm and pointed at the cross. "What's different from speaking to spirits and praying to The Holy Ghost?"

Father gritted his teeth to quell his anger. "If you've come to debate theology, Ms. Callahan, I would be happy to do so another day."

"We might not have another day, Father. The time we have to catch and destroy what's out there is short. The only ones who can do this are you and I. Neither of us can banish what waits for us in the woods by ourselves." Valerie took a breath and stepped back. "I don't like you, you don't like me. We've established that much. I suppose it's my fault for how I've treated you. There's a lot you don't know, but I don't have time to tell you everything. I need you to trust me, Father."

The priest dropped his arms to his sides to alleviate his annoyance. He'd always been a level-headed man, but there was something about this woman that made him want to yell at the top of his lungs. "Ms. Callahan, I really don't have time to play word games."

Valerie fixed him with a steady glare. "This is not a game at all, Father. If you don't help me, more people will die."

Shaking his head, he turned and left. He'd had more than enough of her foolishness for today.

Father Foxland still felt uneasy as he sat at his desk at the rectory trying to decide which Bible passages he should use for his sermon this week. He tried to speak to the things the congregation would have on their minds, things they would worry about, but he could find nothing specific to focus on. The world was in chaos, but to speak about the general malaise of society would serve no purpose. He began to search his well-worn Bible for his favorite encouraging passages. It was always good to have a reminder that hope was possible even in the darkest of days.

A knock on his door startled him. "Father, are you home?"

Pulling away from his desk, Father went to the door to see who it was. Resisting the urge to look through the peephole first, he swung the door wide to find Harold Whitmore standing on his doorstep with a rifle.

"Harold, planning to do some hunting today?"

Running a hand through his short gray hair, Harold rested the butt of the gun on the floor at his side after Father let him in. The pockets of his camouflage clothing bulged with the items he needed for his outings. Father invited him to sit, but Harold shook his head.

"I'll make this quick. Father, I saw some strange tracks out in the woods not far from here. I followed them. Usually, an animal moves away from people, but the tracks I found led me here."

"You mean that because of the storm a confused animal probably thought to seek shelter here instead of somewhere in the woods?" Father thought that was a reasonable explanation. The thunder and lightning would have scared even the largest of creatures.

"No, Father," Harold shook his head. "The tracks don't show an animal running in fear. They show slow, deliberate progress, no hesitation at all. Whatever it is also walked on two legs."

Father Foxland smiled. "Harold, stop pulling my leg."

"I'm not kidding, Father. The footprints look like a cross between a human and a bear. The claws of the foot dug into the mud with every step. There are also claw marks on the building. It doesn't look like a bear, but I don't know what else it could be. I know you would never leave food out for a wild animal, but I wanted to let you know something was prowling around."

Father nodded. "Thank you for telling me. I'll remember to lock the doors and be more mindful of the garbage."

Harold seemed satisfied that his warning would be heeded. "By the way, Father, there was another thing I found strange. Normally when an animal is seeking food, it looks for containers or goes to porches, things like that. The marks I found were on the side of the building where your bedroom is. It's a strange place for an animal to search for food. Don't worry. Me and the boys are going to track it back to the woods and see if we can find it." Harold smiled. "It's been a while since I put a new trophy on my wall."

The priest nodded and smiled. Father Foxland had opinions about killing for the sake of killing but kept them to himself. He thanked Harold again and then tried to settle down to think about his sermon again, but couldn't. His thoughts drifted to how hard it had been for him to move back here and how he kept having a feeling that he needed to for some reason.

He had requested to come here and Father Jacobson wanted to leave. The Bishop had denied both requests without explanation. When the Bishop went on special assignment the acting Bishop reviewed the requests and approved them. Father Jacobson left quickly, only two days after his replacement arrived.

Father stood from his desk a half hour after Harold left, the sermon still a stark white page on his laptop. He couldn't dismiss what the hunter said, but couldn't process it either. The weather outside was nice, but Father felt a chill he couldn't shake. Curiosity drew his attention and made him walk out the door in search of the marks Harold spoke of.

The ground was still muddy and slick in some areas, but he was determined. He rounded the corner and could see the marks on the wall. They were grooves in the wood that were spaced apart larger than a man's hand. The sight of it deeply disturbed him. What on Earth could cause something like this?

A bird call startled Father out of his reverie and prompted him to leave. Using the garden hose to clean off his shoes, he leaned against the wall warily searching the forest that backed the church grounds. He told himself it was just nerves, leftover anxiety from the creepy cabin and the storm. After the nightmares he'd been having, his imagination was running wild. He took a breath, wiped his shoes on the doormat and went inside to finish his sermon.

Once content that his words on Sunday could be useful for those who attended, Father went to the kitchen to fix a late lunch. It was mid-afternoon by this point. It had taken some time to settle his mind enough to work. His thoughts kept wandering to the strange things he'd learned in the past few days. None of it made sense, and it seemed the only person who could help him clarify things was the one person he didn't want to speak to: Valerie.

Martin hadn't contacted him since the day they went to the cabin, but that wasn't unusual. Martin was a man always on the go, researching, asking questions, and digging for answers. Father was certain Martin would let him know if he found out anything else. In the meantime, Father had no choice but to visit the town psychic and try to get her to tell him what was going on without spewing a lot of New Age babble.

Leaving the rectory, he chose to walk. It wasn't very far, and the walk in the woods had taught him that he was in dire need of exercise. Taking his time, he took deep breaths as he walked. He could always find someone to give him a ride back if he was overtired. The day was chilly but sunny. A drastic change from the state of the sky only yesterday. The weather was becoming as changeable and unpredictable as the human heart.

The area was lush and beautiful in the way untamed things are. The people here were resilient, and stalwart. He was born in the area, but taken away so young, he had no memory of it. In asking the old-timers about what they remembered of his family, none could recall anything about them. He'd thought nothing of it, but Valerie's insistence that it was related had him wondering. The psychic's shop was about a mile and a half from the church. The way was flat, and he was able to walk there only stopping occasionally to say hello to someone he passed. Sweat made his collar cling to his neck. He slid a finger along the rim to allow air to circulate. He felt he had adequately exercised today, he hoped it would be enough to help him sleep well.

Valerie's shop was small, but well lit and had a friendly feel to it. She did readings there as well as sold a few pieces of jewelry, candles, and incense. If interactions with her hadn't been so unpleasant, he would have found the place charming.

Stepping up to turn the doorknob, he felt a strange pressure on the front of his body, as if he was walking through something. The bell above the door chimed and Valerie peeked around the corner of a tall bookcase with a broad smile that soon faded when she recognized who it was. "You're the last person I expected to see," she said.

"This is the last place I expected to be," Father admitted. "Yet, here I am with the need to clear up whatever this is."

Father Foxland blew out a breath and shook his head. "Ms. Callahan, I have no hard feelings toward you. I understand that you must be grieving. I am very sorry for your loss. Joshua's death was a tragedy, but I don't know what it has to do with me."

Father watched as Valerie closed her eyes and breathed in the cold air swirling in the room from the air conditioner. Father waited until she opened them again and spoke to him. "Let me turn the sign and close the store. We'll go in the back to talk."

Father stood to the side and waited for her to complete her tasks then followed her to a back room that had a small wooden table and two chairs. A refrigerator, sink, and microwave accompanied it. A few shelves and a couple of cabinets were all the tiny room could hold. Valerie gestured for Father to have a seat and he chose the one facing the door. She busied herself by taking two mugs from one of the cabinets and filling them with water from the pitcher in the refrigerator. Father shivered slightly feeling the cool air when the door closed.

"Father, have you never wondered why you weren't allowed to come back here?"

He surprised himself by answering. "It's not my place to question the Bishop's decisions. I'm sure there are things I was unaware of at the time, and he thought it was in my best interest and that of the church to go where he chose to send me." As he spoke, he wondered how she knew his initial request of coming here had been denied but kept speaking. "We always have our preferences, but to make sure that all of the faithful have access to the clergy, we need to obey the orders of our superiors." Father felt confident in his answer and wasn't a bit surprised to see a sneer cross Valerie's face when she turned to face him. He wouldn't expect a woman like her to understand the depth of his commitment to the calling.

Valerie sat and placed a mug in front of him. "Did you want to be a priest, Father, or did they tell you it was your only option?"

"Ms. Callahan, I've come here for clarity, not further confusion. Now please tell me what all of this is about." Father didn't bother to keep the annoyance out of his voice. The nightmares had robbed him of his sleep, and the strange prickly feeling during his waking hours had kept him on the edge of hysteria. It was too much.

Valerie sighed and leaned back, her blonde ponytail jerking behind her head. The bracelet around her left wrist scraped the table and her face held an impatient expression.

"Father, there's not enough time for me to tell you every detail I've learned, but let me make it as clear as I can. Joshua's death is directly tied to you and your family." She held up a hand to prevent him from speaking. "Let me finish, or we'll be here all night."

Father nodded for her to continue. "You know your family is from here and you were taken and put in an orphanage when your parents were killed. After high school you went into the seminary, right?" Father nodded again, not trusting himself to speak.

"When they took you away, they lied to you. Your parents weren't killed in an accident. Your mother was murdered, and your father was a suspect, but he disappeared. None of your relatives living here at the time would take you in so the priest here, Father Mason, sent you to the orphanage in Seattle.

"Due to the circumstances of your mother's murder, they thought it was best that you were placed as far from here as possible and still be under the care of the diocese. They convinced you of the death of your parents and kept an eye on you while keeping you away. Forcing you into the priesthood was the only way to protect and control you at the same time."

Father Foxland stared at the woman seated across from him. Her words had so inflamed his temper, he was gripping the mug tightly in his hand. He couldn't understand why she would say such despicable things. He didn't believe for a moment that his father would have killed his mother. The few memories he retained were of people who loved one another and him. "I don't know who's convinced you of such lies, but my parents were not that way," he insisted.

Valerie took a sip from her cup while his remained untouched. "Father, you were five years old when they took you. Do you really believe the memory of a child so young can compare to the facts? Dig into the newspaper archives, see what was reported back then. If you still don't believe, then get ready Father. There are going to be a lot more funerals in Mirror Point."

Valerie turned away from him, disgusted, and Father could see that she had no interest in discussing it further. He stood from his seat and left without saying anything. Father took his time walking back to the rectory even though what he wanted to do was walk over to the building that housed the local newspaper and start digging through their files. The best person to do that without drawing suspicion was Martin. He would call him as soon as he arrived home.

The day was waning. He was running out of time to do things he needed to before he had to open the church for those who chose to pray the rosary in the early evening. Out of breath, the priest went directly to the phone to call Martin to explain what he needed. After promising Father he would get the information, Martin hung up. Satisfied for the moment, the priest began preparing to pray the rosary with those who would attend this evening.

With the church locked up after the evening prayer, he walked the few feet to the rectory in the dark feeling uneasy. The quiet around him that used to be comforting now held only dread. He stood in the silence listening to the movement of the trees in the light wind knowing that the difference wasn't due to his surroundings, but in how he felt about it. Tiredness weighed on him. Even while praying, thoughts of the dreams, conversations with Valerie, and images of the cabin, flashed through his mind breaking his concentration and ruining his devotion. It had never been so difficult to block out the world and focus on his faith before. Today was Wednesday. He had a few more days before he would stand before the congregation on Saturday night for Mass. Whatever this was needed to be taken care of by then.

Stepping into the rectory, Father locked the door behind him, twisting the handle once more to assure himself that it was secure. He then went to check every room and window to make sure that each was soundly fastened. He felt sure that anything he found out of the ordinary would cause him to be awake all night.

Stripping off his coat and shoes, Father walked in stocking feet to the kitchen for a light supper. His stomach had growled unmercifully at prayers. He'd been too busy thinking about what Martin might find that he'd forgotten to eat until it was too late to do so. A warmed-up can of soup and a couple slices of toast were all he had the energy to make for himself. It was still early, before nine, but his jumbled and paranoid thoughts frustrated him. It was best to go to bed. Changing into his pajamas, he crawled into bed. He chose to leave a light on in the hallway and left the door cracked open to allow it to break the darkness in his room. He closed his eyes and fell asleep.

He opened his eyes. Father sat, fully dressed at the small table he saw in the cabin. It had been moved to the center of the circle on the floor. Candlelight chased away the shadows to the edges of his vision. He looked up to see the symbols on the wall. They seemed to glow, but with a light brighter than the candles could provide. It was eerie.

"I'm sorry, Father, we can't wait any longer. There's no more time for explanations."

Father turned at the sound of Valerie's voice in the shadows.

"I'm sure you're wondering what's happening here. I'm using you as bait, Father," she said. "Your family and mine suffer an intertwined fate that locks us together between life and death. Heaven set us up to be natural enemies."

The priest balled his fist on the table. Even in dreams, he couldn't escape this absurdity. He needed to wake up. He stood from his seat assuming that he would be awake and fuming in bed, instead he was still in the circle staring at Valerie who had entered it with him.

"Why can't I wake up?"

"Because you're not dreaming," Valerie answered. "Listen to me. Our guest will be arriving soon. We need to prepare. You'll hear and see some strange things, but don't leave the protection of the circle no matter what."

"I don't understand." Father gritted his teeth and balled his fists trying to control his need to scream. He took a deep breath and focused on relaxing his body, unable to fathom why everything this woman said to him grated on his nerves. There was something about her that made him manic. Thinking through every interaction with her left him befuddled as to why he had such a reaction.

Valerie left the circle and walked around the cabin lighting more candles. Father couldn't understand why as it was nearly as bright as daylight inside already, but having her be focused on anything other than him gave him a moment to calm himself. The door to the cabin was wide open which seemed odd. If something fearful were about to appear, they should use every physical barrier they had to protect them from it.

Through the open door, Father could hear the wind blowing. The gusts whistled through the pines and rattled the leaves on the other trees. It was reminiscent of the documentaries he'd seen of rattlesnakes right before they struck. What he heard was nature's rattle, a warning that death was close.

A loud thump on the side of the cabin startled Father. Valerie gasped, inhaled hard. Moving back into the circle, she closed her eyes and took a deep breath. "Remember what I said, Father. Don't leave the circle for any reason. It's for your safety and mine."

Scratching along the outside wall drew their attention. There was no window for them to see what could be causing that sound, but as it moved closer to the front of the cabin, it couldn't be something ordinary.

The cabin would have been warm and cozy had fear not slithered up Father's spine. Beads of cold sweat broke over his skin and he shivered. The flickering of the candles cast fearsome shadows on the walls, giving the impression that things were closing in. He placed a finger at his throat to pull his collar away from his neck. He couldn't breathe.

Whatever it was moved closer to the door. The small pieces of darkness cast by the light elongated as the flames suddenly shrunk, as if hiding themselves. Father feared they would wink out leaving only a single trail of smoke signaling the end of life.

"Breathe, Father. It will be over soon. I promise," Valerie said.

Father's heartbeat threatened to burst from his chest. He forced himself to stand still despite the burning desire to run. What was left of his reason reminded him that there was only one door and whatever was coming would be standing there shortly.

It only took a moment before the darkness outside the door became even darker. Something was there. It was sentient and waiting. A soft guttural cry issued from the doorway. Father felt something like sorrow hitch the breath in his chest. He stared into the darkness outside not noticing that it was getting darker on the inside. Some of the candles around him had gone out, leaving the scent of melted wax.

"James." Father's name drifted to him in a gruff whisper. He looked at Valerie thinking it was she who had called his name, but she turned to him, shook her head and pointed at the doorway.

"That's right, it's James," Valerie said speaking for the first time. Father wiped his sweaty hands on his pants and tried to steady his breathing.

Whatever it was took a step forward into the light. Father stumbled back unable to take in what he saw. It was a creature. There was no other word for it. He'd never seen anything in nature resembling what appeared. It was no more than six feet tall, and it was covered in a combination of fur and scales. Its eyes were black with yellow slits, sharp teeth lined its elongated jaw, and thick, curved claws protruded from the hands and feet. It took a step forward. Father looked at its face. It was covered in fur but had a human-like quality about it.

"James," it whispered. The raspy voice was also human, it caused a shiver up the priest's spine. Hearing his name, Father felt as if all the air in his chest had been sucked out. He was unable to catch his breath.

"Stop," Valerie said.

Father watched the creature turn his head and see Valerie. A vicious growl rattled the cabin, startling Father with its ferocity. Valerie didn't even flinch.

"Mine," the creature said.

"You can't have him," Valerie replied.

The monster roared, and Father fell to his knees in the circle. The sound rolled through him, taking his legs out from under him. The creature got down on its knees near him and Father could feel the heat emanating from it. The circle separating them felt solid as if he would have to fight his way through it. He recoiled from the edge of it. Why would he want to get closer to a walking nightmare?

"Come to me, James." It reached out to him, and Father felt his heart ache. "Come home," it said.

"No!" Suddenly Martin was there shouting. He threw out an arm in front of the priest and pushed him further away from the edge of the circle. Father hadn't realized he was leaning forward.

Another roar sounded in the cabin and Father covered his ears. His mind fell apart then. Everything was strange and familiar at the same time. Old memories surfaced. Images flashed in his mind. The house he grew up in, blood on the dock by the lake, a warm cave a few miles away, his mother's open eyes, and his father's changed form.

Father fell onto his side with his eyes screwed shut. Pulling his knees into his chest, harsh sobs burst from his body as he hugged himself, his hands digging into his arms, so deep was his desire to hold onto reality.

He cried out the anguish that filled his soul. More images assailed him: blood, screams, terror, loss. Buried emotions destroyed him from the inside out. He'd been holding a grenade inside him, and the pin had been pulled. The explosion of feelings devastated him.

"My son," the creature said.

"No," Father screamed, "No!"

"James, James," Valerie shook his shoulder.

Father felt himself rocking. It was what he used to do when he was a child to make it stop. "No, no, it's not true. I'm a priest, I'm good, I'm not evil, I'm not, it's not true."

Muttering to himself, Father Foxland rocked on the floor of the cabin while Martin, Valerie, and the creature called to him. He was no longer able to answer, he had receded into himself seeking the silence he desperately needed.

"What do you think, Martin?"

"We may have lost him for good this time," Martin answered. "I thought that by playing into it that we could finally help him, but it's worse."

"We tried everything else," Valerie commented. "Joshua's death was too much for him."

Martin shook his head. "Yes, but look at him. He's catatonic, trapped in his delusion. We've taken a man terrified of his own demons and locked him inside with them."

Valerie sighed. "We did what we thought was best. Other therapies weren't working. We had to do something. There was no intention to hurt him."

"I know that," Martin replied. "But how does anyone atone for such a grievous mistake?"

Drs. Martin Wilson and Valerie Callahan turned and left. Martin closed the door, hearing the heavy lock engage. Looking through the tiny window, he saw his patient staring blankly with open eyes, mouth locked in a silent scream, his frail body rocking back and forth. Martin silently prayed the former priest would once again find his way out of the nightmare. In the meantime, Martin would work on getting an explanation for the claw marks on the outside of Father Foxland's door.

The Grey Bride

by Deron Sedy

You can see me? Oh, praise the maker!

Oh, dear, but … I'm sorry. That means you're lonely. Only lonely people can see me.

I'm getting ahead of myself.

Welcome to Chesterton Manor of Way's End, Washington. I'm the Grey Bride. Maybe you've heard of me? No? Hmph. In my day, a haunted manor was something special. Mortals aren't impressed by anything anymore. I blame mobile phones.

Yes, I know your technology. The Innkeeper often falls asleep with the television on. I may have been born in 1882, but I'm completely caught up with the Kardashians. (You have no idea how much I wish he would pick a different channel.)

And that, the typing machine, it's called a laptop, right? You can use it for … um. Bogging? You could make a bog post, and people would see it on laptops of their own?

I must share the story of my death with seven thousand, seven hundred, seventy-seven mortals before I may leave this realm.

That's the curse, if one is partly responsible for one's own death. Ancient rules, do not ask me. No exceptions, no consideration for circumstance.

It has been at least a decade since anyone has heard my voice. I had eight brothers and sisters, always someone to talk to. This existence– you have no idea how terrible.

My husband, married to me two years only, told me he needed to come into town for grain. I finished my cleaning early and decided to follow on horseback to surprise him. But no one in town had seen him. I asked everywhere, finally going to the saloon. That's where we are, you know. This was a saloon, originally.

In this very room, I found my husband on top of a prostitute. I promise you, my actions were not my own. My world went red. I flew at him, nails… teeth. That's when the man I loved, calm as you please, put his hands around my throat and …

I thought he would stop. That was my last thought:When will he stop?

They let this room out so seldom. You're only the sixth person to hear my story. But we could tell so many people, so much faster, if… Will you type it for me?

I don't have money … I thought … I can't touch – But, I could … undress? I saw what you were doing with the laptop earlier. Please don't be mad! I would be better than that, right? You could … Tell me what to do?

Please?

WAY'S END OBSERVER
COMMUNITY PAGE

ESTATE AUCTION SATURDAY –
PROCEEDS BENEFIT THE
CENTENNIAL FUND

The Herschel estate auction will take place Saturday afternoon at the town hall community room in Way's End and all proceeds will go to the Centennial Fund. Artwork, tools, photographs, furniture, and a large collection of papers and journals are included. Participants may arrive as early as 2 p.m. and the auction will start at 3 p.m. sharp.

A Modern-Day Nostradamus
by Chloe Holiday

"Forty-two! Do I hear forty-five?" The auctioneer glanced around the room at the estate sale in Way's End. "Forty-two going once, forty-two going twice! Sold for forty-two dollars to the young lady in the green suit."

Delighted, Sophia made her way to the organizer's desk to arrange for payment. It would also keep her from spending money on a hot dog she couldn't afford now or looking at any of the other antiques.

"Sophia Sorensen," she told the man at the table, as she dug out her credit card.

"Ah, yes, the writings of E.M. Herschal." He called the holding room, and a few minutes later a young man came up, pushing a dolly laden with two boxes, each the size of a small suitcase.

He smiled at her. "I'm Greg. Can I help you load them in your car?"

Sophia swallowed. "Yes, please." She hurried to bring her car around. He was cute—and maybe flirting? She stood tongue-tied as Greg lifted the boxes into her trunk.

"Anything else?" His eyes touched her lips, her neckline.

"No, thanks." Blushing, she climbed into her eight-year-old Volvo and drove to the ferry terminal, kicking herself. Always too shy to talk to men, even the ones that seemed interested, while her friends always were talking about their hook-ups—not that she was interested in that. *I'd give my life for real passion, though.*

She shook her head as she eased into the line for boarding. That sort of thing only happened in fairy tales, anyway. That's why she collected books and old writing—almost her whole paycheck went to them. But little towns like this were great sources, too far for the Seattle and Tacoma competitors to drive. She earned enough selling the things she could market to supplement her meager salary as an archivist, dreaming of a big score: a trove of love letters from Jimmy Hoffa or a confession from the Boston Strangler. When she got home, she carefully transferred the boxes inside to equilibrate and went to bed.

The next evening after work, she donned gloves and opened the first box. The first piece was called "Inferno," and dated April, 1888. The spidery writing on onionskin paper was a first-hand account of the Great Seattle Fire. Rapt, she finished it and carefully laid the pages aside. Maybe she could market it to the Seattle Museum. She went online to check. *Wait—the Great Fire was June 6, 1889. Whoa.*

Had to be a mistake. She shook it off and started on the next piece, "Mudslide in Oso." Dated February, 1888, it was a perfect account of the tragedy, right down to the time it hit—in 2014. She double-checked the date. *Holy shit! Has to be a coincidence.* She shook her head and continued through the box. The Wellington Avalanche from 1910, predicted one hundred years before it happened.

Frowning, she rolled her stiff neck. Had she blown her money on fakes? But the boxes had been sold as original, and the phrasing, the faded ink, the age of the papers looked authentic, with none of the signs of a hoax she'd been trained to spot. She carefully picked up the next document.

The Heppner Flash Flood of 1903, detailed in a scrawl dated May, 1887. The hair stood up on the back of her neck. The eruption of Mt. St. Helens in 1980. It went on and on – all in the Northwest, all eerily accurate. Hands shaking, she finished the box. *He's like a modern-day Nostradamus.*

The other box, labeled "Love Stories," taunted her. *What could be the harm in those?* Sophia went to eat some soup and changed into her nightgown, then returned to read. The first story was a gentle romance between an elderly couple, Maude and Stan Gershwin, the kind that gave warm fuzzies but probably wouldn't sell, although the prose was strangely modern. The next manuscript was sizeable, almost a novella-length. "Love Me To Death." That sounded promising.

The heroine had a boring job and was named Sophia! She almost stopped reading, then shook off her unease. *Get a grip.* She got a muffin and continued, flipping ahead ...

"Ciao, bella." The man at the door grinned insolently, his eyes traveling over her curves. "My name is Alessandro. I just moved in next door and wanted to meet my neighbor." His olive skin and dark hair set off his sexy smile, and a dimple flashed ...

Sophia yawned – it was getting late, but this might be marketable. She started to skim to the good parts ...

Alessandro's hungry gaze took in the pulse at her throat and the expanse of pale skin above her deep neckline. "Amore." His voice was husky as he advanced.

"You were made for this. For me." He sandwiched her against the wall, as his lips brushed hers, then roved her neck. His hand cupped her breast, hot through the thin fabric, and his pelvis trapped her in place, his undisguised need a stark declaration of desire. He swooped her up as her knees buckled ...

Okay, that one fades to black. Sophia flipped ahead ...

Sophia trembled at the tickle of Alessandro's stubble on her thighs. He was going to – she gasped, her fingers tightening on his hair. "Alessandro, I –"
"Be still, cara.*" His hands pressed her thighs flat, while his tongue lapped like fire, a conflagration that spread inward, incinerating her resistance as heat swept over her. When her ears stopped ringing, she lay melting and liquified beneath his hard planes, as he murmured Italian in her ear and reached down to guide his entry. Perfect bliss filled her, building to another wave ...*

Good Lord. Maybe I'll keep this one. Sophia went to get a drink. She stayed up all night to read it twice: a torrid tale of passion, of grand love, jealousy – and murder. It was fascinating – and horrifying. It would be a bestseller. It'd make a great movie. *I'd give anything for a love like that.* If only they'd talked, they could have straightened it out, instead of the heroine being killed in a jealous rage. Exhausted, Sophia stumbled for bed at nearly 4 am.

The next morning, she swatted at her alarm. She awoke an hour late and rushed to shower. As she fixed breakfast, her eye fell on the papers from last night. *I wonder ...*

Clamping her toast with jelly between her teeth, she booted up her computer and looked up Maude and Stan Gershwin. *Holy shit!* There was an obituary for a couple by that name, from just last year. And the details were accurate, as far as she could tell.

She lay down the toast with trembling fingers. There was no last name for either Sophia or Alessandro, but she did have a boring job. *Get a grip – you don't know any Alessandro, and you don't have a new neighbor. Even Nostradamus must have gotten some of them wrong.* She was just tired from the late night and spooked by the eerie pieces that foretold such tragedy.

Laughing at herself, Sophia grabbed her bag and headed out her apartment door. She locked it behind her, dropped the keys into her purse and turned, almost bumping into a tall stranger with dark skin and eyes.

"Ciao, bella." His dimple flashed. "My name is Alessandro. I just moved in next door and wanted to meet my neighbor."

"... be warned I will only tell you once and that's it."

Spirit Lake
by Celena Davis

"Hello, my name is Jake, and I would like to borrow some of your time for an interview," Jake said as he pulled out a recorder, along with a note-pad and a pen.

"Well alright, if you will for once listen to what this old hermit has to say and warn others," replied the hermit as he invited Jake into his old hut that overlooks the lake.

"Can you tell me about Spirit Lake?" Jake asked.

"Now what in tarnations makes you think you can go around asking people about the lake?" Hermit Joe asked in surprise to the question.

"For the high school's newspaper and journalism class."

"Well, I suppose I can tell you pesky youngsters, but be warned I will only tell you once and that's it," Hermit Joe said.

"Of course, Hermit Joe, so tell me about the lake, and what makes it unique?"

"For as long as we've had technology, and even far before, Spirit Lake has always been very mysterious. That's why we've always had a rule since people visited and lived by this lake, is to NEVER go in at night...EVER!"

"What do you mean by mysterious?"

"If you cross the lake at night, there's no telling what will happen to you. Many have tried and only very few made it to the other side alive or in one piece. There are strange fish, that scientists have found but don't know how its possible for them to be alive. Like there are: fish that glows, fish small like a pinky finger that if touched with bare hands can kill you with poison, and ancient fishes from the dinosaur times that not only will eat plants growing in the lake, but fish, animals, and humans."

"That's a little disturbing," Jake said quietly.

"The lake during the day looks crystal clear on sunny days, but at night and stormy days it's dark water; so dark you can't even see your own skin a couple inches away from you. The only safe part of the lake is on the shore or on the island. At night there is a fog that comes over the lake, only the water gets covered. You would have to be on land. You can cross at night, but it can be dangerous. If you are exposed to open air on the lake at night you could potentially go insane and harm yourself and others till you get to land. That's why there's a rule on no crossing or swimming on the lake at night without an air mask.

"Every hour there's a ferry that crosses the lake between the two towns, and at night everyone was required to wear air masks so they wouldn't breath in the fog. But it has been known that at every half hour ghost ships are seen on the lake and at the docks, you can even hear people on them as if they are real.

"Under the prison on the lake, is a bunker, with tunnels connecting to the towns with a huge vehicle port in the lake itself with a hidden button on one of the trees so you can get your vehicles inside. That door is half the size of the lake. The bunkers was made in the 50s for the nuclear shelters."

"There must be lots of spiders, rats and rotting food in there."

"Listen up!" Hermit Joe said being annoyed that Jake wasn't completely paying attention.

"Okay, okay, go on."

"In the bunkers are bodies with multiple stages of decay, and a strange goo like substance dripping from the ceiling. Some areas look as if it has been blocking something or someone. The bunker in total is big enough to hold all the people, animals and some vehicles from both towns, with tunnels connecting the towns in cellars and basements. The bunker, is stocked with canned foods, instant meals, and any necessities to survive underground.

"Every so often Spirit Lake washes up feet of unfortunate souls who try to escape the prison or swim in the lake at night. For some reason the Hangman's Island that holds the prison has been reportedly seen moving around the lake but never close enough to shore. There is one special boat that takes prisoners to the island at night for others safety, and on special occasions one of the two ferries will make a stop to the island only for an hour, usually during the day when it's safest."

"Well, thank you Hermit Joe, you won't be disappointed," Jake said as he grabbed his things and rode his bike home to type up the interview.

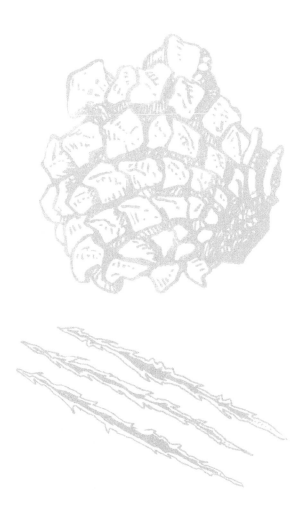

The Honeymooners
by Toni Kief

Finally, there is peace. I'm comforted by the warmth of the rain and the gentle rocking of the water. It wasn't my idea of a romantic honeymoon, but I agreed to go. Derrick wanted to share his love of hunting, and in return, we would investigate the haunted village I read about in the National Geographic.

I never anticipated the incredible discomfort of a two-person tent in late October. He loves the forest and nature, and the least I could do was suck it up and make the best of it. A cold, wet, and dirty five days of communing with nature and tracking through the forest was a torture. I love him, and I tried to share his passion, but I cried myself to sleep. I was grateful the only thing he had killed was my enthusiasm.

Yesterday, with two days left before we had to head home, we broke camp and drove to Mirror Point. I rejoiced with the restaurant, a warm shower, and a bed for the night. Maybe I enjoyed the indoor bathroom too much.

Today started as a beautiful morning. We caught the ferry at seven a.m. and started to sail across Spirit Lake. I was hopeful that Derrick's mood would improve as we were served a lovely breakfast on the deck. I was enthusiastic as I retold the stories about the small town, Way's End. There were years of unexplainable sightings and stories as far back as the founding of the little town at the other end of the lake.

I shared the brochure for the Best Way Inn and the room I reserved at the famous haunted mansion and spirits they say reside there. I was ecstatic and anxious at the same time to explore the town. I wanted Derrick to share in my interest with the supernatural.

Right after our food arrived, I could feel a drop in barometric pressure and the cold assaulted us. I pulled my sweater closer and took a sip of coffee.

Derrick stood, I assumed to go inside, so I walked over to his side of the table, next to the rail. He had been silent for the entire morning. I spoke, "Thank you, darling, for doing this with me, it means so much."

I remember clearly, Derrick rolling his eyes and the venom in his voice. "I hope this makes your woo-woo ghosties happy." He knocked his coffee mug off the table and glared out at the water. Freezing rain started to pelt us, I moved closer to him. He suddenly shouted, "I think this is stupid and a waste of money."

I reached to embrace him. "Don't be mad, I suffered through your trying to kill Bambi."

Now, I watch from afar as the icy lake embraces my body. An agonizing wail assaults the air. I don't know how I arrived at this place above and beyond the ferry, no longer cold. I expected this day was to start a new life with my forever love. Instead, I see the ferry slowly turn, and people filling the decks. The embrace of harmony comes over me, and realization that I'm just a body in the lake, another story for Way's End.

There is a loving light and it calls to me, but I'm not going. I won't give up on my part of the honeymoon. My ethereal essence turns to the bridal suite reservation for the Best Way Inn Bed and Breakfast.

... wondering for the hundredth time what I had gotten myself into.

Lola's Cottage
by Yazz Ustaris

"'Get your own place,' they said. 'It'll be great!' they said." Harley tilted his head at my rant, a soft whine escaping as if echoing my sentiment. As I knelt on the kitchen floor and continued scrubbing at the citrus scented bubbles, I couldn't help wondering for the hundredth time what I had gotten myself into.

Moving to the small town of Mirror Point was supposed to be the start of many new and happy changes. Instead, I couldn't shake this feeling of foreboding, like I had made a big mistake in coming here. The people were nice enough; that wasn't the problem. It was this *place.*

At first, I felt so lucky to have found such a great place to live in because the rent was so cheap! A quaint little cottage nestled between the coffee shop and the diner, with a cute little trail that led from the back door down to the water's edge. The location was killer since the trail was perfect for walking Harley, and living further away from Seattle, I could breathe in as much fresh air as I wanted.

Just not at the moment. I wrinkled my nose and coughed into my elbow. I couldn't explain it, but there was a weird phantom smell in the cottage. I was working on my second pass through the house, scrubbing and sanitizing each room so that I could finally unpack and enjoy my new home. But I just couldn't do that until I was able to identify where the bad smell was coming from. It was starting to drive me crazy.

I had opened all the windows to air out the cottage, so the place should've smelled lemony fresh by now ... except it didn't. There was a strong smell of rot and decay and it didn't seem to be centered in any one room. If I didn't know any better, I'd swear that the smell was following me around. Quirking my head towards Harley at the thought, I asked, "Is it just me or am I being overly paranoid? Do you smell that?"

I really wasn't expecting an answer, but the hair on the back of my neck stood up and goosebumps crept up both arms when the smell suddenly intensified around me. I coughed and started fanning my hand in front of my face, but that really didn't help the situation much.

Setting my sponge aside, I was just preparing to climb to my feet when Harley began loudly barking. I jumped, my hand clutching my chest in shock as Harley began to snarl at the corner of the kitchen. Leaping up, I pivoted around, fully expecting to see an intruder in my living space, but when I stared in the direction that Harley was barking, there was nothing and no one in that corner to be found.

"Hey! Stop that, Harley!" My heart was still pounding from the sound of Harley's initial barking in the silence of the kitchen. He was such a mellow dog and seldom made noise. It was one of the best things about his temperament, so I was truly baffled at his behavior. I placed a comforting hand on his fluffy back when his ruckus subsided to a low-pitched whine, but his gaze remained fixated on the corner.

And because my right hand was still resting lightly on his back, I actually felt Harley's entire body jolt before he let out a loud yelp, almost as if he had been painfully struck. Before I could react, Harley continued his loud yelping as he turned around and dashed out the open front door.

The sight of my dog's furry butt bounding outside finally spurred me into motion, and I cussed as I scrambled to slip into my sneakers. Leaning down to grab my purse and keys from the floor in front of the TV, I looked up and was shocked to see the reflection of a person standing behind me. A little shriek escaped me as I whirled around, but I was met with nothing when I looked. Automatically, I jerked my head back towards the TV, fully expecting to see the image, but only my reflection peered back in the glossy black surface.

"Oh my God! What the hell is going on?!" I demanded in the silence. Unnerved, I stomped around behind the TV and leaned down, reaching for the cord that I knew hadn't been plugged into the wall yet. Raising the cord up to inspect it, I dropped it almost immediately before muttering to myself, "Aarrgh! I don't have time for this crap!"

Not bothering with my jacket, I dashed out the door, pausing just long enough to lock it before darting out to the street. A quick glance left and right showed no signs of Harley.

Damnit! Knowing I'd have to take a guess, I decided to turn left to head deeper into town. We had stumbled upon a park earlier that morning during our walk and I hoped that Harley decided to take refuge there.

Jogging a little faster when the sign to the park came into view, I followed a trail leading into the heart of the park and started scanning in all directions once I broke into a clearing. The park appeared to be empty. Cupping my hands around my mouth I shouted, "Harley!" A feeling of pure panic was starting to set in when I realized Harley wasn't in the park. *Where the heck is he?!*

Sprinting down a back trail, I screamed, "HARLEY!!" as I rounded a corner and discovered the playground. I came to a sudden stop when I spied a girl sitting alone on one of the swings, head bent low over her phone as she texted. The sight of her surprised me, but the girl merely stared back, her eyebrow raised expectantly.

She looked to be in her early 20s, attractive, with long dark hair, pale skin, and intense eyes. She was also decked out in black leather pants and a black crop top with a skull on the front. Everything about her screamed *goth*, including her thick black lipstick. I realized her lips were spread in a wry grin as we continued to play the staring game.

Stopping to catch my breath, I greeted the girl. "Sorry for disturbing your peace ... but, by any chance have you seen a large gray and white dog come through here recently? Very fluffy ... sparkly gray collar?"

Wordlessly, the girl shook her head.

Devastated at her response, I continued, "Well, my name is Lola, and I just moved into the cottage down the street. Harley is my dog and he's never run away before ... until about 20 minutes ago. If you happen to find him, can you please, please let me know?"

The girl's expression filled with compassion before she nodded at me. "You got it. I hope you find your dog."

Murmuring my gratitude at her, I darted off again, intent on finding Harley. It wasn't until I was back out on the street again that I realized I hadn't even caught the girl's name. *Well, that was rude, Lola.*

Outside the high school, I finally ran into a group of teenagers who verified that they had seen Harley running down the sidewalk in the direction of the movie theater. I shouted my thanks as I took off down the street in the direction they were pointing. A few blocks later outside the movie theater, I was finally out of breath and needed to take a break. Slumping onto a bench on the sidewalk, I leaned over to rest my forearms on my thighs as I noisily tried to catch my breath.

Turning my head to the left at the sound of approaching footsteps, I saw a girl with brown wavy hair and a folded apron tossed over her right shoulder. I noticed she was staring straight back at me with her left eyebrow raised, probably because I was still breathing hard.

When it looked like she was going to march right past me, I lifted my hand to gain her attention and wheezed, "Sorry ... have you seen a gray and white sheepadoodle run past here recently? I lost my dog."

The girl smiled at my question before shaking her head at me and laughing. "Yeah, I've seen your dog; my boss has him right now."

"Oh, Thank God! Holy crap was I worried!"

The girl's expression softened at my obvious relief and she pointed in the direction she had just come from. "You'll find him at the diner. He just walked in the front door and sat down like he belonged there. My boss is busy cooking him some chicken cutlets as we speak."

The girl followed up that statement with a laugh, but I just covered my face in embarrassment as I groaned, "Oh my God, my dog is a diva."

Popping off the bench, I was preparing to give my thanks when the girl held out her hand to prevent me from dashing off. "My name is Phoebe, by the way."

"Nice to meet you. I'm Lola. I just moved into the cottage down the street."

Phoebe's eyes grew big before she mumbled, "The haunted one?"

That stopped me in my tracks and I stared back before asking, "What did you just say?"

She shrugged nonchalantly before rushing on to say, "Nothing. It's just a silly rumor around here. You know how it is with rumors. Anyway before you go running off, I just wanted to ask you if you've seen my friend Amie while you were out running around town looking for your dog. She's tall, thin, pale skinned, long dark hair? I can't get a hold of her; she's not answering her phone."

Phoebe was clearly trying to brush off with her earlier haunted house comment, but since I was anxious to get back to Harley, I let her get away with it. "I didn't catch her name, but I saw a girl who matched that description. She was by herself at the park, sitting on the swings."

With a relieved grin, Phoebe clutched one of my hands between both of hers in a genuine handshake before dashing off to find her friend.

Once I arrived at the diner, I found that Harley was indeed being pampered relentlessly by Clyde the cook, who not only insisted on sending me home with a doggie bag of chicken cutlets for Harley, but he also packed two slices of fresh apple pie to take with me, stating that unpacking from a move was hungry work. He refused my money when I insisted on paying, instead making me promise to bring Harley by for another visit in the near future. I heartily agreed before slipping $20 into the tip jar when Clyde wasn't looking.

On the walk back home to the cottage, my thoughts centered around Phoebe's comment of it being haunted. Based on what I had experienced so far, I was starting to believe it was probably true and *not* a rumor.

As we neared the property, I decided to err on the side of caution and I reached over to clip Harley's leash to his collar. "You're not getting away this time, buddy." Harley just looked at me as we walked, his tail wagging happily in the breeze. The sun was just starting to peek through the clouds and it cast an innocent-looking halo behind the cottage, making me wonder if everything I had previously experienced was just all in my head.

As I unlocked the front door and unclipped Harley's leash, I looked around the living room to see if anything looked out of place. And then I laughed at myself when I realized the only thing to see was a wall of unpacked boxes that I had yet to tackle. Stifling a yawn, I watched Harley stretch before plopping himself down on his doggie bed.

Deciding to follow his lead for a much-needed nap, I kicked off my sneakers before heading for the couch, stopping in mid-stride as I passed by the TV. For good measure, I snagged my jacket off a nearby box and draped it over the front of the TV screen before collapsing on the couch. I was asleep almost instantly.

The only way I knew I was dreaming was because it felt like I was having some kind of trippy out of body experience. One moment I was lying on the couch sleeping; the next I was standing in the doorway between the kitchen and the living room. But when I looked in the direction of the couch, I saw myself lying there asleep.

Out of curiosity, I walked to my sleeping self and leaned over to poke my shoulder ... only to have my finger go through me. *Hmmm.* When I straightened up to my full height, I looked up and jumped with a shriek when I saw a woman watching me from the other side of the couch.

She was about my height and the clothes she was wearing were definitely dated; her blouse just looked old. Her hairstyle was also from decades past ... it reminded me of the bouffant style from the '60s that required too much hairspray to achieve that height.

But none of these details were terrifying. The terrifying part was the huge red gash across her neck. Especially when she opened her mouth and tried to speak. Nothing came out ... except for bubbling red blood from the gash in her neck.

Covering my eyes, I moaned, "Okay ... I wanna wake up now."

When I peeked through my fingers, I was surprised to see that she was gone. Exhaling in relief, I turned around and came face to face with her directly behind me. I let out a terrified scream. She was less than two inches from my face! The intensity in her black, soulless eyes was frightening. I couldn't look away as she stared silently back at me.

"I don't know what you want ... I'm scared," I whimpered. Without blinking, she pointed to the direction of the hallway. "You want me to go there? Okay, I'll go." Slowly edging my way around her, I exhaled a shaky breath once I reached the hallway.

Suddenly, a door opened.

Walking to the door, I looked down at the light that suddenly flashed on at the bottom of the stairs. I was looking into the basement of the cottage.

As I watched, the mystery lady instantly materialized at the bottom of the stairs and continued to stare up at me. "You want me to go down there? But I don't want to go down there. I draw the line at basements."

It didn't shock me that I was met with silence—what *did* shock me was the solid, brutal push that swiftly catapulted me down the stairs. I screamed the whole way down, not realizing until I landed at the bottom that I felt no pain. I mean, I should've broken my neck from that fall, and just that thought was terrifying enough. Dazed, I sat there and looked up when I saw movement. The mystery woman just stared unapologetically back at me as she stomped her foot on the concrete floor and pointed down.

Without taking her gaze from me, she repeated the motion and just watched me. "Okay ... I got it. There's something down there that you want me to get. Is that it?"

Shooting me a sinister glare, the woman slowly walked towards me before reaching behind her for something in her back pocket. When she pulled a wicked-looking knife out and started slashing the air in front of me, I screamed again and tried to crab-walk backwards out of her reach ... but I wasn't fast enough.

With her next slash, I felt a painful sting to my throat before the feeling of warm, thick blood began oozing out of the gaping cut. *This* was painful.

I tried to gasp in air. I couldn't catch my breath. Was I dying?

I lay on the ground and stared up at the ceiling, trying to make sense of it all. The last thing I saw before I fell unconscious was the cold, dark glare of the woman's eyes.

She slowly bent down to stare at my face, ensuring that *her* face was the last thing I saw before darkness claimed me.

I woke up with a loud gasp, my hands instantly going to my throat to check for the gaping cut. Harley was already awake.

He sat next to me, licking my face as if to tell me that everything was going to be okay. The dream was so realistic though, that I felt somehow obligated to follow through on my word and check beneath the basement floor. If I didn't find anything, then I'd have the peace of mind to put the dream behind me and move peacefully forward. Either way, I couldn't rest easy in the house until I acted on the dream.

Looking at my phone, I saw that I still had a few hours before the hardware store closed. After a quick call, I had arranged for the hardware store to drop off an electric jackhammer for rent. It was dropped off about twenty minutes later by a hesitant teenager named Jacob, who hovered uncertainly in front of my door with a million questions in his eyes.

Cutting to the chase, I explained, "So—I heard the rumor about this cottage being haunted. I've only been here for a day and a half and I have to say, Jacob ... I'm starting to believe the rumor is true. I also just had a crazy dream earlier where some unknown woman wanted me to dig beneath the basement floor. I'm afraid of what I'll find down there, but I decided I can't rest in my own home until I find out the truth to whether or not there's something under the basement floor. What do you think? Should I be worried?"

I chewed nervously on my bottom lip while I waited for his response, but was pleased nonetheless when Jacob responded with an enthusiastic, "So you're tearing up the floor? Cool! Can I help?"

When Jacob didn't return to work in a timely manner, the hardware store sent his older brother Jason (who also worked at the hardware store) to check on him. Jason's girlfriend Claire happened to be visiting when he was on break, so she decided to tag along on the quest to find Jacob. And that's how we all ended up in the basement thirty minutes later.

Harley was sitting on the floor between Claire and I while we watched the boys taking turns with the jack hammer. Claire had filled me in on the story about a woman named Rose who was a seamstress and lived in the cottage.

She had disappeared about 50 years ago but no one had been able to solve the mystery of what had happened to her. Some of her blood had been found in the driveway, but other than that, there were no other clues.

When the jackhammer finally turned off, the sudden silence was a blessed relief. Claire and I stared at one another before leaning forward to see what the boys had found.

"I think we found something!" Jacob exclaimed. The four of us stood looking down at the sizeable hole.

Through the debris we could see a flash of blue. Jason reached down to lift up a chunk of concrete.

We all jumped back and screamed.

There were remnants of a blue blouse, and beneath that, decaying skin and bone.

Desperately wanting out of the basement, we all tried to make a run for the stairs at the same time. We stopped when a loud booming voice demanded, "What the HELL is going on down here?!"

Blessedly, Deputy Sheriff Andy and his deputy, Chuck, had arrived. Their timing couldn't have been more perfect. The sheriff initially looked peeved that I had decided to damage the basement floor of a rental cottage based off of a "bad dream," but then exchanged an indecipherable look with his deputy after looking down at the obvious remains of a dead body. Shaking his head sadly, he muttered, "Well, now I guess we know what happened to poor Rose. May she finally rest in peace."

Deciding that I had had enough, I tossed my cottage keys to the sheriff and stated, "I decided that country living is not for me after all. I think I'm going back to Seattle. I'll return with a moving truck in the next two days to pick up my stuff."

And without a backward glance, Harley and I jumped into my SUV and drove off into the sunset, away from the town of Mirror Point.

WAY'S END OBSERVER
CLASSIFIEDS
OCTOBER 2019

SPECIAL – CENTENNIAL WEEKEND
Due to an unexpected cancellation the Bridal Suite
is available for the Centennial Week and the full
moon Halloween festivities.
Room includes the customary bottle of Champagne
and Fruit basket.
Be one of the first to welcome our new haunt,
Jennifer. She is friendly and looking forward to
meeting you and seeing the sites.
Breakfast starts at 7 a.m. and is included.
We are also offering a new brunch for you late sleepers.

BEST WAY INN BED AND BREAKFAST
400 Main Street, Way's End
Call 360-666-1111 ask for Norma

Dark Art
by Sonya Rhen

Detective Raymon Ramírez stared at the portrait of the dead girl. It was really one of his finest works. Last season's berries produced the perfect shade of blood red.

He'd only been sheriff a few years now after the tragic demise of the last one. He suspected the town's citizens were divided into two groups. The first group admired him for his easy charm and the good looks he had inherited from his father, and the fact that his sister, Rosalind Sánchez, was a longtime resident. This group dropped off baked goods at the sheriff's office for him. The second group distrusted him for his brown skin and the slight accent that he couldn't get rid of no matter how hard he tried. This group probably voted him into office hoping he would meet the same fate as his predecessor.

He felt a bump against his leg. He reached down to pet the black fur of Spook, the unofficial sheriff's cat. Spook had been around long before he became sheriff, would probably still be here long after he was gone. He walked to the "evidence room" at the back of the sheriff's office to grab the shoe box. It was, in fact, just a locked door which held rows of shelves containing shoe boxes. There were a few boot boxes for when they needed to hold bigger things. The shoe boxes were left over from the old Buster Brown Shoe Store that had been in this building before the sheriff's office.

You could still read the faint outline of the letters "Buster Brown" on the front of the building and Buster Brown and his dog smiled out from behind the Way's End Sheriff's Office sign. The town of Way's End couldn't afford to build a new sheriff's office and the shoe boxes were ideally suited for storing any evidence they needed, so there was no real reason to change.

He pulled out the box labeled for last October. It was a size 13 men's and felt heavier than it should, considering. It had been a full moon and he had plenty of reasons to worry that something bad would happen. He returned to his desk and opened the lid.

The scent of earth, fallen wet leaves and blood took him back there.

The call had come in early. A late season group of hikers was missing a member of their party. They had returned to the Way's End Campground the night before, stayed up late at the campfire drinking and eating s'mores. The next morning they packed up their tents early to catch the first ferry. Only one single-person tent was still up.

They found her later that day in the woods: mangled and mutilated.

"Bear attack," he said. "Sorry for your loss."

He knew better.

He took a picture with the official sheriff's office camera. (It was an old one that still used film.) Then he put her tennis shoes and any leaves and a small pile of dirt that held her blood into a size 13 men's shoe box and labeled it with the date.

Since that day, he returned to the spot and gathered moss, twigs and berries that grew there. He was even fortunate enough to find a raven's egg. He had to climb the top of a tree for that one. The raven still hadn't forgiven him, even though he left her the other eggs and brought her a rabbit he had trapped. Well, you couldn't please everyone. Occasionally, he still tried.

He burned the twigs. He had to do it several times. The black cat seemed to laugh at him. On the fourth try he managed to make charcoal instead of ash.

"Beautiful, huh, Spook?" he said. The cat blinked slowly. "You know it's not easy making charcoal. Different wood. Different drying times. Spontaneous combustion."

He opened the Altoid tin and selected a stick of charcoal. This one felt right. It was heavy and dark. He took his canvas and sketched the ground, the trees and the outline of the body.

Raymon got out the size 13 shoe box. He put the dirt and leaves with the dead girl's blood and mixed it into a plastic jumbo-sized ice cream container left over from the holidays. He poured in holy water and let it soak. Earthy browns with a hint of red brushed over the background giving the ground and trees depth and shadow.

"Hungry for eggs?" he asked Spook a few days later. He got eggs from a local who raised chickens that fed from the land. Raymon placed a dish of scrambled eggs on the floor for the cat. He used the rest of the eggs to make paint. He mixed it with more holy water from the Way's End Presbyterian Church. The minister was a good friend by now.

Raymon picked berries that grew almost on the exact spot where the body had lain. He dried them and because Spook was there, dried some rabbit meat after.

"Meow," Spook said.

"Yes, I washed the dehydrator after the berries," Detective Ramírez said. He hated being admonished by a cat. He held out a chunk of the meat. The cat's black nose sniffed it all over. Sharp teeth chomped down on the edge, nipping Raymon's finger. He wiped the blood on his trousers as he watched the black tail swish out of sight out the front door. He put the rest of the rabbit in a ziploc and stuck it in the fridge.

He ground the berries into a paste with some holy water and returned to the canvas. He painted the blood on the ground red with some of the brown from the other day. The girl's lips he painted red like they probably had been in real life.

"Es muy hermosa," he said. He painted red on her throat, chest and arms as he remembered it, as it was in the picture that sat on his desk for reference.

He was just getting in from his daily hike, when he saw the short Asian woman standing in front of the door to the sheriff's office.

"I baked you a lemon meringue pie," Mrs. Williams said. He suspected it was a thank you gift for driving her husband home from the bar the other night.

"It looks delicious. Thank you," he said as he took the pie she held out. He balanced it in one hand as he dug for his keys with the other. He twirled the keys on his pointer finger until he found the one for the front door. "I'm looking forward to seeing Dave play in the first football game."

She beamed proudly. "Yes, he likes playing football."

He waved goodbye and set the pie on the counter near the fridge. Spook snuck in before the door closed and sat on the floor eyeing the pie.

"You think you're getting my pie?" Raymon asked the cat. He pulled a raven's egg from his pocket and set it in an empty coffee mug. "You're not getting this egg either. Do you know how high I had to climb for this? You're lucky I didn't break my neck."

"Meow."

"Who would feed you, if I broke my neck?"

Spook blinked. "You are fickle, my friend. I'm sure everyone feeds you as soon as you leave here." He sighed, scooped a big spoonful of meringue onto the saucer he kept for the cat and held it up.

"Meow."

He placed it on the floor. "I thought that's what you'd say." He knew Spook had a sweet tooth. He licked his finger. Mrs. Williams made good pies.

He cracked the raven's egg into a bowl, separating the yolk. He plopped the golden yolk into a tray and mixed some of the moss-colored holy water he had prepared the day before. The green was very light and he cheated by adding some store-bought paint to the mixture. He painted the dark needles on the evergreens and the scant clumps of grass. The globules of paint seemed to bulge and pucker the canvas like the scales of a living thing.

On another day, he took the dried-out eggshells, including the one from the raven, that he had been saving and ground them to make an off-white. By that afternoon, blonde tresses spilled across the canvas. It fanned around the dead girl's face and reached out to touch the red splashes of color. The painting was nearly completed.

He could feel the pulse of dark energy emanating off the image before him. The shapes held it. The essence of each natural element held some part of it.

The canvas bulged at the head and the heart. The tiny dark fingers poked at the paint trying to spear through to touch him.

"No you don't," he said. Raymon picked up the spray bottle and misted holy water on each bulge until it flattened out.

He made the finishing touches to his painting and wiped his brow with the back of his thumb. He could feel the headache starting to throb and quickly tried to wipe off the paint.

Spook leapt into the window box on the side of the building. He pushed his nose through the tear in the screen and dropped down beside the painting. The hair stood up on his back.

"Hiss!"

The detective's large hand reached out to soothe the cat.

"Ow!"

Razor sharp claws left a trail on his arm for the effort.

"Perfect. Now I know it's finished."

He fed Spook in the back room away from the painting.

When it was dried, he put several coats of varnish on it. The painting was heavy: heavier than the mere canvas and paint should have been. He had captured part of the evil that flowed into Way's End. It wasn't enough. It would never be enough.

But it was something, and it was his job. At least he considered it to be part of his job as sheriff. He took care of crime. If evil wasn't criminal, then it should be.

Detective Ramírez shook off the memories. He placed the photo of the body, broken and angular, back in the size 13 shoe box. The leaves and dirt now gone, but remnants of them lingered in the scent of the soiled cardboard. Her tennis shoes caked in dried blood and dirt were the only things that had been found near the body. She had been cremated in her clothes and this was all that remained.

He closed the lid with a resigned finality. Sometimes evil permeated a place. It lingered and there was not a lot you could do about it. The little that he could do, he did do.

Raymon turned on the ancient computer with its fourteen-inch monitor the size of a breadbox. After the few minutes it took to warm up, he logged in to the online auction website with his user name, MalDeOjo. Spook seemed to give him 'the evil eye' and he glared back. The sleek black body squeezed between the bars to the cell on his left, turning his back to the whole thing. Spook didn't care for his plans.

Sometimes when you couldn't defeat evil, you could disperse it. Like a beautiful weed, you could scatter it to the farthest corners of the world.

¡Dios mío! He could only guess at the kind of person that would bid on his "masterpieces." Maybe it was wrong of him, but it was the only thing he knew to do.

He read through all the bids. He wasn't supposed to know where they were from, but he had installed software to show him that global intel. He selected the farthest one. Shipping would be expensive, but he had included that in the price. It looked like the Way's End's Sheriff's Department was getting a digital camera with these proceeds.

Detective Raymon Ramírez stared at the portrait of the dead girl on the computer monitor and clicked the button: Bid Accepted.

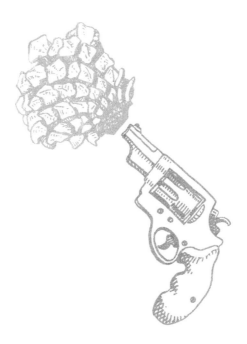

Everyone in the café turned to stare at her.

Venus Flytrap

by Susan Old

"A Venus Flytrap by any other name would kill the same." I drew a line through that sentence as soon as I wrote it. It was slow at the all-night cafe, so I worked on something for my creative writing class. It also helped take my mind off Amie who had disappeared three days ago. We had been besties since third grade. We covered up for each other, always had each other's back, and hated the same blonde cheerleaders all through high school.

A few days ago, out of nowhere she said she didn't need accounting classes, dropped out of the community college and called in sick to work. I really missed her snarky sense of humor at one o'clock in the morning. When she didn't answer her phone, I got worried. She was always on that damn phone.

I made up some missing person posters but then decided not put them up in town. Her parents were in Las Vegas for a weekend. I didn't want anyone to contact her family and upset them for nothing, but the feeling something was wrong was hard to shake.

A few guys from the AA meeting at the church wandered in. They ordered caffeine and sugar bombs. I filled their mugs and left a plate of donuts. It was the same every Tuesday night. After a few minutes one of the sober guys called to me trying to be polite. "Hey hon, some more coffee here! Please." Working the steps made them much more self-conscious. I left a pot on the table. They would be here for hours.

A few more people wandered in when the cinema closed. Townies refused to drive into Seattle unless they couldn't avoid it. They always studied the menu, even though it hadn't changed for twenty years. I gave Clyde their orders for loaded fries and sat back down by the register. I tuned everything out as I tried to figure out what to do about Amie.

Earlier today I had gone into Seattle to the goth club she had talked about for months. I had brought my missing person posters and put them up around Pioneer Square. As it got dark, I stayed away from the more poorly lit alleys. Of course, the only entrance to the club was down one of the darker ones. A small wooden sign with Funeral Pyre written in dark red script hung above stairs down to the club's entrance. Pretty creepy!

Clyde yelled, "Phoebe! Order up!"

He startled me out of my thoughts. "I'm not deaf," I muttered as I picked up the plates. I could have said anything because Clyde could barely hear cannon fire. He was eighty but looked eighty-five. I tried to force a smile as I put the grub on the table. The 'Friendly' in Friendly Café was a town joke. Now that I had taken care of everyone I tried to focus on what to do about Amie.

I had taped the missing person image of Amie from a high school photo she hated on the wall at the bottom of the stairs to the club. It was the creepiest, scariest place I had ever been in. I jumped when someone came up behind me. I moved to put my back against the old brick. A tall, sexy, handsome guy with Jamaican dreads and black leather looked at me like he was pissed. "Take it down!" he snapped. I thought my heart was going to explode.

"My friend is missing. I think she was here recently." I stammered as I clutched my few remaining posters tightly. "Have you seen her?" I was about to give my Nikes a work-out when he responded.

"I'm sure you'll hear from her soon." A smile barely softened his hard stare. "This is my club and my building." He tore Amie's image off the wall. "It's getting very late. You should go home. Now!"

I shot up the stairs, took off running and did not stop till I got to my car on the third floor of the parking garage. I locked my doors twice and almost crashed my Prius as I spun out of the structure and onto the street. WTF! Who was that? Did he know my friend? I was more worried than ever.

Clyde broke my train of thought again as he leaned over the grill counter and pointed to a corner table; it was Herbert Selinger. He was sort of old, skinny, and balding. Amie nicknamed him Sleazinger, because of the way he always stared at her. Amie was tall, skinny with long dark shiny hair, but I was chubby with brown frizzy hair. She had broken a few hearts. I'd had a few broken.

I walked over to his table, and in my most professional waitress way asked, "What do you want?" He turned his phone over as I looked down. It was pics of women I bet he would never have a chance with.

"You the only one working?"

I ignored his question and just stared.

"Cheeseburger and fries, no onions." He put down his menu and took hand sanitizer out of his pocket. The café was a nightmare for a clean freak. As I walked away he called out, "And Diet Pepsi."

Clyde took the order and I knew I'd have a few minutes of peace. Since I got back from Seattle my paranoia had only increased. I was about to call the cops when I got this text message from Amie. *It's all good, chill. I'll be in touch.* WTF! I tried calling but no answer. Whatever. I guess I just had to trust her. I mean that text sounded like her.

Clyde yelled, "Order up!"

I chuckled because he had ignored what I'd written about no onions. I dropped the plate in front of the creep and walked away. It took about five seconds before he groused about his meal. Sometimes I found satisfaction in my work.

A stranger walked in and sat at the counter. He pulled back his Dodger's hoodie and said, "Black coffee please." He was a young, outrageously handsome Latino with straight dark hair pulled back in a ponytail.

I put the mug on the counter and managed a natural smile. "Anything else?"

His eyes showed amusement. "No." He lightly touched my hand as he handed me a twenty and said, "Keep the change, hon."

That was a first. I briefly considered framing that twenty-dollar bill. "Thanks!"

"Hey, Pheebs!" Amie walked in. Everyone in the café turned to stare at her. Herbert's eyes almost popped out. She was wearing skin-tight black jeans and a tiny Joan Jett T-shirt that showed her midriff. In place of her usual skull necklace she had a menacing bat pendant. Black eyeliner emphasized her large brown eyes.

I came from behind the counter and hugged her tightly. "I've been so worried about you!" I tried not to tear up. "Are you okay?"

"Clyde!" Amie yelled, "she's taking a five-minute break!"

He nodded and got back to cleaning his grill like everything was normal. We sat down at the far end of the café away from the others. I saw Sleazinger take a pic of her with his phone.

"I went to Seattle looking for your sorry ass. This big guy in leather sort of threatened me."

"You're lucky he realized you were my friend. That was Henry. You were in the presence of greatness," she whispered. "He's in the band Carnage."

"Great what? Why are you whispering?"

She grinned. "You won't see me again for quite a while, maybe years. I'm making a major lifestyle change. I left a letter for my parents. I wanted to tell you before I left. I waited in the park the other day, but I was afraid you'd guilt me into staying. When you came by the club, I knew I had to tell you in person."

"What are you talking about? Did you join some religious cult?"

She tried not to laugh. "They have never been called that. You know that crap about my rare blood type, you know, HH. I always thought it was kind of a pain, but it turns out it's my ticket out of this shitty town. I've been invited to join an organization that does hematology research."

"You flunked out of chemistry. C'mon, really? Who are these friends?"

She looked over at the guy at the counter. "Angel!"

He strolled over and joined us. If they all looked like he did I could see why she was eager to be with her new friends. He glanced at Herbert then back at Amie. "Is that him?"

Amie nodded. "He'll follow me out. He always does when I take a smoke break."

"Are you from Seattle?" I wanted to ask if he had a brother.

Angel looked at me and I felt warm and fuzzy all over. "Los Angeles. It's why they call me Angel." He turned to Amie. "We must leave. The ferry has stopped running, it will take a couple of hours to drive back across the bridge and get to the city ." He smiled. "Good night, Phoebe," he purred. "Perhaps we'll meet again."

I died. I mean literally died, but somehow my heart kept beating. "Yeah, sure." I mumbled. His cologne lingered. I breathed it in and sighed. I watched him walk out the door.

Amie chuckled. "You really need to leave Mirror Point. Get a job in a coffee stand or a bookstore somewhere. Maybe Olympia or Portland, where you can find some gamer guy and live happily ever after. You're the only one I'll miss. Some night you'll understand."

That was the last thing she said to me. Then she pulled an envelope with my name on it out of her purse and put it on the table. As she left, Amie tore a poster about the town's centennial off the wall and dropped it on the floor.

Herbert shoved the last of his cheeseburger in his mouth, threw some money on the table and followed close behind Amie.

I opened the envelope. It was three thousand dollars in hundred-dollar bills. "What the hell?" I counted it again. She gave me relocation money. I looked out of the Main Street window, but all I saw were the tail lights of a sports car breaking the speed limit as it left town. Herbert's car was still there, but I did not notice him. It had been such a weird night I didn't give it much thought.

When I got off shift at six, I was ready for bed. It had been pretty quiet after Amie and Angel's visit. Clyde was pissed when I told him she had quit. He banged the pans around a little louder than usual. I wondered if Amie and her new friend had robbed a bank. I held on tightly to my purse as I started to walk home.

A piercing scream startled me. A woman with her dog on a leash stood near the dumpster behind the café. I rushed over ready to help. Then I saw the mangled body. Herbert was on his back covered in blood. His bottle of hand sanitizer placed on his chest. Herbert's eyes stared blankly at the world. I grabbed the woman's arm and pulled her back as I called the cops.

It took fifteen freaking minutes for someone to pull on his pants and drive a couple of blocks. When Chuck, the youngest of our three finest, saw the grisly scene he was like a kid at Christmas. His reaction made me less grossed out and more excited. It was his first murder and it was grue-some.

Someone had slashed Herb's throat and left him to bleed out like a pig. Soon the fire volunteers showed up with their ambulance even though it was pretty useless, unless some townie fainted. It took an hour for the sheriff to arrive sirens blaring. Half the town gathered around.

Clyde, not one to miss an opportunity, sold some coffee and donuts to the bystanders. Herbert was left untouched for the coroner. Some people stared at the body, a few even took out their phones to take pictures, but I had seen enough of Herbert to last a lifetime.

I gave all my information to the deputy, so I could go home. What a night. I was halfway to my apartment on top of the beauty shop, when it dawned on me that Amie was probably the last person to see Herbert alive, besides the killer. I mumbled, "No way," as I opened the door to my place. I collapsed on my bed certain she had nothing to do with it.

At the god-awful hour of noon, someone pounded on my door. "Phoebe Gaskins, it's the police!"

I sat up and yelled, "Coming!" Then walked over to the door. "What?"

It was Chuck. "We've got a few questions about last night."

I looked past him, but he was alone. "Sure, whatever, just make it quick so I can get back to sleep." I grabbed a glass of water. "Want some?"

"No thanks." He looked at the collection of dirty glasses on my counter.

I sat across from him at my two-chair kitchen table. He was very bland looking. Chuck was blond enough to be part Norwegian. We had a lot of them in town.

"What do you want to know? I told you I didn't hear or see anything."

He stared at me intently and asked, "Who was at the café last night?"

I told him about all the usual customers. I knew I would have to mention Amie, because Clyde would have. "My friend Amie Brown came by for a few minutes with her boyfriend. She's moved to Seattle, but I don't have her new address. Her boyfriend's name is Angel. She just told me she decided to quit her job. That's all. I was bummed to see her go."

"Did she or her boyfriend talk to Mr. Selinger?"

"Herbert? No. I was the only one he talked to, and I just took his order."

"Hmm," he frowned. "What's Angel's last name?"

"No clue, but he was nice. Gave me a big tip."

"Did they all leave the café at the same time?"

I was lucky he didn't say 'about'. "No, Amie and Angel left before Herbert. Do you have any idea who did this?"

"No." He looked down like he was hiding something.

"What's going on? That Herbert was always weird, stared at women."

"Good instincts. If you ever get that feeling about anyone else, let me know. This will be on the news tonight, so I might as well tell you. It turns out Herbert Selinger was a serial killer. He retired from a large aircraft manufacturer and moved here. That's when young women started going missing around U.W. We found evidence hidden in a trunk in his house. Souvenirs of women he murdered going back ten years."

"Amie?" I uttered. My hands trembled.

He kindly reached over and patted my hands. "No evidence of any local victims. The only blood at the scene last night was his, and about half of his blood was gone. No fingerprints or weapons. Coroner can't figure it out. I shouldn't say this, but whoever did this, I won't lose sleep if they aren't apprehended."

After the deputy left I lay in bed as thoughts of grisly murders filled my head. Sleazinger had killed ten women that they knew of. I didn't even want to think about the pictures of women he had on his phone. It gave me a sick feeling in my stomach. I had served cheeseburgers to a monster.

From now on I would be nicer to the customers. Amie was alive, but what kind of hematology research were she and Angel involved in? I flashed on an old vampire movie, then shook my head. No way. Right?

I sat up and started working on my Creative Writing assignment, "A Venus Flytrap by any other name would kill the same ..."

The Costume
by Hugh Mannfield

Roxy struggled to control the swerving SUV. Gravel flew as her tires dug into the shoulder and then bit into the pavement. She groped blindly for her phone as the headlights swung wildly, casting stark shadows into the forest along the road.

"Come on ... pick up!"

"Hello ..."

"Andy! Andy! I just saw it!"

"What?"

"That thing!"

"Huh?"

"That thing everybody's been seeing all month!"

"Holy shit! Where are you?"

"I don't know! A mile or so out of town on Four Mile Road. Are you on duty?" The SUV tires squealed as Roxy sped around a curve in the road.

"Roxy, are you driving?"

"Of course I am!"

"Well, pull over if you're gonna talk."

"Oh no, it was huge ... I ain't stopp'n for noth'n! It came out of the trees right in front of me ... it had these red eyes ... I nearly drove off the road!"

"How fast are you going?"

"About ninety!"

"Jesus, Roxy, slow it down! You caught me on my way to the station, I'll head out on Four Mile Road right now. Lucky I was still in the west end of town. You should see my lights coming up in a minute or two."

Richard smiled to himself. This was a good stretch of road, nothing but single cars with lots of space in between. One more and he would pack it up for the night. The trees along the roadside began to glow faintly and he could hear the low hiss of tires off to the east. He crouched down beside a large tree trunk.

Richard tensed as the lights drew near. At fifty yards, he rose and lumbered out of the brush toward the shoulder of the road and turned toward the oncoming vehicle. Tires squealed as the car swerved and flew past, dropping two wheels off the opposite shoulder. It skidded for twenty yards, bounced back up on the road and sped off at full acceleration.

"Ha! That was a good one! I bet he shit his pants!" exclaimed Richard as he watched the car disappear into the night. He wheeled around at the sound of squealing tires from behind. A pickup truck was skidding to a stop a hundred yards back up the road. A bank of lights mounted above the cab flashed on, catching him in a blinding glare.

"Fuck!" Richard darted for the trees. As he got under cover, he glanced back to see a man jump from the truck, rifle in hand. Richard pelted down the trail as fast as his oversize boots could go. The first shot whizzed overhead, splintering the bark of a nearby tree. He dodged down the winding trail at breakneck speed. He could hear running footsteps and voices at the trail head.

"Did you see that thing!"

"Yeah, it went into the woods right about here."

"Come on ... Let's get it!"

Richard dove head long down the trail into the ravine. No time to stop and remove the costume. He came to the suspension bridge. Just across it would be a short run to the shack, but he would be totally exposed for too long. He would never make it across alive. *Better take the long way down and up, at least there's cover.* Skipping the bridge, he plunged on down the trail.

As he neared the stony creek at the bottom, Richard tugged at the zipper under his chin only to be reminded how earlier that evening, while donning the suit, he had to secure it with a zip tie to keep it from sliding open. Now to remove it he needed the clippers which were in the shack. He looked up through the dense cedars. Flashlight beams played back and forth across the suspension bridge.

"Do you think it crossed?"

"No … it went on down the trail."

"Okay you take that side and I'll take this … We'll catch it between us."

Richard swore to himself. *I didn't think about that … now what?* He yelled up at the hunters, "Hey don't shoot, it's only a costume!" But the voice modulator in the headpiece turned his words into garbled animal noises. This only invited a hail of bullets. With no other options, Richard left the trail, following the creek downstream.

The cold dark water swirled around his feet, filling the boots and slowing his progress. When he judged he was just about below the shack, he crossed the stream and started zigzagging up the opposite bank of the ravine. The beam of a flashlight swept across his location and then snapped back onto him. He scrambled for the thicker cover above.

"Bill! I saw it coming up your side! It moves pretty fast for its size."

"Okay, Doug, you work your way above it on your side and I'll try to flush it out."

They're going to hunt me down like an animal. He hunkered down behind a large tree trunk between an outcropping of fern covered rocks. Each breath he took was amplified into the huffing of a great beast. He tore at the zipper with all his strength but it wouldn't budge. All he could do was twist his head away from the microphone because the voice modulator off switch couldn't be reached until the head piece came off.

Sweat trickled down the back of his neck.

Flashlight beams played over the area where he hid. As they moved off, Richard made a scramble for another hiding place.

The rock he planned to climb was larger than he thought and his first grab came away with only a handful of moss. The light beam from across the ravine found him, but he quickly leapt and scrambled over the rock.

The crack of a rifle split the night and he felt the tug as a bullet ripped through the padding above his left shoulder. Richard fell in between two rocks where a large tree sprouted.

"STOOOOOP!" he yelled, which came out as a loud angry bellow.

"Bill, I think I hit it!"

"I think you pissed it off. How many rounds you got left?"

"About a dozen. You?"

"I got five."

Tears welled up in Richard's eyes. This was not the fun he had planned. He could hear his mother's last words in his ear, "*now be safe*," and began to sob, which remarkably came out sounding like sobbing.

"Listen to that. Bill! Is it crying?"

"I don't know what it's doing, but at least we know where it is."

Richard sprang up and scrambled for a cluster of trees up the ravine to his left. Just as his momentum carried him into the cover, a bullet ripped into his right shoulder blade. He fell howling among the tree trunks.

"I got it that time! Bill, can you get a shot?"

"Yeah, give me a minute to get into position."

Richard's mouth went dry and his stomach turned. In a few moments his life would be over. The sickening dread of death enveloped him. Strangely, his breath stilled and his senses heightened. There was an odd musky odor in the air, skunk-like, but different. He lay on his back looking up through the trees, waiting for the slam of the final shot. In a small clear patch of sky above he could see the wisp of a cloud move off, revealing a cluster of stars in the night, possibly the last he would ever see. He could hear each footstep above and across the ravine. He could hear the snap of each twig as the hunter drew close.

Up above, a shadow passed over the patch of sky. Something moved in the night. Something huge. Something fast, but strangely graceful.

A scream from the hunter nearby split the night but was cut off short. The hunter's rifle landed in the brush not far from Richard and then something else crashed and tumbled down the slope to the bottom of the ravine. The shadow passed over him again. It paused, hovering, just for a moment. Richard lay frozen, holding his breath. He could sense a thing of awesome power and size hidden in the shadow, standing above him. It seemed to be regarding him. In an instant it disappeared into the night, as if it never had been.

"Bill? …. Bill? You alright?" Silence. "Bill! Answer me!"

Richard dragged himself up and peered out between the trees. He could see the swinging light beam of the other hunter's flashlight as he beat a hasty retreat back up the ravine. A hellish nightmare of clawing through brush and dragging himself up the slope followed before he reached the trail. Richard managed to get to his feet and stagger the last few yards to the door of the shack.

A shaking left hand eventually managed to snip the zip tie and the headpiece flopped back. Richard gulped a breath of fresh air. He worked his left arm free of the costume, but the right, crusted in blood, dirt, and twigs, wasn't going anywhere. His phone was there on the workbench where he had left it. Richard dialed 911 and collapsed on the floor.

As she swerved around another corner, Roxy spotted Andy's red and blue flashing lights coming up the other way. She finally lifted her foot off the accelerator. A passing lane opened on the right side of the road and Roxy swerved her vehicle to a screeching stop. Andy circled his patrol truck around, came up behind her, and stepped out.

Roxy sprang from the SUV and flung herself into his arms, clinging tightly. "Oh Andy, I've never been so scared in my life! I never believed such things really existed in this world."

Andy held her trembling body. Whatever had happened had shaken Roxy to the core, not an easy thing to do to this tough mountain girl. Roxy, a volunteer for the sheriff's office, had helped out the department more than once at some pretty horrific highway accidents and never flinched. "Okay, you're gonna be alright. Get in my truck and I'll take you to the station to file a report."

"Hold me, a little longer … please."

Andy sighed. He was already late reporting in for the night shift, what were a few more minutes? He brushed the tears away from Roxie's cheeks. Her trembling continued.

"You ever seen a monster, Andy? A real monster?" she choked.

"Can't say that I have."

"Well, I never thought I would, but they're real. Real! D'you hear me!?" She shuddered.

Andy walked her around to the side of his truck and helped her in. Settling in behind the wheel, he backed his truck up and swung out into the road, driving slowly back to town. Roxy had calmed down quite a bit by the time the pair walked into the Mirror Point Sheriff's Station.

The sheriff checked his watch as he spotted Andy enter the office. "Late again, Andy … what was it this time?"

Andy hesitated. "Uh … Roxy … I mean Roxanne has a monster sighting to report."

The sheriff snorted. "Ha! You're a day late and a dollar short … again. That's all over an done with!"

"Huh?"

"When did you wake up?"

"About half an hour ago."

"And you didn't turn on your radio?"

"No."

The sheriff slapped his knee and burst out laughing. "Boy, you sure missed out tonight! We've had our hands full the past three or four hours, and you slept right through it!"

Andy looked around. "How's that?"

"It turns out the Johnson boy thought it would be a hoot to dress up like Bigfoot and scare people along the road at night. Seems like he's been doin' it all month."

"The high school track star? How did …" Andy was cut off by the sheriff's upheld palm.

"Well, tonight he got more than he bargained for. He ran into a couple of hunters and managed to get himself shot."

"No!"

"You can see for yourself, we've got the costume in the evidence locker, bullet holes, blood stains, and all."

Andy looked dumbfounded. "Is he dead?"

"Not quite, he's up at the hospital in surgery. He'll probably live, but he may never compete again. Stupid boy!" The sheriff walked over to the coffee station and poured a cup. "That's more than I can say for one of the hunters. Now he managed to fall down a ravine and break his neck." He looked Andy in the eyes. "Yes, that one is dead."

Andy slumped into his desk chair. "But this doesn't make any sense."

The sheriff settled into his chair. "The boys are fishing the body out of Cook's Ravine east of town right now. You might consider going out to lend a hand, if that ain't too much for you."

That was it. Roxy stormed up to the sheriff and squared off. "You just leave Andy alone! He does a fine job around here and you know it! He gets all the shit jobs no one else will take and never complains a bit!" The sheriff rocked back in his chair, a bit stunned. "Besides that, it's *you* that has *your* facts mixed up!"

"How's that Roxy?"

"Well, *I* saw that thing crossing Four Mile Road *WEST* of town not *FIFTEEN* minutes ago!"

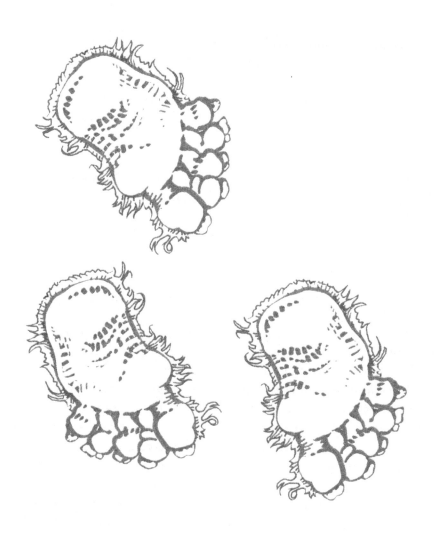

MIRROR POINT ECHO
HEADLINE NEWS

Hunter Falls to Death; MPHS Track Star Shot

Mirror Point resident and avid hunter, Bill Williams, died last Friday night from massive trauma he suffered resulting from a fall down Cook's Ravine. Sightings of the "Mirror Point Monster" apparently inspired MPHS decathlon hopeful Richard Branson to create a costume he used to frighten motorists along several roads leading into Mirror Point. Reports indicate that Williams and a partner attempted to hunt down what they thought to be the monster. Richard is recovering from surgery for a bullet wound to his right shoulder at Mirror Point General Hospital. His prognosis is good, but his decathlon hopes may be finished. See section D4 for obituary and service announcements for Mr. Williams. The Sheriff's Office has not released the identity of the second hunter, pending investigation, but has declared the "Mirror Point Monster" a hoax. The Echo, however, continues to receive reports of sightings post-dating this incident.

She picked out a spot, sat cross-legged on the ground ...

A Good Family

by christine Gustavson-Udd

The car squealed around a corner, shifting Jane against the door. "*Cheese-whiz!* Could you slow down please! That sign said twenty-five!" Jane dug her nails into the arm rest, her eyes glued to the road, willing the car to stay on it.

"That's only for the tourists." RJ smirked. "I've driven this road a million times, and much faster. I was goin' slow 'cuz you're in the car."

Her grip loosened after they were through Dead Man's Curve. "I think I saw a sign back there for a museum. Could we go tomorrow?"

"Nah, we're going to be too busy waterskiing and taking out the ATV's to do any of that tourist trap stuff." He dismissed her idea with a wave of his hand.

Jane's shoulders slumped. She murmured, "I've never water skied before. I'm willing to give it a shot, but I don't know how good I'll be." She sat up straight and smiled hopefully. "Maybe we'd have a little time afterwards to go into town?"

"Maybe, but I have to study this weekend too. Don't you have homework?"

"Yeah, I have to do a painting. I was thinking there would be some good scenery here I could paint." Her eyes turned towards the car window, scanning the landscape they passed.

"No, I mean don't you have any *real* homework? Like math or science?" He gave her a side-eye glance.

"Um," Jane tried to not get mad at his snarky comment; she didn't want to have their first fight. She took a breath and chose her words carefully. "I'm not taking any math or science this semester, I'm taking art. A painting is my homework."

"Ah." He frowned and shook his head.

"I'm really nervous about meeting your parents. I hope they like me." Jane looked at him hoping for reassurance.

"Don't worry about it. I have friends up here all the time," RJ said offhandedly.

Jane's heart sank. "Friends or *girlfriends?*"

"Friends. I've never brought a girlfriend up here before." RJ put his hand on her leg.

Jane smiled, grabbed his hand and held it.

They pulled into the driveway of a very rustic-looking cabin. Red gingham curtains rustled in the window. A chubby middle-aged man wearing khaki's and a button-down shirt burst out of the door.

"Uh-hmm, here we go," RJ said just before they got out of the car. Jane gave him a puzzled look.

"Jane, this is my dad, Rich Goodman," RJ said. Mr. Goodman stuck out his hand and flashed a gleaming white smile. Jane shook it.

"Great to meet you. I'd like to say my son has told me a lot about you, but he hasn't." Rich chuckled. His son shot him a dirty look.

Jane smiled shyly. "Pleased to meet you, Mr. Goodman." She tried to take her hand back.

"Please, call me Rich. Here, let me give you the tour." Rich led her by the hand towards the cabin.

"It's a basic cabin, but there's indoor plumbing now. I had it put in a couple of years ago. I would've done it myself, but I'm too busy with my businesses."

That explains the 'business casual' outfit on a weekend at a lake cabin.

Rich led her around the side of the cabin. "Here's the well— I've had that water tested. It's better than any bottled water." Jane smiled and nodded, trying to look interested. "My grandfather built this place with his own two hands." He smiled and puffed up with pride. Jane smiled back. "It was one of the first on Spirit Lake, long before all the tourists came in. We owned most of the property on this side of the lake, so they had to build the hotel up north of us. We sold *our* land only to *good* families. Those cabins have been passed down through the generations. We know everybody on this lake. Every Sunday after church, we host a huge bar-be-que for the cabin crowd."

Still hand-in-hand, they walked past a wooden building. "What's that? A bunkhouse?"

"It's a smoke house."

"Wow! It's huge!" Jane remarked.

"You bet! You could lay down in there."

Jane made a silly wide-eyed scared face. They laughed.

"Patience makes the best smoked meats you'll ever taste! She has a secret she won't tell anyone, not even me." He winked at Jane. She smiled.

"It's really no secret," a petite blonde woman wearing an apron came out the back door of the cabin. "I just use the best meat— free range. Hi. You must be Jane. I'm delighted to meet you. Welcome to our home away from home." She held out her dainty hand in a way that made Jane wonder if she was supposed to kiss it or shake it.

Mr. Goodman finally let go of Jane's hand, so it was free for his wife to shake. Jane was relieved and hoped she wouldn't have to hold hands with *Mrs.* Goodman too. Patience gave Jane's hand a quick gentle squeeze.

"Would you like to bring your things in?"

"I haven't showed her the boat house or the lake yet," Rich complained.

"Plenty of time for that later. Go get your things out of the car. I'll have you sleep in the kids' room. Rich Junior can sleep on the couch in the family room."

Jane stifled a giggle. *Junior.*

"Mom, we're in college. I think we're old enough to share a room," RJ insisted.

"Not in my house!" Rich put his hands on his hips. "Not without being married!"

RJ rolled his eyes at Jane. She shrugged. "Whatever. My parents would've agreed with that." Her hand went to the locket that hung next to her heart.

Jane got her bags from the car and brought them into the cabin. Stepping through the door was like going back in time. On the old-fashioned wood paneling hung framed yellowed newspaper clippings, black and white photos, stuffed ducks, and blue ribbons.

Rich waited inside for her. "My dad, RJ's grandfather, shot all of these ducks. Here, this one is really rare to see around here," he boasted.

"It's beautiful," Jane said. *Too bad he shot it.*

"Are these blue ribbons for the ducks?" Jane asked.

"No, some are for Patience's smoked meats, some her flowers."

"Here's where you can put your things." Rich led Jane to a small room with twin beds. The window looked out over the cool clear lake. "Wow," Jane whispered to herself.

"Get your suit on. We'll take the boat out." Rich grinned like a kid at Christmas.

She nodded and closed the bedroom door to change. She took off her locket and carefully tucked it into a zippered pocket. She dug around in her bag and pulled out a bikini and an oversized T-shirt. She put them on, then tugged at the T-shirt and wished it was longer. She looked down and saw it was her "Meat is Murder" Tee. She yanked it off, wadded it up, stuffed it back into her bag and got a different T-shirt and some shorts. She smiled, satisfied with her outfit.

She opened the door. RJ was standing right outside.

"I didn't bring any sunscreen." Jane looked down at the floor.

"Oh, we have some." RJ led her to a cupboard, inside were several bottles of vintage suntan lotion. She regretted not bringing her own.

"Is your mom coming?"

"She has cooking to do."

Jane looked towards the kitchen, saw his mom chopping on a huge dark wooden cutting board that took up most of the kitchen counter. *I wonder how she washes it?*

"Should we offer to help?" Jane asked.

"Nah, she doesn't like anyone in her kitchen."

"Oh, okay." Jane smiled weakly.

They walked out the back door and headed down the steep rocky path to the lake. Jane wished she was wearing hiking boots instead of flip-flops. When she saw there was no handrail, she wished for hiking poles too. She walked slowly, watching every step until she reached the dock.

"Here, this one should fit you." Rich handed Jane a lifejacket.

Jane slipped it on. "It's pretty loose. How do I adjust the straps?"

"Hey now, that one's mine!" Rich smirked at her. "Blame Patience's cooking."

Jane found the end of the strap, pulled it tight. "Wow, look at how much slack I had to pull in!" Jane giggled mischievously. RJ shook his head.

"Ha-ha. Be serious now. I'll drive the boat, RJ can help you get the skis on," Rich said.

RJ got her feet in the waterskies and handed her the rope. Rich hit the boat's accelerator, yanked Jane out of the skis and face first into the water. She came up coughing and spitting out lake water.

Rich circled the boat back around. From the driver's seat he yelled, "You're supposed to bend your knees! Try it again!"

Jane braced herself but was dragged face first through the water again. "Are you trying to *drown* me?"

"RJ will show you the right way to do it!"

RJ made water skiing look as easy as walking. He was an old pro, having spent every summer of his life at the cabin. His dad circled the boat back around. RJ sent a single ski skidding towards Jane whom he'd left standing in the shallows. She jumped out of the way of the projectile.

"Hey!" *Show off.*

When they circled back around again, RJ tried to drop the other ski and ski barefoot, but he fell.

"My dad slowed down too much. I can barefoot ski going faster and out in deeper water."

Rich pulled the boat up to the dock and got out. "Watch me and try again," his dad said.

Jane's arms and legs quivered. "I'm exhausted. I'd like to go in for a hot shower."

"Here. We keep soap and shampoo on the dock. This lake is as clean as the well water. You might as well get cleaned up down here, as long as you're soaked already. Then you'd better get out of the sun. You're fried to a crisp!" Rich chuckled.

Jane washed her hair in the lake and felt sorry for herself, having to rough it.

"We should take the ATV's out. My brother broke his collar bone last year flying off of one, but he had a helmet on, so he's OK."

Jane's eyes opened wide. "You're not getting me on one of those things!"

"Ah, come on! It'll be fun!"

"I really don't want to. Couldn't we go into town? I'd like to see the museum and look around."

"*Come on!* We need the daylight to drive through the woods! We can go into town later."

"Nope. Nuh-uh!" Jane shook her head.

"Suit yourself. I'm going. You do what you want."

Jane paused, frowned and thought about giving in. "I need to do a painting. I'll work on that while you're gone."

"Knock yourself out."

RJ got an ATV out, revved the engine a few times. His dad came out to scold him about the exhaust fumes. He put on a helmet and sped away.

Jane took her paper and watercolor paints outside and strolled around the cabin. She'd been so attentive to Mr. Goodman's tour, she hadn't noticed the blood-red flowers growing there.

She picked out a spot, sat cross-legged on the ground and began to lightly sketch.

"Oh," she smacked her forehead with her hand, "I forgot water." She went back into the cabin.

In the kitchen, Patience hacked up meat with a cleaver that was impressively large for a little lady.

Jane averted her eyes. "Is there a glass you don't mind me using for painting?"

Patience held up her blood-soaked hands. "Please help yourself, dear."

"Thanks." Jane took a glass from the cupboard, filled it with water, and scurried back outside.

The flowers were breathtaking. Jane inhaled deeply and caught a whiff of something rotten. She wrinkled up her nose. *Fertilizer? Or maybe a squirrel or chipmunk died nearby.*

She finished the picture, took it inside and put it on the dining room table to dry.

"Why, isn't that lovely? Could I keep it? I'll frame it and hang here at the lake."

"I need to turn it in for a class, but after it's graded, I'll give it to you." Jane grinned, pleased that Patience liked her painting.

"I look forward to that very much." Patience smiled back. "I'll hang my blue ribbons around the painting."

"Thank you! I'm so honored." Jane blushed. "Your flowers grow so big. The blooms are stunning. How do you make them so lovely?"

"I grind up what remains after I make my award-winning smoked meats. It makes a nutrient-rich fertilizer. *Waste not, want not.*"

"Doesn't it attract animals?"

"Not usually, but sometimes I get lucky and the flower beds entice something tasty."

Eww! Like racoons and possums? She fought to keep her feelings hidden, so as not to appear rude. *Judge not least ye be judged,* her mother always said.

"RJ said you prefer to do things yourself, but would you like help in the kitchen?"

"Oh, no thank you, dear. There's a method to my madness." Patience smiled sweetly.

"I'm glad you said no. I saw my mom cut up a chicken once and I can't eat meat anymore." Jane's face turned a little green, remembering the sight.

"That's a pity. I do hope you're tempted by my award-winning cooking."

Jane smiled weakly. "I have a little required reading to do for school. I guess I should do that."

Patience nodded.

She went to her room and dug a book out of her bag. Walking to the front porch, she sat down on the wooden seat. It swung gently as bees and butterflies floated by on a warm breeze. A chipmunk skittered past her feet. *You better run, little guy. Mrs. Goodman will smoke you.* Jane pictured the little lady chasing down a chipmunk and giggled.

An ATV thundered up the driveway.

When RJ took off his helmet she asked, "Did you have a good time?"

"Oh yeah, it's always fun on the ATV. You should try it sometime."

"Mmm. Maybe if I could go really slow." She smiled.

"Nah, you gotta goose it." RJ mimed twisting the throttle. "Vroom, vroom!"

"No thanks, then." *Better safe than sorry,* Jane remembered her mother saying.

"You're not really livin' if you don't live dangerously." He untied a tarp from the back of the ATV. Something was wrapped in it.

"What's that?" Jane asked.

"Something for my mom."

"Oh?" Jane said, not sure how to react. She glanced around and hoped there were free range cows there.

"A fawn. Its mama got hit by a car. Little guy wouldn't have survived on his own. He doesn't have to suffer. We get young fresh venison. It's a win-win." He walked around the side of the cabin.

Jane shivered. She couldn't help but think about the poor little deer and his mama.

RJ returned. He ran his hands through his helmet hair.

"Could I borrow your car and go into town? Do you want to go with?"

"Sure, I'll drive."

"Can we go to the museum?"

"Our family stays away from the tourist traps, usually."

"Have you ever been?"

"No."

"Then you don't know if it's touristy or not."

"Ok. Let's go."

They hopped in his car.

"Please slow down! Are you trying to kill me?"

"Relax, I've done this a million times."

The museum was a small old-fashioned house, a museum of the history of the town. Not very exciting.

"See? What'd I tell ya?" He smirked.

"Is there a bakery? I'd like to pick up something for your mom. Maybe they have a good dessert for after dinner?"

They went to The Piehole: Pies and More Bakery and Café. The baker was a round, rosy-cheeked man.

"RJ! Great to see ya! How's college?"

"I'm killin' it." RJ smiled a smug little grin.

"Is this your girlfriend? Say, she's delicious!"

"Yeah, Jane's special."

Jane blushed and looked down at the display case. "I'd like to buy that pie, please."

"Cherry, great choice! I'll box it up for you."

Jane stepped to the register where a young girl took her money. Jane smiled. The girl looked away.

"Here you go." The baker handed Jane the box. "So great to see you RJ. Great to meet you Jane. See you at the barbeque!" The baker grinned ear to ear.

They walked out of the bakery and heard a wolf-whistle. A man yelled, "She's scrumptious, RJ!"

Jane was taken aback. "People here are sure, *friendly*. Could we head back to your cabin?"

"Yeah, we'd better get back. Mom will have dinner ready soon and she'll kill us if we're late."

"Could you please take it easy? I don't have a death wish."

"Sure," he said and grinned.

Jane held on tight as he sped through the curve.

"A lotta people go over the edge," he frowned. "Stupid tourists."

Something smelled wonderful as they entered the cabin. "Oh good, you're back! I hope you didn't spoil your supper," Patience said. The platters of meat and bowls of vegetables were already on the table.

They sat, then passed around the food.

"What do your parents do for a living?" Rich asked.

"My dad was an accountant and my mom was a secretary," Jane answered.

"*Was?* Are they retired?" Rich asked.

"No. They died in a car accident." Jane looked down. "Here are their pictures." She opened the locket and leaned in. Rich glanced at them.

"It's not our place to question God's plan," said Patience.

"How are you getting along without your parents? You didn't get stuck caring for a house full of brothers and sisters, did you?"

"It's just me, and I do just fine on my own."

"Good, good," Patience muttered.

"You're taking art this semester? No wonder you're so thin—*starving artist*, as the saying goes." She looked at Jane's plate. "You didn't try the meat yet."

"Oh, I'm good with the veggies," Jane said. "They're delicious!"

"Thank you, dear. I grew them myself," Patience said.

Rich went to the cupboard and poured some drinks. "I'd like to make a toast." He handed a glass to each person.

"I'm good with water. I don't usually drink," Jane said.

"It's a special occasion, it'd be rude to refuse," Rich insisted.

Everyone raised their glass.

"When we drink, we get drunk.
When we get drunk, we fall asleep.
When we fall asleep, we commit no sin.
When we commit no sin, we go to heaven.
So, let's all get drunk, and go to heaven!"

Rich beamed. They clinked glasses and drank.

"Oh! We bought a pie today. Let me…" Jane tried to stand, lost her balance and plopped back onto her chair.

Patience smiled sweetly. "Looks like it's almost time to take out the trash."

Jane fought to keep her eyes open. Her head bobbed then dropped to her chest.

Jane moaned. Her head throbbed and stomach ached. She vomited and opened her eyes. It was dark, except for a dim light across the room. She lay somewhere cold and hard—porcelain—a bathtub.

"She's waking up. You didn't use enough!" a familiar voice said.

"Too much spoils the meat! Just knock her head against the tub until she's out," said another voice Jane knew but just couldn't place.

A shadowy figure walked toward her, a man.

Jane put her hands on the sides of the tub and tried to pull herself up.

Rich chuckled. "Don't bother trying to get away." As he neared, he slipped on the vomit and bashed his head against the tub. He collapsed in a heap. Blood formed a pool around his head.

Jane dragged herself up and out of the tub. She used the edge to steady herself.

"You *stupid* girl! You killed my husband!" Patience screeched. She came at Jane with a knife. Jane looked around for anything she could use for a weapon. Patience slipped on the pool of blood and fell on her own knife. She lay lifeless on the floor.

Jane found a door, stumbled out of the building and into the night. It took a moment for her eyes to adjust, then all she saw were trees. She plodded from tree to tree and leaned on each one for support.

She heard twigs snap beneath someone's feet. She looked for a hiding place. There was nowhere to go, even if she could run. She crouched behind a tree.

"You might as well give up. If you go for help, all you'll find is our lifelong friends and neighbors. No one will help you." RJ strolled through the forest, searching for her.

Jane heard an animal scurry in the brush. Then a gunshot. Jane's heart beat out of her chest.

"You have no one to live for, no family. No one will miss you."

She tried to calm her breathing, afraid he'd hear her.

"You were never going to amount to anything anyway," RJ sneered.

Jane saw him walk past. She tip-toed in the other direction.

A twig snapped. RJ turned and fired the gun. The bullet hit a tree near Jane.

Jane bolted and stumbled blindly into the night.

Another gun shot. The bullet ricocheted off a rock, part of the stone staircase that led from RJ's family's cabin to Spirit Lake. A smug grin oozed across his face.

"I know where you *ah-are.*" He taunted her. "We can still salvage the Sunday barbeque. Your worthless life will have *some* meaning then." He crept towards the staircase. A motion detector light snapped on and startled him. He turned and shot at it. Jane popped out from behind a tree and shoved him. He tumbled end over end, down the stone staircase.

Jane strolled across the college campus, earbuds in. She stepped to the beat of the music.

A young guy who wore a backpack motioned at her ears. She removed her earbuds.

"Hey. Jane, right?"

"Yeah?"

"You go out with RJ don't cha?"

"No. Well, we went out a couple of times. We decided not to keep seeing each other."

"Oh, that's too bad."

"Mm. Not really. We didn't really have anything in common. Why?"

"He hasn't been coming to class. Have you seen him?"

"No. Not since we broke up." Jane was as cool as a cucumber.

"Well, if you talk to him, let him know he's gonna get kicked outta school if he doesn't start coming to class, would ya?"

"Sure, but I think he said something about transferring to another college."

"Oh, okay. That's probably what he did."

Jane took a tinfoil wrapped package out of her backpack, opened it, broke off a piece of something, popped it into her mouth and chewed. She held it out towards the guy. "Jerky?"

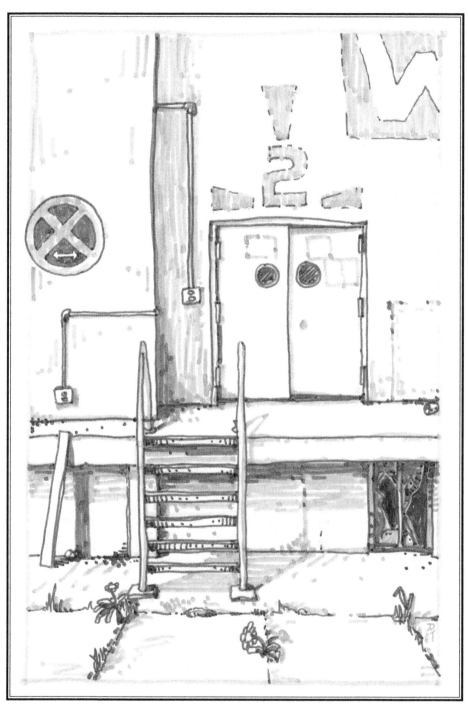

... to explore the penetrating roots of humanity, or so they said.

Overturned
by Matthew Buza

Lucio watched the empty loading dock at the base of the concrete enclosure at the end of first avenue just a block over from the Mirror Point Mortuary. There were empty lots lining the street with overgrown alder stands and thick piles of brambles for picking sour blackberries in August and hiding teenagers smoking weed after school. The remnants of the old produce packing plant had long been a hangout for bums and drug addicts. Anything to give cover or warmth from the cold winter rains. Fall was coming, and the first cold dips of air began rushing down from the Canadian border. The first shade of yellow crept along the edge of the green leaves and gave a blurry feel to the overhanging trees. Old burn barrels reeked of heavy oil and tickled his nose.

It was nearly dark and Lucio stood transfixed. Somewhere in the distance metal struck metal and beat like a clock tower sounding the hour. What he was standing in front of was a rumor, an iceberg conspiracy thread at the end of the dark web. The *Bara Crypt*, a moving castle there to explore the penetrating roots of humanity, or so they said. An origin story of self-reflection and fear. Never in the same place. Always moving. As elusive as sand held tight in the fist.

Months had passed as Lucio watched the sunrise with spent energy drinks piled in the corner and dried jerky serving as the only reasonable morning meal. All for a riddle pieced together from forum posts and cyberstalking. He had spent long nights outside of the gated houses that spanned the inlet along Maple Grove. He waited for targets to stumble out of private dinner parties into his waiting Uber. Recorders in the leather headrests. Cameras embedded in mirrors. Their stories backfilled his notes, popping one theory while inflating the next. County and state records were a gold mine. His data cross-referenced against business records and title searches.

Clues were everywhere if you knew where to look. It was painstaking, but that's what his small online community of fifty-six anonymous individuals expected. A big reveal. A journey they were promised to control. He had teased this night for weeks and he was not one to disappoint. And like all quests, there was a gift at the end of the *Crypt*. Maybe a deeper truth for both Lucio and the community, or maybe it would be an empty room filled with used needles. He didn't know, but he wanted to find out. He needed to find out. If only to purge this obsession.

Lucio had modified a failed parachute vest he found for free in the classified section of the Observer. The cold ferry ride across the lake and the long walk through Way's End to the broken-down hunting trailer was worth it. The black canvas straps fit perfectly around his thin shoulders. It had taken nearly three days and hours of YouTube videos to figure out his mother's sewing machine. The pouches he had sewn had ended up lopsided, but the phones sat flush and that's all that mattered. Two battery backups rested on his hips and the white cables ran under his shirt and connected to the phones, one resting between his shoulder blades and the other on his chest. The cameras faced out. He turned them on and launched *Twitch*.

CiousCommader logged in. The message read.

The cameras shared the split screen. The community had been waiting for hours and now they had become Lucio himself. The street was empty and the afternoon light was beginning to fade. Lucio clipped the tiny microphone to his shirt collar and spoke.

"How's the audio?" he said.

He stared down at his wrist. A third phone sat in a black wrist band and displayed the chat window. Streams of comments and emote images scrolled by. He smiled and felt the warmth of his community alive on his wrist. His fingers moved quickly and he launched his pre-programmed bot. The chat window began to stream with the night's rules.

This is CiousCommanderBot.
You will be banned if you brigade.
You will be banned if you share.
Only approved members will be allowed to view.
The Admin will trigger all polls.
Voting will end after 5 seconds.
You have been warned.
I follow your votes. I am your destiny.
I'll see you on the other side.

Streams of 'lols' and emotes filled the chat wall. They were ready and primed.

When Lucio was twelve he had wandered into a local gaming store just down the way from the High School. Long tables were filled with young and old men rolling dice and diligently marking character cards. At the head of the table, a man sat behind a cardboard box telling a twisted story of demons nestled amongst the labyrinth's shadows. Lucio fell in love. Dungeons and Dragons; Paper-based crawls; Text-based video games. He could still remember the day he torrented an old copy of *Colossal Cave*. He played it for days, pouring over the possibilities. Mapping out the paths and decisions. The game was never the same. There was always a different path through the maze, but only one true path to the end. He loved the feeling of discovery, that every movement and every decision was life or death. And to make it to the end required the act of dying. To make it through unscathed would be akin to guessing a thousand coin flips in a row. Possible but not probable.

Lucio first heard of the *Bara Crypt* from an obscure classified at the end of the Mirror Point Echo. With his initial investigation, he learned that some of the classifieds were syndicated, a way for local papers to earn ad revenue. The classified mentioned the *Bara Crypt* and was followed by a series of numbers. It became an obsession. The numbers and their meaning. He poured through old microfiche in the public library, looking through past papers. Old classifieds referencing the *Bara.* After all his work Lucio was finally here. Just feet from the entrance. He felt his chest tighten as his hands began to shake.

"Going in," he said. The microphone pulled his words and transcribed them into the chat window. The community cheered.

Lucio stepped over dense clumps of weeds that protruded through the cracked concrete. The building had been stripped of its scrap metal, likely sold off for drugs and alcohol. The concrete facade remained, framing a long loading bay that dipped into a subterranean dock. He moved down the ramp and drifted to the near wall. His wrist buzzed. It was his community admin.

I'm flipping the feed to night mode. It's getting dark out there.

An iron doorway climbed overhead. He could hear water draining somewhere in the walls. The openings looked like produce chutes where millions of pounds of potatoes or carrots would stream into semi-trucks. The loading bay ended and he saw an alcove around the side. A faint glow of neon red reflected across a narrow puddle. There was a doorway with a sign overhead, *Enter Ye.*

Two women flanked the entrance. A chill ran up Lucio's back. Somewhere deep inside he imagined that all of this was a fantasy or a delusion. And that same part prayed for failure. It would be easy to walk around a handful of rooms and call it a night. But it was more terrifying to be right. These women confirmed the *Bara* was real. And that changed everything.

"Hello?" He called out.

The chat log came alive.

Did he say hello? He's going to die. What an incel.
I'm screen capping this. Straight to liveleak.
Think hot Thots Commander.

"Hello," the two women responded in unison. They stood up. Two chair bottoms had been welded into the wall. They wore short chessboard dresses with alternating black and white squares. One woman was white and half her face was painted jet black, the other a black woman with half her face painted chalk white.

Lucio felt the buzz, a vote had been cast.

Admin (Vote): Go in?

The women watched. Their eyes piercing black. After five seconds his wrist buzzed with the poll's answer. *"Yes"*

It had been nearly unanimous, *55-1*.

"Someone's a pussy," Lucio said into the microphone, trying to ignore his own nerves. "Is this the *Bara Crypt*? I would like to know."

"It is what you think it is," they answered in unison.

"I want to enter then."

"Only if you want to?"

He swallowed hard. "I do."

"Keep to your path. Watch and listen, but you cannot touch."

Lucio nodded accepting the women's warning. The iron doors clicked and a puff of warm air surged. There was a raw smell, like freshly tilled earth. He could feel the dust and grit in the air. His teeth ground through the material. It tasted like charcoal. Both women stepped back to reveal the corridor. They reeked of it, too. Like they had rolled in a bonfire.

Gas lights flickered behind iron cages and water dripped from moss that grew between the cracks of the concrete supports. The roof arched overhead. The keystones had been replaced by an iron grate. It looked like a floor drain placed into the roof and backlit by a row of red lights forming a crude path to guide him along. An overwhelming sensation to touch something took hold. His fingers were inches away from the wall before he stopped.

... you cannot touch ...

He pulled back and looked down at his chat log.

What an idiot.
That would have been fast.
I'll give you two eth to change your mind.

115

"Yeah, yeah, I know," Lucio said. The chat log mocked him, popping with laughter. "I'm moving down the hallway now."

Ahead the red roofline turned around a narrow bend. It grew cold and damp with every step. The water condensed into running capillaries and gathered in a narrow channel. It was moving with him, a black channel foot river.

There was a sound of metal jingling against metal. It was rough and rhythmic. As he turned the corner the sound of chains vibrating filled the hallway. A doorless brick opening glowed with a green light. The smell caught him, a mixture of chemicals and filth. A horrid taste clung in the air. More clinking of chains, this time violent, as if someone or something were pulling or trying to break free.

"Do you all hear that?" Lucio asked.

They did. The chat flow slowed on his wrist. Eyes were watching eyes. Minds locked on the big reveal.

Lucio's nerves battled the urge to run. To escape. To flee. But his responsibility to the community was ever present. If he left now, they would abandon him. He would have to find his way out alone. That fear of failure, of humiliation, pulled him along with every step.

He came to the doorway. Inside the room a fat man rested on a narrow stool, his belly spilling over the small wood surface. His white skin was streaked with red lines of irritation that appeared from underneath thick folds. Heavy chains were connected to leather straps tied tight to his wrists. His bloodless hands were white like chalk. A black eye mask covered his sweating face and a small puddle of perspiration collected on the ground, fresh drops cascaded off his forehead. He was gagged and he moaned. Lucio couldn't tell if it was twisting with pleasure or pain or possibly both.

A black curtain hung from the ceiling and blocked the rear half of his body. The man's body shuttered and his skin and fat rippled. The curtain was hiding something. Another shake and the man lifted his head back and let loose a raspy moan.

The curtain was hiding something, or someone. Lucio froze. What little he could see of the man's face was enough. Lucio had cataloged most of the powerful and rich who lived in the surrounding area. This man didn't fit any of their descriptions. But somewhere beyond the walls of the *Bara* he was someone's son, husband, or father.

The screen buzzed again.

Admin (Vote): Go in?

Another five seconds and his wrist buzzed. "*Yes*"
105-1.

"At least one of you has some sense," Lucio whispered. His footstep echoed as he entered the room. The man stopped shaking and spit out the mouth gag.

"Who's there," he cried.

Like the community, Lucio stared blankly at the stage show. The man was horrid. Grotesque. Lucio fumbled for any words. He looked around the room and then back to the curtain where a shadow moved. Something was hiding behind the curtain. Short footsteps. Something sliding along the ground, the sound of raspy breathing, like an asthmatic sucking their last breath through a straw.

The chains shifted and the fat man cried out, "Identify yourself. We're not going to sit here and wait, you hear me? There's work to be done."

"What work?" Lucio coughed out.

"We're digging for the soul. That's what we're doing."

"We?"

"No, not you, you idiot. You're here to watch. Is that what you want? Who are you?"

"Nobody," Lucio answered. "I'm nobody."

"You're something to someone. What's your name?"

Fake names streamed by, but Lucio remembered who he was. He wasn't himself, he was a stand-in. "I'm CiousCommander and I represent a team. This is the Bara Crypt?"

"The *Bara*...you are the *Bara*. Do you think there's something here for you? It will take away what you value most. Do you know what that is?"

My community, Lucio thought. "No, I don't."

"*No, I don't. No, I don't.*" The fat man's face turned. "Say that again?... know that voice. I know you."

"No. No, you don't."

"Are you here to watch, *again*? Well, no bargain. No double dipping."

The shadow behind the curtain moved again. Someone was there. "*Again*? I don't know. I don't want to," Lucio said backing away. His wrist buzzed.

Admin (Vote): Stay?

The answer buzzed. "*Yes*"
345-1.

"No, I don't want to," Lucio pleaded. "We're leaving."

The first fingers curled over the black curtain. They were black and covered in a shiny film, a latex film. The fat man began to laugh, his rolls shook and quivered. The fabric pulled back and a head emerged, at least that's what it looked like. The face was covered in black latex and blended in with the dark brick wall, black bulbous plastic cups covered its eyes and a respirator covered its mouth. A breath. The raspy breath and then a squeal. It was laughing. The fat man was laughing. The mocking laughs weren't the first Lucio had heard. They had become commonplace. Years of torment in school. The laughing. Now here in the *Bara*.

"There you are. I see you now." The fat man cackled. His eyes were still covered but he was looking directly at Lucio. Somehow he could see. He could see Lucio. "I want you to preach against it. The wickedness is on your chest."

Lucio moved between the two. His face began to quiver. "I don't want to."

"You're a living mirror. You're a hollow little boy."

Lucio took a step back. The figure behind the curtain stepped out. His bent hand clutched a dead snake. His feet were rounded stumps, flat at the bottom and covered with latex. Everything was latex.

"Go out boy," the fat man cried.

The Latex man pounded the ground, rushed at the doorway. He reared back and threw the snake carcass. It struck Lucio in the arm and fell to the ground. A hidden door slid across the brick entry. The last thing Lucio heard was the sound of laughter from the fat man as he sprinted away. On the ground, the snake came to life. It curled quickly before skulking through a gap in the wall.

Lucio felt like an elephant was sitting on his chest, the heavyweight pressing down and threatening to splay him out over the crypt floor. The chat was quiet on his wrist. It had been an incoherent stream after the latex *thing* closed the door. A blur of profanity and acronyms spaced by images and gifs covered the wall. In the excitement of the day he had forgotten to reset his meager tip jar. It was overflowing. Dollars and crypto mounted with every passing minute.

His mind had fogged over and he walked like a silent ghost deeper into the *Bara*. He continued to follow the red line, what else could he do.

...I want you to preach against it...

What was it, he asked himself. *Preach against what?*

His wrist buzzed. It was the admin.

> *You alright? You haven't talked in twenty minutes. Do you know where we're going?*

It only seemed like a minute had passed. His fingers worked the keyboard.

> *I'm g8. Shit my pants there.*
> *Did you bring more? (smiley face)*
> *I wish. How's the stream?*
> *Crystal. Where are we going? Their asking?*
> *I have no idea. Just following the path I guess and wait until a decision is needed.*

Lucio coughed and looked down the hallway. His voice was dry and cracked, "Thanks for the tips, you nerds. Felt the butthole clench hard. Turning shit to diamonds after that. We follow the path. That's what was promised. It's a crawl. We keep moving no matter what."

They moved further into the *Bara*. He stopped periodically to capture etchings hand-carved into the concrete walls. Some resembled figures bent at the hip, others appeared to be stampeding animals. He passed a line of twisted and crooked spirals, each getting larger until the center spiral was nothing more than a circle covering the entire wall. He tried to imagine who or why? Was this supposed to be art or the ravings of a mad man lost in the *Bara?*

The hallway bent and he felt the air grow colder. Midway down the red line running along the ceiling broke and fell to the floor. The path had flipped. Lucio felt the world flip upside down. He felt his stomach settle into his chest cavity, the weight of his organs pressing against his lungs. It was hard to breathe as his abs tightened. His feet stayed on the ground, but gravity was pulling him up. Lucio reached out and steadied himself. One foot followed the other and he began to walk up the wall, slowly spinning the world right side up. He reached what had been the ceiling and he felt his body fall into place like a puzzle piece. His hair laid flat across his ears once more and the blood seemed to drain back through his body. Just for a moment, he felt light headed and dizzy.

> *Did that just happen?*
> *Yes. I can't explain it. It just felt right.*
> *I wouldn't know where to begin.*

The walls seemed to stretch away. The *Bara* was growing or he was shrinking into an abyss. The *Bara* gave way to a spherical room. A meeting point for five separate paths and their respective entrances. Only Lucio's path was lit with the red line that now dead-ended in the center of the floor where a ten-foot monolith was fixed into ornate stonework. The stone pattern of the hallway ended abruptly in an arching circular design and seemed to swirl like a whirlpool. The room was covered in long rectangular shadows fed by the oil lights from the hallways. The monolith caught Lucio and he froze in fear. Two naked feet, up to the calf, hung out the back of the stone structure. Someone had been cast in a tomb. Midway up, he saw the supple curves of a buttocks pressing out. It was skin and stone mixed together.

He looked down at his wrist and the chat log blazed with a renewed adolescent energy.

Braaaaap.
Who dis.
(emote image).
shockedpicacho.gif

A new vote was needed and his wrist buzzed on queue.

Admin (Vote): Go in?

The buzz said, "*Yes*".
The vote, *453-1*.
Lucio shook off the one and the rising voting totals. He didn't have time to deal with the rules that seemed to have been ignored. He crossed into the room and watched the feet. He tried to keep quiet but his shoes clicked. The feet twitched.

"Jesus," Lucio let out in a gasp. He moved around the room. There were arms hanging from the front of the monolith. Pale and white. The elbows were locked in stone leaving her fingers to twitch in space. He saw her sagging breasts and protruding thighs. The skin was wrinkled and old. Brown splotches covered her arms.

At the foot of the stone base was a heavy hammer, head down, handle up, only feet away from Lucio. Her face pulled back, the head tilted to the sky leaving only the end of her nose and the outline of her mouth. Her jaw was closed shut, but her lips moved and danced.

She heard Lucio. Each step, every vibration was like an earthquake inside the stone monolith. She struggled to speak. A shallow shot of air pressed out a garbled moan.

She was in pain. The edges of her skin were irritated and red. The stone scraped and dug into the flesh. The *Bara* was contorting in front of him. This tortured innocent was testing his will to continue. A diagonal scar ran down her lip from a late-life cleft surgery. Her hands were soft and smooth with lines of freckles moving down her thin fingers. He wanted to reach out and touch her. How long had she been there? How many hours had she spent reaching out into open space for the chance to feel the touch of skin, that physical connection we all desire.

Lucio stumbled forward, his face was close to her hands. The smell of raw herbs filled the air.

"Are you OK?" Lucio mumbled. He wanted to reach out. The hammer inches away. "I can help you. Just tell me what to do."

Her lips trembled. "Lucio don't."

"What? How do you know my name?" Everything had been a secret. Not even the community knew the *Bara's* final location. But she knew him. She knew his name. This wasn't a coincidence. She had been placed here because of him. She was his responsibility. "How do you know me?"

"Lucio ..." she mumbled. "Don't"

Admin (Vote): Help her?

The vote read, "*No*".

The vote, *1455-1*.

"No!" Lucio screamed. "No, I'm not doing that. Revote. Rerun it."

Admin (Vote): Revote: Help her?

The buzz said, "*No*".

The vote, *1921-1*.

"This is wrong," Lucio screamed. "You're wrong. This isn't right. She didn't ask for this."

Don't do it. We voted. You said.

"I'm not going to let someone else get hurt. You hear me?"

That's not what we agreed to.

"This ... are you looking at this?" The woman's hands shook in fear. The sound of Lucio's voice was like a loudspeaker in her ears. "Are you? I'm not going to let this happen to her. Whoever she is."

This is a game. You're part of it. Don't break our rules and don't break the Bara's rules.

"Fuck the rules." Lucio lifted the hammer and brought it down on the stone face. With each strike, powder swirled and chips fell to the ground around his feet. He worked, sweat pouring off his face. On the other side of the monolith, the red line that had brought him to the room began to retrace. Lucio was oblivious, filled with defiant rage.

A sharp metal lock sounded and gears, somewhere beyond the walls, began to spin and twist. Pulleys lifted ropes and a stone base began to lower. The ground shook at his feet and Lucio stumbled back dropping the hammer to the floor. Like a missing frame in a movie, the encased image of the woman vanished into the ground. Dust rose up in a plume and rained down around the room. A new circular stone replaced where she had been. Lucio picked up the hammer.

"No! Bring her back!" He screamed into the room and his echo wrapped around the walls and appeared behind him. He twisted. Fear rising in his eyes. Lucio jumped on the new center floor and smashed the hammer down on the stone. "Let her out! Please!"

Why did you do that?

"I'm not listening to you."

That was the deal.

The sound of grinding gears and heavy doors opening and closing sent Lucio in a panic. Another echo rang out. The sour smell of dust filled the air and sounds wrapping around him like a vice. Lucio braced himself expecting to plummet into the depths of the *Bara Crypt*. He gripped the hammer tight. It was his only weapon.

WE told you no.

"I don't care right now. I really don't."

Admin (Vote): Does he stay?

The vote read, "*Yes*".
The vote, *2478-1*.
"You don't run this show! You hear me?"

You're losing control.

"I'm losing control? You're not here. I'm here. I'm overriding."

Ahead, through one of the many entrances that emptied into the spherical room appeared a demonic red ambient light. It illuminated a hallway that he hadn't seen, one that circled just beyond the center room, like a ring around Saturn. He turned, looking at each entrance. A shadow moved off the corner of his eye down one of the hallways. Right to left. It was swift.

"Are you seeing this?" Lucio said to his community. The chat log had gone dark. Their anger that Lucio would defy them seemed to melt away. Thousands of fingers sat frozen above keyboards, paralyzed by fear and excitement. He repeated. "Are you seeing this?"

Down one of the hallways, Lucio saw the first silhouette of, *It. It* was like nothing he had ever seen before. The body of a man, naked, his arms and legs attached to stilts sharpened to fine points. He walked like a spider, skulking through the outer hallway, circling like a shark that smelled the first drop of blood.

Its voice was clear. "Those who turn to worthless idols turn away. Do you hear me? Flesh and stone and steel. You were told not to touch. You disobeyed."

Each step rang like a bell. Lucio followed the figure, keeping his chest and the camera's eye focused. The images streaming from the camera multiplied across computer screens around the world.

"Do you hear?" *It* said again. There was a wave of dark anger in his voice.

"I hear," Lucio answered.

The figure disappeared behind a wall but did not reappear at the end of the next entrance. Lucio watched and waited. His head trembled. His wrist buzzed. Lucio looked down.

Run.

He looked back and saw *It* pounding down the hallway behind him. The arms and legs striking the ground and scraping free fresh chips of stone.

Lucio saw a flash of *Its* face. A smooth featureless creature. No eyes. No mouth. No holes for *It* to breath or speak. The skin was pale white and covered in a thick mucus. *It* came quickly. Lucio took flight down the original hallway. The red line was gone. Only the cold narrowing walls were left behind. He felt the ground tremble as *It* closed on him.

The path moved uphill. Lucio waited for gravity to shift, but it never came. A new path had emerged. The same as the old, but now he was running on what had been the ceiling. The oil lights burned upside down. The carvings etched into the wall had flipped.

He struggled against fatigue, but the fear of death pushed him. He reached the top of the path, expecting the hallway to level out. It was gone leaving an empty opening in the floor. Had he missed this before? Was this new? His momentum and fatigue carried him forward. He tumbled down into the black opening.

As Lucio fell he saw the mucus face of *It* reach the opening, the pegged arms striking out at him. They missed and Lucio tumbled into the darkness.

The shallow ripples extended out and bounced off the edge of the black room only to return and lap against Lucio's face. The water was barely a half inch thick and jet black. He lifted himself to his knees and checked the camera. It was still running. His wrist throbbed and was beginning to swell.

"I think it might be broken. I don't know where I am. It's a room. Like the previous one, round and spherical. I don't want to touch anything."

The hammer had fallen with him. It was laying on the far side of the room. A small amount of stone powder remained on the edge. The sadness returned and his face sunk away. His hand still rang with the reverberations of each strike.

"I don't know where to go."

Do you want me to call for help? I just need to know where you are. What town? Location?

Lucio thought for a moment. Who was listening or worse yet watching?

Lucio looked down and struggled to type into the phone on his wrist.

I'll see if there's a way out.

There was a pause and the response appeared.

Whatever you need. The board is burning down with comments. I can't keep up. My fingers are tired from banning so many.

Overhead the opening in the floor reflected light over the smooth black walls. There had to be a way out, an opening somewhere or a ladder. Whatever *It* was that chased him down the hallway had abandoned him, or maybe *It* was waiting for Lucio to somehow climb back into the *Bara Crypt*. The walls were smooth and black like obsidian. There was nothing to grip onto.

"This feels like a bird cage. I just don't know who's out there watching," Lucio said.

He could see his dim reflection. The disheveled outline of hair and dark wells for eyes. He touched his nose and wiped away a line of blood. There was a copper taste in his mouth mixed with fine grit. He spat into his hand. It was red and spotted with white speckles. Small bits of teeth had chipped off and collected against his cheeks. He spat again and sprayed the wall. It dripped down and touched the edge of the water. Small ripples grew out and a yellowed light appeared underneath his feet. The light stretched out in an arc across the floor.

"No. No. What is this ... a new path?" He cried out.

He followed the light as it quickly branched and branched again, exploding like a fractal underneath the shallow pool, like a television screen projecting an image. It curved and formed an image of a tree. The branches thinned and small buds appeared. Leaves sprouted and grew out. The image reflected off the walls and he felt surrounded.

The blackness had been pushed away and a small forest took its place. It shaded him and for a brief moment, calm stretched over Lucio. He all but forgot the image of the woman trapped in the stone monolith. He forgot about the black birdcage, or *It*, or the Latex Man. The *Bara Crypt* seemed to wash away. The tree's reflection grew up towards the ceiling. It seemed to move and sway as if a breeze were blowing through the walls. It smelled like a forest, the rotten earthiness, fresh fruit ripening on the vine. He felt alive. The pain in his arm and face melted away.

Lucio stood in a stupor enjoying the projections along the walls when the light at his feet shifted red. The trees slowly began to die. The leaves burned yellow and then orange before breaking off and sliding along the ground. The forest was disappearing and the blackness swelling in behind. The branches and trunk snapped and tumbled to the far side of the room, collecting in a small kindling pile. As it burst into flames Lucio began to tremble. There was no heat, only the cold. It was back. The *Bara*. The fear and terror were like hands reaching up out of the ground to pull him into a crevasse.

A line rose up from the base of the kindling pile and split the wall in two. It was a door and it opened to reveal a figure on the other side. Lucio looked for the hammer. It was next to the opening. He was too far away to fight his way out and his arm hurt too much to grapple. Lucio looked past the figure to see the sun setting through a line of trees. There was a street and a car. His car. His town. Where the whole journey had started. It was an exit, or an entrance, depending on how you stood.

"Who are you?" Lucio cried out.

The figure stepped into the room. It paused at the foot of the hammer, fingers danced in anticipation. There was something strapped to his wrist, a light, a screen. Lucio looked him over and he saw a vest with cables running down his shoulders.

"Who are you?" Lucio asked again.

The figure lifted his arm and typed into the small screen.

Lucio's arm buzzed.

Admin (Vote/Paredo): What do I do?

The response came quickly. *"Top Answer: Kill him."*
Number of voters, *3395.*

"I didn't ask for a vote," Lucio said.

The figure looked down and typed into the screen.

It's not your job to ask. That was the deal.

A horror stretched across Lucio's face as the screen illuminated the figure's face. He nearly collapsed.

It was him.

Lucio.

Like a reflection in the mirror. The paranoia locked in. This was the *Bara* at work. He knew it.

"They voted," the voice said.

"What? What is this! Who are you?"

"Respect the vote."

"Kill who? How?" Lucio looked at the hammer. It was ten feet away. He could have the jump. The street beyond was even more enticing. Slide by this person, whoever they were pretending to be, and escape.

"I'm not killing anyone. Do you hear me? I'm going ... I'm not playing this game anymore. If you get in my way I'll go through you," Lucio growled.

"Is it right for you to be angry?" The figure responded. Lucio looked in wonder. It must be a mirage. The *Bara* had sent one last trick.

"How fitting of them to send you to stop me," Lucio said waving his arm.

"I'm not here to stop you. You've already done that." His face was clean, smooth, and his body thick with muscle. It was Lucio but a different Lucio, from a different world. One that didn't torment him or leave him behind. Like something out of a dream. A future vision that never matured. Just looking at what he couldn't be sent Lucio into a fit of rage. They were teasing him.

"You think this is funny. Sending *this* at me?"

"Are you angry?"

"I am. Is that what you want?"

"What do you wish for?"

Lucio's lips quivered. "I wish ... *you* ... were dead."

Lucio broke into a sprint, fighting through fatigue. He dove, reaching for the hammer, but it seemed to vanish in front of him. The figure had snapped it up. Lucio crashed into the water and slid against the wall, the burning fire projecting just over his shoulder. He turned to see his face standing above him. Two faces. Two separate lives. Two communities watching each other. The same person. The hammer hovered overhead.

"You're the admin?" Lucio said. "Did you vote?"

"I always voted. You just didn't listen. I was the *one*. What did it say?"

The one, Lucio thought closing his eyes. "It said to kill him."

The hammer dropped and smashed through Lucio's forehead collapsing bone into brain. Blood dripped from the depression and he slumped to the ground. A quiver escaped and he stopped breathing. The figure, the new Lucio, dropped the hammer and the dark water splashed over the dead body. He reached down and turned off the phones and the wrist chat. He pulled the vest off and left through the opening and out into the street. The old packing plant and loading bay stood behind him. He crossed the street towards his car.

"So many cycles to get it right. Good night," he said into his microphone. His words became text and scrawled across his wrist. A quick flip and the chat window and live stream ended. Across the internet, thousands of black screens left a community of ghostly faces in shock wondering what they had just witnessed.

... everyone knew how he liked to drive too fast.

Sometimes Nice Girls Do

by Sonya Rhen

She sat on the frozen ground. A ball of her own hair enmeshed on her lap. The cold could not penetrate the numbness. She did not feel.

In her hands she held two sticks: one straight and one 'Y' shaped. She turned the 'Y' upside down and crossed the straight one over the tail of it. Her fingers worked deliberately, twisting the strands of hair in a crisscross pattern around the two sticks. Her body rocked in a gentle rhythm as she chanted.

> *Blood of Earth work through me*
> *Give breath of life to this dead tree*
> *Power of mortal flesh and bone*
> *My mind's eye image here be sown*
>
> *Blood of Earth work through me*
> *Give breath of life to this dead tree*
> *Power of mortal flesh and bone*
> *My mind's eye image here be sown*
>
> *Blood of Earth ...*

She could see him as he was the first time they met. She hadn't even really been interested. He was eye-candy, but she didn't go for that sort. Still, something about him attracted her.

Sara glanced toward the noise. Two boys stood near; nothing that would make that high pitched squeaking sound. She looked away and continued to sway to the music.

"Eeeee!"

She heard it again. It sounded like feedback from a mic or the DJ's sound system, but it didn't seem to bother anyone else. Looking around, there were only those two guys standing close to her and now one of them was making a show of not looking at her.

She stared at him as he glanced at: the wall, the ceiling, the floor, the other wall. She wasn't here to play games; she was here to dance. She turned her back on the pair.

"Eeeee!"

She didn't bother to look over this time. Sara scanned the dance floor in the rival high school's gym. Mirror Point was the more affluent side of Spirit Lake aside from the few houses on The Bluffs in Way's End. Not that there weren't poor kids here, too. Not that her family was poor, exactly, but they certainly weren't rich. It was all relative anyway. Her shoes were worn and her clothes were a little outdated. Regardless, she did her best to pull together a look that she wasn't too embarrassed by.

Mirror Point High School was hosting a back to school dance for all the schools. She had been here a few times, but this was her first dance. There were so many kids here she felt a bit lost, but the familiar music put her at ease. The other kids were all in pairs or groups. She loved to dance and she could do that alone or with a partner. She didn't mind flying solo. She still scoped the room for cute guys.

"Your shoes are untied."

She glanced down over the edge of the table she was resting on, to the buckles of her shoes as they swung back and forth. "How'd you make that noise?"

He pretended not to notice her again, so she kicked his shin, not hard, just enough to let him know she was annoyed.

He grinned.

"What's your name?"

She debated whether to pretend she didn't hear him. She wasn't into his games. She gave him a suggestion of a smile and said, "Sara."

"I'm Chip. He's Dale." He jerked his head toward the shorter dark-haired boy. "Together we're Chip en Dale." He winked.

"Hey," Dale said. He smiled, but looked slightly uncomfortable.

She could hear the beginning strains of a song she liked. Her feet were itching to dance. She looked at Chip. "You wanna?" She nodded her head toward the dance floor.

"Nah." He shrugged.

Sara glanced at Dale and raised her eyebrows in question. He eyed Chip and shook his head.

"Suit yourself." She slid off the table and danced her way across the floor. She passed a few kids she knew, engaging and disengaging along the way. She was on a mission from the dance gods and nothing was going to stop her. She wasn't the best dancer, despite her mother's efforts. She didn't really care, which was part of the problem. She just wanted to do her own thing. She'd done everything Way's End had to offer: ballet, tap, jazz, hip hop and even zumba (not that she considered that really dancing). Group choreography was not for her. Here on the dance floor, she just let her body move and feel the music.

At last she was near the front by the DJ. She could feel the music vibrating up through her toes, rattling her shoe buckles. She'd been dancing most of the night and wanted to get a few more songs in before she left. She caught the DJ's eyes and swayed her hips to the rhythm as he bopped his head along, one hand on the controller, the other on the headphones around his neck. She noticed Chip was watching her. She turned her back to him and performed some of her best dance moves. His loss. The DJ winked at her and she beamed. The dance floor was pumped with energy.

She hadn't noticed when Chip had joined her. They danced several songs and she could feel the sweat forming on her skin. He was a good dancer and she played off his moves in equal measure, occasionally catching and holding the gaze from his brown eyes with her blue ones. The DJ seemed to sense their vibe and played high-energy music until Sara felt she would drop. A slower song came on and she waved bye to Chip.

She mouthed a quick, "Thank you," to the DJ who nodded back. She danced her way back off the dance floor and went in search of a water fountain. She didn't look back at Chip. She hadn't come here to pick up guys.

The vending machines in the back corner had over-priced sodas and water. She didn't have any cash left. She only brought enough to get in. Her keys and ASB card were glued inside her bra with sweat. She pulled her white top away from her and shook it to cool off. There had to be a fountain around here somewhere. She found it outside the bathroom. The water felt cool. She finally stopped gulping when she felt other people waiting behind her.

After using the toilet, she stood at the sink and tried to freshen up. Wadding up some wet paper towels, she dabbed at the sweat on her brow and chest. A few girls from Mirror Point High were fixing their makeup in the mirror, laughing and talking about some absent friend that had just been dumped. She looked at their perfect hair and makeup and wondered how they managed to keep from sweating. Very likely they hadn't even been dancing.

She threw the towels in the trash and ran into Dale by the vending machines.

"Hey, Sara," he said.

"Dale, right?"

Behind her the group of girls emerged from the bathroom, giggling. "Marco, come dance with us," they called.

He averted his gaze and let the girls take him out on the dance floor.

"Huh." She had no idea why he would say his name was 'Dale', but when she thought about it, he had never actually said that was his name. It was Chip, the one with the golden brown hair. Maybe his name wasn't even Chip. Besides, who in their right mind named their kid 'Chip.'

She pulled her phone out of the waistband of her skirt. She had a text.

Kate: *Don't miss the ferry.*
Sara: *Plenty of time. You don't miss it.*
Kate: *I'll be there.*

She was about to turn off her phone when a hand reached around her and took it.

"Hey!"

Chip was holding her phone and typing something. He turned his back when she tried to retrieve it. Finally, he handed it back to her. The phone in his back pocket buzzed. He pulled it out and grinned.

"What?" She looked at the screen and saw 'Chip' and his phone number. She was about to hit 'Delete' when the scent of his cologne hit her. It was musky and sweet. She inhaled deeply. Dang, if he wasn't kind of cute. He was her definition of pretty boy. Her finger hovered over the phone. She clicked the button. The screen went black and she shoved it back in her waistband. It vibrated. Expecting a text from Kate, she was surprised at the words.

Chip: *Let's get out of here*
Sara: *I hardly know you.*
Chip: *but you want to*

She felt stupid texting someone standing within arm's reach, but somehow it was easier.

Sara: *Maybe.*

She was still looking at her screen when he whispered in her ear. It jolted her. She felt the buzz of connection and followed as he walked toward the door. She grabbed her jacket from among the coats lined against the wall and let him lead her out of the building. He headed across the parking lot to a yellow sports car. He unlocked his car and made for the door. Her mother's warning about getting in cars with strangers broke the connection and she stopped.

"I'm not getting in your car."

He leaned against the trunk, folding his arms across his chest. "Fine. We'll talk."

"I don't know you. Is your name even Chip?"

"It's a nickname. All my friends call me Chip."

"But what's your real name?"

"Tavin."

He began telling her about his father, Edsel Hellman, who ran the service station in town. How he helped out when he could. He told her about his brothers. She drew closer and leaned on the car, feeling the connection again. His voice was soft and warm as he talked about growing up in town.

"You must be new here," he said. "I haven't seen you around before."

"Not new, but I'm from Way's End. I just don't get over on the ferry very often," she said. She smiled and leaned toward him. His elbow now resting on the trunk as they talked. She opened up her jacket and held up the back showing the large black bird printed there under the words 'Way's End High School'. "I'm a Raven."

"I believe it," he said reaching out and touching her long dark hair.

When her phone vibrated she tossed her jacket on the car with the bird staring up at them. Was that the time?

> **Kate:** *On the Ferry. Where are U?*
> **Sara:** *On my way.*

"I have to go."

"Stay. Let's go up to Madd Falls. You can catch the next ferry."

Her mother would have a fit if she went up to the falls. She would call Sheriff Ramírez if she missed the ferry. "I have to go." She reached in her bra and removed the key for her bike lock.

"Text me," he said as his eyes followed her hands.

She waved over her shoulder as she headed for her bike.

A black sports car drove by. A boy leaned out the passenger side and yelled, "Hey Tav, we're headed to the falls."

Tavin yelled back, "Meet you there."

He was in his car and out the lot before she was on her bike. She watched as the two cars speed down the street, the yellow one catching up to and passing the black car. She peddled to the ferry terminal as the black car was side by side with the yellow on the two-lane road. When she turned the block for the terminal past the statue of the town's founder, Julian Brioc, and the sign for the upcoming Centennial, she could see the black car ahead of the yellow one as they turned onto the road for the falls. It curved into the trees and she lost sight of the cars.

Sara boarded the ferry and stowed her bike. Then she went out on the deck in search of Kate and her boyfriend, Ritchie. Glancing toward the mountain, she saw that the road was higher up but followed the curve of the lake for a while. She saw the black car appear from the trees, then the yellow. The yellow car sped up in the left lane as they approached the curve.

Her heart was racing. She didn't want to witness a car crash, but she couldn't look away. Apparently, Tavin liked to live on the edge. The yellow car sped around the curve and whipped in front as the black one slowed. She saw taillights round the corner as they sped out of sight. A second passed and headlights appeared from the other direction as a blue car drove toward town.

"Hey, Sara," Kate called. She was sitting with Ritchie near the front of the ferry and had an open seat next to her.

She joined her friends.

"How was the movie?" she asked.

Kate blushed. "Uh, we skipped the movie and drove up to the falls. It's nice up there. You should come next time."

"You know my mom would kill me," she said.

"No, she wouldn't," Ritchie said. "She knows I'm a good driver."

Sara shook her head to disagree.

"How was the dance?" Kate asked.

She wanted to tell her about Chip, or rather Tavin, but there was so much wind it was hard to talk and she didn't want to shout it. Plus Ritchie was here. She zipped up her Raven's jacket and shrugged. She stared out at the white crests of the waves. "It was fine."

It had taken a while to collect her hair, pulling the strands from the brush every day and stashing them in her dresser. She wandered in the woods looking for the perfect sticks, no bigger than her hand with the fingers outstretched. She discarded many that didn't feel right, were too brittle, too thick, too narrow, did not sing. The book had been specific. Its yellowed pages describing the ancient voodoo power. It had to come from the Earth. Its vibrations felt.

The sticks bound by her hair were a crude skeleton, but she felt it. Her fingers smudged with dirt felt the humming like a long-forgotten song. It trembled in her hand. She needed something just as strong to hold it in. It was many days before she found it.

The faded words told her of Earth Magic in moss. The faded pictures showed green growing on rocks and hanging from trees. She wanted something stronger, darker. Stronger things needed more life; darker things required death. She had been afraid of the dark. She could no longer feel it, fear it.

It had been a mercy killing, she told herself. Put the crippled thing out of its misery. She didn't think her mother would notice the blood on the car tire. She took the plastic sack from the trunk. The printed words said, "Thank you. Come again."

She took the remains of the Raven, its eyes open and unseeing, and stuffed the bag. Its feet and wings stuck out. She placed the bag in the trunk of the car, covering it with an old towel. Unbidden tears streamed from her blue eyes down her face.

Now it lay on the ground surrounded by trees and melting snow. A shovel lay beside a shallow hole of half frozen Earth.

A light inside her repelled what she wanted ... had to do. She pushed it down and away. She grasped the black feathers and pulled.

They resisted.

"Ahh!" she cried out, pulling with her whole being. Her knees digging into the mud, her hand flung from her and a handful of black feathers fell from her bloodstained fingers. She felt the hum of magic through her legs, flowing into her hands. Felt it as strongly as she had felt connected to him.

When she rode her bike up the drive her mom was standing in the living room window, a dark silhouette against the bright lights on throughout the house. She was late, but only a little. Kate's house was before hers and they had been in the driveway talking.

"Hi, Mom. Sorry I'm late," she said.

"I told you eleven fifteen," her mom accused.

Sara said, "I'm only five minutes late."

"I was worried."

"You worry too much."

"You'll know when you have kids."

"Yeah, I'm never having kids," she muttered under her breath.

"What?"

"Nothing. I'm going to bed."

"Goodnight. I love you," her mother called to her as she headed for the bathroom. She could hear her mother locking the front door and moving around to turn off the lights. She didn't say it back.

As she brushed her teeth she got a text.

Kate: *You in trouble?*

Sara: *A little*
Kate: *Sorry. Next time, we won't talk so long.*

Sara stared at the phone and didn't reply. She didn't want to do a next time. It had been fun, but she wanted to stay in Way's End. She didn't want to upset her mother. She didn't want to be Kate's excuse to go into Mirror Point with Ritchie.

Kate: *Night*
Sara: *Night*

She was annoyed with her mother and her best friend. She took her phone to bed. She stared for a long time at the number. She edited the name and hesitated briefly before texting.

Kate: *Hey*
Tavin: *Hey*
Kate: *I just got home.*
Tavin: *What are you wearing?*

A pile of feathers lay beside the shallow grave. In a tree above, a cacophonous aggregation of ravens eyed her. She looked up, her eyes devoid of feeling, as a third bird joined the chorus. The cawing of the unkindness echoed in her ear, magnifying in her head.

"I'm sorry," she yelled to them. "There was no other way."

They paused at her words, but soon resumed their cries. She carefully gathered the feathers into the plastic bag. She would need more hair.

"Is she up?" Jenny asked as she flipped another pancake.

"I haven't heard her yet," Scott said. He scrolled through the news feed on his phone.

"Go wake her."

"Let her sleep. I read that kids aren't getting enough sleep."

Jenny put down the spatula. "Do you know what time she got home last night?"

"11:30."

"11:19," she said, picking up the spatula again.

"So?" he said. "It was Friday night. She's young."

"Parents have a lot to worry about these days," she said.

"I worry, too."

"It's not the same. You're only her step-father. You don't know."

At that, Scott put down his phone. "What? What don't I know?"

"She didn't come out of your body. You didn't sacrifice ..." Jenny paused, wiped at her brown eyes and took a breath. "There's gangs, and drugs, and boys ... it's not the same."

"Gangs in Mirror Point? Come on. You know she's not the type to do drugs. Sara's a smart girl," he said, "and I hope she did meet a boy."

"Don't even joke about that."

"Who's joking?"

Jenny pursed her lips. Thoughts of her lost ballet career, a pair of bright blue eyes and the little white sports car did a complicated choreography in her mind. She wanted to snatch them all back, recapture them, but they danced away from her, just out of reach.

Scott came to her. He took the spatula from her hand and wrapped his arms around her. The embrace chased away other thoughts; let her forget. He looked in her eyes and kissed her briefly. "She'll be fine. Don't worry so much."

The body was difficult. She sat – the rocks she placed making a circle around her. The lump on the ground she covered with leaves to keep the dirt from washing away. The unkindness of Ravens had grown to four.

Her fingers held the feathers tightly to the stick. Each feather was wrapped five times with her hair 'string' as she chanted.

Blood of Earth hold here within
Binding body to body, now begin
Power of darkness gather his soul
My mind's eye image let me control

Blood of Earth hold here within
Binding body to body, now begin
Power of darkness gather his soul
My mind's eye image let me control

Blood of Earth ...

The feathers under her fingers felt solid: a thing dense. He felt solid to her, before, once.

Tavin texted her most evenings the next few weeks when she was in bed. If she texted him any other time of day, he didn't reply. It surprised her to get a text Friday morning asking her out for that evening. She already had plans to go see *Girl on a Long Train to Nowhere* with Kate and Ritchie. She was really looking forward to seeing it, as she had read the book and it starred her favorite actress.

Tavin: *Me and you. Tonight.*
Sara: *Going to movie with friends.*
Tavin: *Cancel*
Sara: *Can't.*
Sara: *Come with.*

She received no reply until after school. She hadn't even asked Kate, since it didn't seem like Tavin was going to show. She responded immediately to his "What time?" She didn't need to tell him which movie or which theater, since there was only one in town and it only had one screen.

Ritchie had picked them both up at Kate's house. It seemed like Kate was now trying to go out of her way to make her not feel left out, which somehow made it worse. They were close to the front of the line outside the small theater. The two hundred or so seats tended to fill up fast. The owners, Bob and Kay Meyers, had bought the theater years ago and were happy keeping it just the way it was, including no on-line ticket sales. Mirror Point residents could deal with it, or they could drive the hour to the next town over to see movies in a newer theater.

Sara looked up and down the street. There was still no sign of Tavin.

"Are you sure this guy is coming?" Kate asked. "Maybe you should text him."

She bit her lip. She didn't want to come across as being overly anxious about the date. They shuffled forward a few more steps. They were almost to the ticket window. She smoothed down the front of her pink sundress. She shouldn't have bothered and just worn shorts instead. The September weather was starting to get cooler, but today was warm enough. Grey clouds hung heavy in the air, so she had worn her Way's End High School jacket with the raven mascot across the back. She reached into the pocket and turned on her phone. She started to type, 'Where ar' when she heard a high-pitched girl's voice call out, "Hey, Tavin!"

She looked up, eyeing the brown-haired figure striding across the street. He gave a slight nod in the direction of the shout and Sara's head swung around to the girl in line and quickly back to Tavin. They locked eyes and he headed toward her.

She introduced him. "Kate and Ritchie, this is Tavin, but all his *good* friends call him Chip."

He looked slightly embarrassed. "It's just Tavin."

Kate gave her a questioning look as she said, "Hi, Tavin."

"Hey." Ritchie acknowledged him with a nod and turned to buy the movie tickets.

Sara was unsure of the date status and hesitated. Tavin waved her forward and stepped in behind her, so she pulled some cash out of her phone case and paid for her ticket.

Waiting in line for popcorn and soda, she asked, "Have you read the book? It's really good. I've been looking forward to this movie for a long time."

"I don't read much," he replied.

"But you've heard of it, right?"

He shrugged.

When they entered the theater, Kate and Ritchie were already sitting in the middle of the sixth row with two seats saved for her. It was her sweet spot for watching movies. The perfect viewing angle. She returned Kate's wave and headed toward them, only to be stopped by a hand on her wrist.

"Come on," Tavin said, pulling her toward the back row.

"But my friends ..."

He said nothing, waiting for her to make up her mind. His body leaning away from her. Buttery popcorn scents tinged with a musky cologne wafted up to her. She tugged a little toward her friends. He gave her a smile and she stopped. He grinned wider and pulled her just a bit more. She caved.

Sara looked back to Kate, waved and pointed to the back row. She never sat in the back row. What was the point of that? She paid to see the movie and stood in line early, just so she could get a good seat. Still, she followed Tavin to the farthest corner.

The red velvet chairs were old, but cushy, and matched the curtains in front of the screen. Soon all the seats were filled, except the fourth one in the front row. Even the second one in the third row was filled. Maybe it wouldn't rain.

She put her jacket in her lap being careful not to lose her muted phone. They both put their sodas on the floor, since there weren't any cup holders. Tavin reached in and grabbed popcorn from her bag. "Hey, get your own."

"Tav," a guy in a Mirror Point HS sweatshirt called. He was two rows up with a large group of teens Sara thought were probably all from his high school. "Your dad have time to look at my car?"

"Sure, bring it by the shop Monday."

The lights dimmed and the curtain pulled back to reveal the screen. The previews began and she practically inhaled her popcorn before the movie started, to keep Tavin from eating all of it. She wiped the grease from her hands and reached for her soda.

"While you're ..." the music blared, then adjusted to normal levels as the movie began.

She settled back in her seat and sipped from the straw. "What did you say?"

He bent his head to her ear and said, "Never mind," before gently biting her earlobe.

Soda threatened to shoot out her nose, but she choked it down as her body gave an involuntary shiver. She felt more than heard his chuckle. Her hands shook a bit as she finished her soda, trying to keep her mind on the movie. Tavin seemed to be watching the movie, but every time she got absorbed by the screen, he would blow in her ear.

She finished her drink and set it down. The couple on her other side were making out and didn't seem interested in the movie at all, which was oddly distracting. She couldn't concentrate on the movie, so she turned to glare at Tavin's dimly lit profile.

"Shhh." He put his finger to his lips. "I'm trying to watch the movie."

"No, you're not," she hissed, still glaring at him in the dark.

He turned to face her, his face now inches from hers. She held her breath, lips parted, barely daring to breath. He leaned in.

Under the sweetness of the corn, she tasted butter and salt from his lips. She wanted to drown in buttery saltness. She thought she might and didn't know how long she had been swimming. On the screen, her favorite actress was looking out the window of a train. When had she gotten on the train?

She started when Tavin pulled her jacket off her lap. "My phone."

"Oops. Here it is." He put it back in her pocket and draped the jacket over their laps.

"Are you cold?" she whispered.

"Yeah," he said, reaching for her hand.

She smiled. She hadn't held a boy's hand since roller skating with Dave Williams in the fourth grade.

He smiled back and slid her hand under the jacket onto his lap.

The shiny black figure was grotesque. It was a solid mass of feathers and hair covered sticks. She held the grey material in her other hand. The book had told her an item of personal clothing was the best skin. She needed it to be the best.

She had gone to the garage. He was working. His car was in the lot. She thought she might grab a shirt. He never locked his car. The gods favored her with his gym bag sitting on the back seat. No one was watching as she reached in for a t-shirt or sock. Her eyes kept vigil on the garage door. Beneath shoes, she felt the soft material, quickly gathered it and shut the door.

He appeared. She folded her arms around the item and dropped her head. Her dark hair hiding the theft.

"What are you doing here?" he asked.

"Nothing, I just ..."

"I'm busy. I have to work."

"Okay, I just ..."

He turned and left.

She inhaled the scent of him from the ball of fabric in her hand. Not a sock. She held the boxer briefs up, eyes growing wide. Then urgently balled them up, shoving it in the pocket of her Raven's jacket. She pushed off his car remembering the first time she had been in it.

The movie was long and she was trying to pay attention, but she could practically feel her face burning. She occasionally glanced over at the couple next to her. They were permanently glued to each other. With all that soda, now she really had to pee. "Bathroom," she said, extricating herself. She left her jacket, jostled past the couple (who came up for air) and finally made it to the end of the aisle.

When she emerged from the restroom, she was surprised to find Tavin waiting for her. He handed her her jacket. "Let's get out of here."

"But the movie isn't over."

"You read the book. You already know how it ends." He grabbed her hand, as if she might somehow escape back into the theater.

"I came with Kate and Ritchie," she said lamely.

"You can text her." He pulled her to him, kissed her forehead and proceeded to walk slowly backward toward the exit.

She was still locked in his arms. Her steps were slow and awkward, but they kept heading for the door. She made no attempt at resistance. When his back hit the door, he let go of her. He turned and pushed the door wide open and stepped out.

She felt the rush of cooler air swirl around her as the door began to close. Tavin was standing across the threshold. She could still go back and finish the movie. He stood watching her as the door cut her view: hand, arm, shoulder, ear, eye.

She pushed it and stepped through.

The bright yellow sports car stood out from the rest of the cars in the parking lot. Tavin unlocked the door with his key fob and got in the driver's side. Vague echoes of her stepfather's words nudged at her brain. Words like: dating, gentlemen, and always opening car doors. Sara pushed the word NEVER down, away where she didn't have to hear it, and opened the door.

The black interior was immaculate and smelled like some sort of citrus cleaning solution. Above the gleaming dash a lacy black bra hung from the rearview mirror. She hesitated. He leaned back and cocked his head, so he could look at her. A lazy smile grew on his face and his wink drew her in.

"Nice car," she said as she wondered whose bra it was. She was hoping he bought it himself for show. That story worked for her.

"It wasn't running when it came into the shop, so I got it cheap." He ran his hand across the dash. "Fixed it up myself."

"Cool."

He started the engine and began to back out. Sara panicked and her hand moved for the seatbelt. Then she noticed that he hadn't buckled his. She didn't want to seem chicken in front of him, so her hand fluttered back down to her lap. It made her uncomfortable, but now they were already moving. "Where are we going?"

"You'll see."

They headed for the end of town and took the turn to Madd Falls Road. She gripped the edge of her seat as he sped around the curves. They were nearing the big curve she remembered from the other night. She thought about the seatbelt behind her and held her breath.

Blue lights flashing in the rear facing mirrors drew a curse from Tavin. The yellow car slowed and pulled over at the closest turn off. He rolled down his window and the officer peered in at them.

"Evening officer," Tavin said.

He nodded his head to Tavin and tipped his hat to Sara. "License and registration."

Tavin handed them over. He seemed perfectly calm, but Sara was shaking with nerves.

"You're Edsel's boy, Tavin, aren't you?" he asked as he handed back the papers.

Tavin had on his respectable son face. "Yes, sir."

"Do you know how fast you were going?"

"Sorry, I wasn't paying attention."

"And you're both not wearing seatbelts." He eyed them directly for several seconds before clearing his throat. "Your father's a good man. He'd feel real bad if something happened to you. You know that's a dangerous curve up ahead."

Deputy Sheriff Andy Moran stood tall and tapped his pad against his leg. He seemed to come to a decision about something. Then he leaned back in the window. "I'm not going to give you a ticket today. I'm giving you a warning. SLOW DOWN and put on your seatbelt. I just saved you both a lot of money and probably your lives. Don't make me regret this. Next time, you will get a ticket." He rapped the top of the car and they both put on their seatbelts.

"Thank you, sir," Tavin called.

Deputy Sheriff Moran waved and Tavin waved back. As soon as his back was turned, Tavin's wave turned into 'the bird', which quickly disappeared as the officer got into his car.

The yellow car eased back onto the road. They didn't speak, and Tavin turned the radio up to cover the silence. He took the sharp curve a little too fast, but the car handled it smoothly and Sara's breathing returned to normal.

He turned and looked out the back window. "Good. He's gone."

The car slowed and turned left onto an obscure road leading back into the trees. The headlights of the car showed a gravel path winding up away from the main road.

"Where does this go?"

"Nowhere," he replied.

"I thought we were going to the falls."

"This place is better," he said.

The car crept up the path and finally turned onto an open clearing. Trees hid it from the main road, but between them Sara could just make out the sharp curve of the road below and the lake beyond. Tavin stopped the engine and cut the lights.

"Hey," he said.

Sara swallowed and managed a weak, "hey."

He undid his seat belt and reached over pushing the button on hers. It clicked open and slid across her and out of sight. He beckoned with his finger.

"C'mere."

The silver blades came together, cutting the man shape from the grey fabric. The edges were jagged. It was imperfect, like the man, the boy. Like his soul.

She sat in the circle of rocks on more leaves she had gathered. The quaternary of the large black birds eyed her intently.

The energy from the material buzzed around her. The scissors cut sharp angles as she chanted.

> *Blood of Earth through my hands*
> *Weave your power in these strands*
> *Shape of man formed from raiment*
> *My mind's eye image take in payment*
>
> *Blood of Earth through my hands*
> *Weave your power in these strands*
> *Shape of man formed from raiment*
> *My mind's eye image take in payment*
>
> *Blood of Earth ...*

In her mind the pain of betrayal was a dull memory, cut into her like the pieces of grey fabric falling into her lap.

Sara woke the next morning and stared at her dance trophies and awards on the shelf over her bed. They seemed to taunt her. She was not living up to her mother's dreams. She was not going to be the next Prima Ballerina. But in her case, it wasn't because of a boy. She had already failed miserably at dancing before she met Tavin. Her mother would still use it as an excuse to keep him away.

She wanted him to meet her mom and stepdad, but she would have to work on her mom first. It would be a hard sell.

Her phone buzzed. She reached under her pillow, smiling at the expected text from Tavin.

Kate: *Come over.*

She read the text several times, confused by the unexpected disappointment.

Sara: *Not up yet. Later.*
Kate: *Okay. Hurry. Need to tell you something.*

Her mom placed a bowl of oatmeal in front of her. "You can put it in the microwave. It's probably cold. Your dad and I ate hours ago."

Sara took the bowl to the microwave. She could feel her mother watching her accusingly. Did her mom somehow know about Tavin? It hadn't been that late, so her parents were both still up watching a show when she had gone to bed.

"Sorry. Just catching up on sleep." The microwave dinged and she sat back down with her bowl.

"How was the movie?"

"It was really good," she said, not looking up at her mom. She hated lying, especially to her mother, who had some kind of crazy mom lie detector implanted in her brain. "The book was better." That probably wasn't a lie.

"What was better about the book?" her mom asked.

Sara was spared an answer when her stepdad walked in. "Jen, let's go. I want to get the shopping done, so I can watch the game."

She breathed a sigh of relief when they both left. She'd have to ask Kate about the movie. Hopefully, she was paying more attention.

Kate practically dragged her to the pink room upstairs. The bed bounced beneath their weight as Sara turned to her friend. "You have to tell me everything about the movie."

Kate grabbed her hands. "I have to tell you something about Tavin."

"What?"

"He's dating Sophie."

"Which Sophie?" Sara pulled her hands away and picked at the lint on the bed spread. She didn't want to hear this. "How do you know?"

"At the movie," Kate said, "some girls sitting next to us were from Mirror Point High School. They saw you together. One said, 'Isn't that Tavin? He's dating my friend, Sophie TerVeer.' They texted her before the movie started. When the movie ended, they were plotting to feed him to the Spirit Lake monster. I tried to warn you about him. Didn't you get my texts?"

She folded her arms across her chest remembering the deleted texts asking where she was and not to go off with Tavin. "No. They must not have gone through. You know how bad reception is around here."

"He's bad news. You're not seeing him again, right?"

"Definitely," she lied.

She placed four of the eggs outside the circle on each cardinal point and the fifth egg she buried with her sacrifice. The Ravens flew down one by one, broke the shells and devoured their contents. The book told her five held power to seal the spell.

The needle glinted in the light as she sewed. The two flat man pieces covered the black feathered body. It was difficult to hold and sew together. Her fingers stretched the fabric, but sometimes got in the way. Pricks of blood dotted the grey fabric.

She sucked her finger where the needle had punctured her again. She drew a straight line for his blood red mouth. She finished stitching the skin to the body, the mouth getting darker as she sewed.

She studied the book every night. It consumed her thoughts. The idol before her grew stronger. The book told her it would. She trusted the book from the moment she first touched it.

The next week she frequently brought up boys in general to her mother. She wanted to ease her into the topic, even though her mother always changed it, usually to talk about how she was doing at school. Which lately was not as good as it had been.

She didn't believe Kate, didn't want to believe her. Even if Tavin had been dating Sophie TerVeer, they must have broken up. He wouldn't go out with her and Sophie at the same time. It just wasn't possible. She didn't know Sophie that well. She was one of the few rich kids in Way's End. Her house was on The Bluffs with the scattering of other rich houses. She had seen her around school. Sophie wasn't what everyone thought of as attractive, but she was well dressed in a way that screamed of money.

It wasn't a conscience decision on her part, but she avoided Kate for most of the week. It wasn't hard, since Kate was wrapped up with Ryan.

In art class they were doing portraits. Sara was working on a pencil drawing of Tavin from a picture off her phone. She was trying to capture the wave and shine of his hair when Ms. Quay hovered over her shoulder.

"Take your finger and smooth out the edges. Like this." Ms. Quay ran her finger along Tavin's jawline and softened up the dark pencil lines. She studied the face for a long moment. "It looks good. Seeing how you're ahead of most of the class, would you mind doing me a favor?"

Sara looked around. It didn't seem like she was any closer to finishing her portrait than the others, but she liked Ms. Quay. "I don't mind."

"Good. You know I'm getting married soon. I need this book from the library. We're doing our own vows." Her teacher tore off a sheet of bristol paper and wrote on it. Then she folded it in half and handed it to Sara. "Ask the librarian. She'll show you where it is."

Way's End High School was originally built to be a hotel, but before construction was finished the owner died. After several years, the town purchased the building from the family and made it into the first high school. The outside of the red brick historic building had the appearance of a medieval castle with turrets and spires. The library, office and cafeteria were on the ground floor. The gym was in a separate building, next to the football stadium. In the 1940s there had been an earthquake which shifted the home team end zone six inches to the south. Sara loved this school.

She wouldn't trade this building for the newer one in Mirror Point, even if all their rooms had heat in the winter. She went down the stairs and headed to the library on the other side of the building. Out of curiosity, she opened the folded piece of paper.

The note was written in French or something. The only words she recognized were "Trina Quay" signed at the end.

She pushed open the heavy wooden doors to the library. Behind the desk a new librarian was helping a boy in a football jersey. She could tell by his black hair and the number on the back it was Dave Williams. He was a nice guy, but she knew he would probably need a lot of help. Rumor was he needed to get his grades up or he'd be on suspension from football. She looked around for the head librarian, Mrs. Small, who was ironically on the tall side.

Several girls were studying at a table. As she walked by, she overheard one say, "Did you know Sophie TerVeer is pregnant? Brianna saw her buying a pregnancy kit at the store."

"Shhhhh." The girls grew silent and watched as she walked by. The murmuring started again after she passed. It gave her an uneasy feeling and her thoughts drifted to Tavin.

She headed for a tall older woman with a cart reshelving books. "Hi, Mrs. Small. Ms. Quay sent me to get a book for her." Sara handed her the note.

The librarian read it, looked Sara up and down, and read the note again. "I see," she said, pushing the cart off to the side. "Follow me."

They walked past all the rows of books. On the far wall was a door. Mrs. Small removed a ring of keys from her pocket. The door opened up at the top of a stairway. The lights flickered and buzzed when she flipped the switch and they made the steep descent.

Sara had heard rumors of a secret library. She had never seen it. As if reading her thoughts, Mrs. Small said, "Students aren't allowed down here except with teacher permission. It's where we keep the rare and old books. Ms. Quay trusts you. She said for you to bring back the book she wants and that she'll vouch for you, if you want to check out something for yourself."

"Oh. Nice."

The room was cool but didn't feel damp. The musty smell of old books hung in the air. Ancient wooden shelves lined the walls and stood in rows like soldiers. The very back shelf held books locked behind glass doors.

Mrs. Small noticed her looking. "Those are the rare books. You won't need anything from there. Here we are." She stopped in front of a stack of books with old leather spines and pulled out a thick red book with gold lettering. "This is the book for Ms. Quay. You can stay here for a few minutes to look around, but I should get back upstairs. Just close the door behind you when you leave and it will lock. And remember to be very careful with these books."

"Right, 'cause they're old," Sara said.

The librarian gave her a queer look, then nodded and left.

Sara was passionate about books. Being down here was a dream she didn't know she had. She thumbed through the book for Ms. Quay. It was hand lettered and unreadable. There were a few diagrams, but Sara couldn't make any of it out. She had no idea how this was supposed to be helpful for Ms. Quay's wedding. She placed the red book on a wood book stand and paced the shelves. She pulled out book after book and replaced them. Many seemed to be on plants and animals, but others seemed oddly about magic.

Two covers caught her eye and she pulled out a green book and the black book beside it. The embossed cover read, "The Grimoire of Voodoo Arts" enclosed in a circle of feathers. The green book had no title, but was an unusual shade. It almost matched the green of her shirt. Its pages were filled with grotesque pictures of demons emerging from pits of fire and torturing humans. The pictures were fascinating and a bit unsettling, so she returned that book to the shelf. The black book had fewer pictures and seemed to contain mostly incantations. Maybe there was a love spell in it.

She grabbed the two books and went up to the main library. Mrs. Small was at the front desk and she placed both books in front of her. She was slightly nervous about checking out a book from the 'secret' library, but the Head Librarian didn't blink at the request. "I'll put Ms. Quay's name on this card. You can write your name on this card." Mrs. Small slid a blue-lined, white card across the desk to her.

"I have my student ID card," Sara said.

"Oh, these books aren't in the computer. We still use the card file for them." She pulled out a long wooden tray and filed the card for the red book in it. Sara wrote her name on the next empty line on the other card and handed it to her. "Enjoy your book."

Cotton string had been dyed with onion skins and turmeric. The golden brown of his hair. She had boiled it with some of his hair caught on her ring. The strands, later twisted into the string. The Ravens cawed as she called out to them, laying down more eggs for their feast.

She finished sewing on the hair and brown button eyes above the blood red mouth, now almost black. She could feel him in the skin, see his eye-candy looks in the hideous figure. It resembled him, beneath the skin.

She went to the lake after the boat had gone. No one was around.

She held the grey form under the water. Baptizing it from the book she had borrowed. A sprinkle of Sea Salt from the kitchen. She danced at the edge of the water, holding the doll. Giving it his name.

Overhead a Raven cawed.

That evening after dinner Sara went upstairs to do her homework. She pulled the book from her backpack and studied it. She had texted Tavin, but he hadn't replied. She was sure that he had nothing to do with Sophie and her buying a pregnancy test. It could have been for her mother or something.

She ran her hand across the soft leather feeling the raised letters and decoration. She was fascinated by the idea of voodoo. All kinds of images came to her as she stroked the cover. Love spell. She just knew there was one in there. She thought about calling Kate to come over, so they could both make love spells. The echo of Kate's warning to stay away from Tavin stopped her.

Fine, she would do this on her own. Kate be ... well, darned.

The next morning she was exhausted. The book had kept her up all night. It was difficult getting through a lot of the language, which seemed to read almost like Old English. She enjoyed Shakespeare, so she felt she was picking up the gist of it. One section in particular spoke about destroying someone's aspect and shaping it to a more favorable one by recreating their image. She thought that sounded promising.

She did miserably on the test she hadn't studied for and had to finish a paper during lunch, but she managed to make it through the day. All the while, she referred to the book on the best way to recreate a person's image. She jotted in her notebook.

Sticks
Twine
Hair
Feathers
Clothing (sock?)
Straw, Yarn
Brown buttons
Sea Water (sea salt?)
Baptism (book from church)
Shovel

On the side she sketched out a picture of the finished image with hearts surrounding it. It would be kind of an ugly doll. Maybe she could make it prettier with some ribbon or something.

It had been her intention to cast a love spell, but you cannot cast love on a barren heart. She studied the book and the words and the idea had grown in her. It spread like weeds in the garden of her soul. She had already made a choice and the path lay before her.

She replaced the pink pins she had taken from her mother's pin cushion. Carefully, she selected all the black ones.

Sara collected the first couple of items from home. Then she fretted about the clothing. Still no texts had come from Tavin. After school that day her parents were still at work, so she skipped her last class and took the ferry over to Mirror Point. She just needed to get a piece of clothing from Tavin. Not that she really believed in voodoo or magic, but what could it really hurt.

Her life would be perfect. Tavin would fall in love with her. She would leave Way's End and they would get married. They'd live in a nice house in Mirror Point where he would work as owner of Hellman's Garage and Gas. It would be a pretty good life. She couldn't fool herself enough to believe that he was in love with her now but after next week ... Who knew?

The ten-minute ferry ride across Spirit Lake was not unusual, but today she felt anxious. She had never been to his school while it was still in session. She worried that she might run into someone that would recognize her. Luck was with her as she walked her bike off the boat with only strangers around. She rode the five minutes up to the high school and cruised the parking lot looking for Tavin's car. She spotted it in the far corner.

She got off her bike and sat in the grass near his car. She unzipped her jacket and pulled her phone from the pocket of her red shirt. A text from Kate wondering where she was. Delete. No text from Tavin.

Eventually, the bell rang and she watched the doors. Tavin emerged, bringing a smile to her face. It faded when she saw he was attached to a blonde girl wearing a tight Hellman's Garage and Gas t-shirt. This girl was not her and it wasn't Sophie. With their hands clasped, Tavin pulled the girl closer and they kissed. The blonde left in a different direction and Tavin headed her way.

Sara didn't wait for him to see her. She got on her bike and sped to the ferry.

Stupid boy.

Stupid love.

Stupid her.

She buried the doll next to the sacrifice in the circle of rocks. It would be ready in five days.

Sara tied an old shoe lace around the dirty figure and hung it around her neck. The grey smudged doll with its yellow brown hair sticking up and brown button eyes rested on her gunmetal grey jersey, just south of her heart. The black pins were angled so they didn't stick out the other end and poke her. There were a lot of pins. She covered the ugly thing with her Ravens jacket.

She stood on the prow of the ferry with the wind whipping her face. Rain drizzled from the sky, casting a grey mist around everything. She wondered about the time, but she had tossed her phone in her closet weeks ago and hadn't bothered to charge it since. It didn't matter.

When the ferry docked, she rode through the rain up to the school.

She had heard of another dance. Cars were parked outside, but she only needed to see one. The yellow was a beacon standing out in the lot. She willed it to follow her. She willed it's driver.

She threw the leather gris-gris pouch with the black feathers tied to it over the roof of the car. It fell to earth, binding the magic.

"Follow me," she whispered with forceful breath.

She was drenched and out of breath by the time she reached the clearing. She dropped her bike behind a tree and waited.

On the fifth day she brought five eggs and five black candles. She placed the eggs as before and the candles just inside the circle of rocks, the fifth in the center. The glow from the candles glinted off the shovel as it unearthed the magic she had sown. Metal clanged against stones. She was careful not to dig too close, not to cut off any parts, yet.

The unkindness gathered to watch. They feasted one last time.

She knelt on the ground and carefully shook the Earth from the grey form. The damp half-frozen fabric smelled of a faint musky decay. It hummed in her fingers, singing of connection. The Earth bound to her and to another across the water.

She called his name so loud the Ravens hopped back, startled.

It was just her.

They resumed their feast. The cracking of shells under their beaks a background to her chanting. She swayed with the energy flowing from the ground into her bare feet.

> *Blood of Earth flow from me*
> *Transfer essence to this body*
> *Give power over fleshly aspect*
> *My mind's eye image here collect*

She began to turn, slowly at first.

> *Blood of Earth flow from me*
> *Transfer essence to this body*
> *Give power over fleshly aspect*
> *My mind's eye image here collect*

She spun faster. The doll clutched in her right hand, arms outstretched, her mind in a trance.

Blood of Earth flow from me
Transfer essence to this body
Give power over fleshly aspect
My mind's eye image here collect

She fell to earth. Her eyes closed, but her lips still moved.

Blood of Earth ...

Mud seeped into her shoes. She spun slowly, winding the energy to her, into her. When she could feel it tightly coiled within her, she stopped.

She sat facing the road, the curve below her like a serpent. She pulled the doll from her jacket.

A Raven drifted down and settled in the tree overhead.

She pulled out a black pin and stuck it in the grey cloth of the right foot.

"Come to me."

Another in his left foot.

"Come to me."

A second Raven landed in a tree to her right.

Holding another pin tightly, she pushed it carefully between the brown button eyes.

"Your mind is open. Your eyes do not see."

Several cars drove past. They slowed at the curve. Neither was yellow.

The third Raven perched high above on her left.

She pricked a pin in the center of the 'Y' stick. Twisted it, just to be sure.

"You need nothing else. Race to me."

The quaternary Raven circled above.

She selected another pin.

Its talons latching onto a tree in front of her.

She looked up at it, rain dripping down her face.

Headlights appeared far below.

She drove the pin into the left arm.

"You lose control."

The car swerved on the road. She saw a flash of yellow. The car righted itself.

Quickly she stabbed a pin in the figure's head.

"You do not have control."

The car screeched near the edge, but straightened. She could see his face in the window, hands clenched on the wheel. He was almost to the curve.

She fumbled for a pin.

Dropped it.

Fumbled for another.

Hurry.

The panic in his face echoed hers.

Clutching the voodoo doll in her hand, she plunged the pin in its heart.

"Damn you!"

The head of the pin impacted the grey material; its point piercing her palm. Tears mixed with rain. Yellow and sparks and twisted metal wrapped around the screeching, "Eeeeeeeeee." Crashing echoed into the ghostly cawing of a Raven from across the water.

No one noticed Sara on the return ferry. The air was buzzing with news of the crash. She could still see the red flashing lights on the road near the gaping hole in the railing. The yellow car was upside down on the rocks, halfway between the road and the water.

In her left hand, three fingers curled over a napkin to staunch the blood, two held the rain-soaked figure. She plucked out the black pins and tossed them in the water one by one. The other ferry passengers were inside keeping warm and dry.

She was alone.

When all the pins were gone, she held the figure between her hands and snapped the twigs inside. Her hands hung over the railing of the ferry. Her fingers opened. The doll fell, bounced once off the spray from the boat and churned under the waves, disappearing from view.

She breathed.

At the funeral, it was mentioned, but not to Edsel Hellman or his other sons, how odd it was that the coroner's office found water in Tavin's lungs.

It was almost as if he had drowned and not broken his back when his car had crashed. Of course he had been drinking and everyone knew how he liked to drive too fast. Deputy Sheriff Andy Moran shook his head with regret. Young people thought they were immortal. Didn't they know seatbelts save lives?

In Way's End a few people were saddened by news of Tavin's death. Sophie was seen crying in the bathroom.

Sara was surprised by how much she felt. She cried and Kate had been very sympathetic.

She clutched the black leatherbound book to her as she headed down the hall to the library. It felt heavy in her arms. She tried not to act nervous as she slid the book across the counter to Mrs. Small.

"You're finished?" she asked as she pulled the wooden card tray from the shelf. She thumbed through the cards looking for the right one.

"I'm done," Sara said.

Mrs. Small picked up the book and examined it as if looking for signs of damage. "Good."

"Okay," Sara nodded. "Um, thanks."

She turned and left. Mrs. Small watched as the door closed behind her. She flipped over the library checkout card. Her finger skimmed down the list of names until she saw the "J". The date was right. Seventeen years ago. She thought about how apples didn't fall far, even good apples. "Sometimes nice girls do," she muttered as she stamped the card with today's date, "do voodoo."

The Hitchhiker
by Robin Ridenour

Reba's pickup bumped slowly along the dim lake road that connected Mirror Point to its neighbor to the west, as she peered into the bushes for Wilbur. The drizzly, dark night made it hard to see – a far cry from the dry Arkansas weather – and the former life she'd escaped by moving here.

"Where's that blasted hog got to, you think?" She rubbed Samuel's long floppy ears, and he turned to stick his nose out the window, claws digging into the heavy-duty vinyl spread over the seat. "Can't imagine he knew it was Sausage Day."

She braked hard at a pale shape looming in the shadows. "Good Lord." She gripped the wheel tighter – what was it?

Through the swirling dust, the headlights illuminated a man at the side of the road, carrying ... a gun? A baseball bat? He threw his hand up to shield against the bright lights, squinting. Odd to be way out here, but these young people had no sense sometimes.

"What you reckon, Samuel? 'Do not neglect to show hospitality to strangers, for thereby some have entertained angels unawares.'" His tail wagged as they rolled up to the stranger. "Well, he don't look nothing like an angel to me," she told the beagle. But he *was* handsome, in a hungry – looking way, except for the blood on his face and neck.

Reba fished in the side pocket, then lowered the window a mite more.

"You okay, son? You need me to call 911?" The .45 in her hand didn't waver.

His eyes widened when he saw her gun. He raised both hands – it was an axe he carried, the edge clotted with gore. "No, ma'am, I'm fine – this ain't my blood." He shook his head. "Something come after me in the woods. Squealin' and hollerin' – reckon it was a bear."

Reba laughed. "I'm after a hog – he's a big 'un. It was probably him what got after you. Did you get him? Help me track him down, and I'll give you some of the sausages from my last batch. 'Let him labor, doing honest work with his own hands, that he may have something to share with anyone in need.'"

"I don't know, ma'am." He wet his lips, eyes on her gun. "I could use the work, but I ain't goin' back in those woods, not without a light. But if you got something to share, I'll take it – I'm too hungry to think straight."

Samuel nosed her and then faced the man.

Reba looked at him a long moment. Young. Seemed jumpy – some of them nowadays had no judgment, but she tried to do her Christian duty. She laid her gun on the seat. "Hop in, then. This here's Samuel – named after my late husband. The dog listens better, though."

The man bent to look into the cab, then climbed in and rested his axe on the rubber floor mat. The beagle wriggled and sniffed his sleeve.

"Mind your feet," Reba said. "That's vodka for the hog."

"For the hog?" He hefted the paper bag.

"Yep. I use an ax to kill 'em, then cut 'em to bleed out where they lie. But first I give 'em a party, so they're drunk when it happens." She shrugged. "Guess I'll drink it instead, if Wilbur don't show. I've got another flashlight at my place – let's get to it." She piloted the truck through a 3-point turn to head back.

He glanced again at the bottle.

"Have a swig if you like – paper cups in the glove box. 'Drink no longer water, but take a little wine for thy stomach's sake.' Just a bit, though," she cautioned. "'Specially if it's been a while since you ate."

"Don't mind if I do." He cracked the seal, poured out a tot, and threw it back. His gaze darted to the gun and around the cab again, lingering on her chest – how long since a man looked at her that way? "Nice truck. Thanks for the ride. These days most people would just as soon rob you as look at you. You ain't afraid of me?"

Reba laughed. "I ain't 'most people,' and I've been around a while, son. I try to give everyone the benefit of the doubt 'til I have reason to change.

The Bible says, 'Give and it will be given to you. For with the measure you use it will be measured back to you.'" She eyed the hickory handle in his palm. "And an axe is no good in a small space like this, anyway."

"No shit." He snatched up her gun, pointing it straight at her heart. He licked his lips again. "Pull off here, nice and slow."

"What're you doing, son? You don't want to hurt me. 'The wages of sin is death.'"

His eyes traveled over her breasts. "I ain't gonna hurt you none – I just need a little of your attention. And your truck."

Samuel barked and yelped, whirling in the seat.

Reba turned off the ignition and unclipped her seatbelt. "Well, you've got my *attention*, son, but I don't aim to turn the other cheek, so to speak. 'Like a muddied spring is a righteous man who gives way before the wicked.'" She dropped her voice. "'Blessed be the Lord, my rock, who trains my hands for war and my fingers for battle –'"

"Shut up with that! I've got something for you to *worship*, right here." His left hand tugged at his zipper.

The beagle whined.

"Samuel, *down*." Her blade cleared its sheath before the hammer clicked on the empty chamber.

Blood bubbled gently between his fingers as he clutched his chest, his neck. "Shit." He slumped against the window and was still.

"No judgment." Reba shook her head. "A real shame, that. And the pig gone, too."

Samuel crowded up to the man's neck, licking at the blood, tail going a mile a minute.

Reba turned over the engine. "Maybe you're right, boy. 'Every moving thing that lives shall be food for you.'" She rubbed his ears and glanced appraisingly at the dead man. "Looks like we'll get the same amount of sausage, too."

Dominique should have known better than to bet against him.

The Omen
by Stephen christiansen

"Another body has been found in links to the brutal slayings of ..."
Click.
"The body count continues to climb as another ..."
Click.
"He used to be such a good boy."

Dominique Black stopped flipping through the channels of the news broadcasts and stayed with this particular one. He quickly brought up his hand in the shape of a gun, pointed at his fifth grade teacher, the one being interviewed on the television, and brought his thumb down.

"Bang."

Dominique shook his head. She never really knew or understood him, no one really did, and it was a surprise that these newscasters even dug her up just to have this interview. Perhaps it was for shock value, a good kid gone bad. Well, they had no idea. If they wanted shock value then he would give it to them. At least he was good for something if not a riveting story for their headlines. At least now he was somebody.

He couldn't remember his first kill. They all said that he would never forget, but there had been so many that they were now starting to blend together. He was sure that the first one had a motive, and that the second one was simply easier, and by the time he made his third then it was more out of habit.

He had strangled them, shot them, and had even stabbed them. He had shoved more than one off of a tall building and not more than a few were drowned. He had even burned a woman alive in her building just to increase his thrill and be more creative. A smile came across his face when he thought of that one.

But no matter how he had done it, he had always left his calling card, a message written in the victim's blood. It had been different every time; it didn't matter. It was just something for the media to grab hold of and announce his creative outlet. He was proud of his calling card, but it had almost cost him.

The investigators were getting close, too close for comfort. They had almost caught him in the last run down hotel that he stayed in. It was time to move on, somewhere else, where no one knew him. The stolen car had broken down just outside of town and with the night quickly approaching, this place was as good as any.

The small town of Mirror Point was tucked in the mountains and was well off the beaten path. No one would find him here. As long as the car that he pushed off the side of the road and into the forest wasn't found, then he could stay here as long as he wanted. He might even be able to pick up his "hobby" once again, at least as soon as the heat settled down. He wondered how many of this town could go "missing" before he had to pack up and move on.

Dominique gave a yawn. It was getting late, but despite this fact, he had to admit he wasn't tired. The prospect of a whole new town available for his taking was an excitement that chased away any form of doziness. It was time to see what Mirror Point had to offer.

Dominique clicked the remote one more time. The television went off and plunged the room into darkness.

Leaving Mirror Point B&B, the rustic old place where he had taken up lodging for the night, Dominique set out to wander the streets. The cool crisp air of autumn hit his lungs. The coming of winter in this alpine setting was like an omen of things to come. He could imagine the whole town shutting down for a month or two during the winter months before the roads would be cleared of snow and the pass would reopen. There would be a time where life came to a standstill before resuming once again.

He had to laugh at that. He was becoming far too poetic for his new outlook at life. But perhaps it was true. Perhaps it was an omen of things to come. Perhaps the oncoming bitterness in the air was a warning to the people of this town that something was coming for them, something that they should be afraid of. But there was nothing they could do now. He was already here and it was too late.

Dominique passed a small library, a fish and tackle shop, even a small bakery called The Piehole: Pies and More Café. The buildings came and went as he turned from one street to another and none had caught his attention until he was about ready to turn back. Then he saw it. It called to him. He heeded its call.

The Grey Wolf Casino was everything he had expected it to be. There was a totem pole outside. Most of the animals were so faded, he couldn't make them out, with the exception of the raven on top. The building itself was rustic, with a rock base half way up followed by planks of cedar with full wooden logs for accents. Dominique was sure that the stone was merely a facade.

The inside was just as cliché as the outside. The decorations were fairly cheap. There were several round tables where various card games were being played. A few slots lined the walls. A teller was in the far back. There was a small bar off to one side. As for the clientele, there weren't many, and at this hour it wasn't surprising.

Dominique walked toward the teller, acquired some chips and made his way around the room. There were a few old ladies playing bingo, an older man looking half drunk at the roulette table, and a few other patrons that didn't fit the profile of the person he was looking for. There was no point in coming here if he couldn't pick out his next victim.

The table at the far end seemed promising. There were no players, only a single dealer. There would be no one in earshot and no one to disrupt his conversation.

"Sharon?" Dominique asked looking at the name tag of the young man.

"It's Cha-ron."

"That's an odd name."

Charon shrugged. "I've had it all my life. Did you want to play? We close at midnight."

"Sure, why not."

The dealer dealt the cards and Dominique was surprised at how good his hand was. Without taking another, he let the game play out.

"Bust," Charon stated. "Player wins."

Dominique smiled. "Let's play a few more."

Time passed and Dominique found that he had won far more often than lost. Chips were stacking up. But he had received far more than just a bunch of chips. Conversation had picked up. Charon lived alone. This was good. No one would miss him for a while at least. He wondered if the dealer would walk out some back door, if there was a back alley, and if there was a dumpster large enough to deposit the body.

"Just a couple minutes left," Charon said. "Time for one more hand?"

"Why not?" Dominique mused. He felt lucky. Even if he lost everything, it wouldn't matter. He had only bought a small amount of chips to begin with. He pushed his pile of chips into the middle of the table.

"Let it ride. I bet it all."

"Everything?" the dealer asked.

"Yes, everything."

Dominique watched as Charon dealt the cards, one up and one down to both of them. A smile came across his face knowing that his first kill from this town was only minutes away. His first victim was only a few feet away. He had been dealt a nine showing; the only question was what he had turned down.

He gasped at the card.

This wasn't a card from the regular deck, this was something else entirely. The picture was that of a skeleton in armor on a pale horse. Behind him was a river with a boat upon it and above that, a moon.

Dominique knew what this card was; he didn't have to be a reader of the cards to understand what he had in his hand. This was the card of Death. The rider was the Grim Reaper and the boat behind him was the ferry, complete with the ferryman, on its journey through the River Styx. He shook his head. This had to be a sick joke. He was going to complain to the dealer. He was going to complain to the manager. He was going to ...

Dominique gasped again. He swore he could see the picture on the card moving. The horse breathed; its tail flickered. The boat upon the River Styx could be seen bobbing toward him. The moon glowed. And worse yet, yes worse yet of all things, the skeletal rider turned to face him.

The sounding of the clock on the wall caught Dominique's attention and pulled him back to reality. The sudden noise that cut through the air made him drop his card, face down, on the table.

The clock struck again.

Pain shot through Dominique's chest. He brought his hand up as if to comfort his own heart, but it was to no avail. It grew worse with each sounding of the clock. He could feel his heart stopping. He could feel his soul leaving. He broke out in a cold sweat and a shiver of cold came about him.

The room spun.

The clock struck twelve.

Darkness came upon him.

"Well, my initial finding is that he had a heart attack," the doc said as he drew the sheet over the body. "I won't know for sure until I do an autopsy."

Sheriff Thomas nodded. "That fits the stories of the eye witnesses. He grabbed his chest and just keeled over."

Out of curiosity the sheriff flipped over all the cards that had been in play. "He had an ace of spades and a nine. Dealer has twenty-one. Looks like he lost everything."

Sheriff Thomas turned toward the dealer. "That'll be all for tonight. We may have more questions for you later."

"I'm always around," Charon said as he grabbed his coat and made his way toward the back door.

Once in the alley, Charon brought up the hood from his jacket. His facial features changed. His skin melted and his muscle tone pulled away like wax until all that was left was bone.

Charon shook his head. Dominique should have known better than to bet against him. He always won, one way or another; there was no cheating him. Besides, he never did like competition. He looked upon the wall of the nearby library. He needed to hurry. He had a 12:30 ferry to catch. Charon, the personification of death itself, the ferryman, turned into the night and disappeared in the darkness.

"... but the legend says before anyone ever finds the cage ..."

Exchange Werewolf

by Hugh Mannfield

"What are you … some kind of a wuss?" Brandon leaned in as Viktor pressed his back hard against the lockers.

"No … I just got here, give me chance to settle in."

"So why don't you join the team? You look big enough." Brandon backed off slightly while his cohorts chimed in with, "yeah, yeah."

"I don't even know this game," replied Viktor.

"You got any muscles in there?" Brandon squeezed Viktor's arm hard through the sleeve of the loose hoodie.

"I bench press 150 kilos."

"Really? What the hell does that mean? You Russian dork!"

"Ukrainian."

"Whatever!"

Viktor hesitated. "Is over 300 of your pounds."

"So then why don't you join the team?!"

"I don't much like your recruiting technique."

A voice a short way down the hall half shouted, "And I'm live streaming! Here we have the star quarterback and a couple of team members bullying the new foreign exchange student … at least that's what it looks like to me."

Viktor looked over to see a skinny kid holding up a smart phone. Brandon released the handful of hoodie he had clenched over Viktor's chest and backed up a step. "Get lost, nerd!" he sneered.

"No way ... I owe my hundreds of followers a good story."

"Come on, guys, let's move on." Brandon and his lackeys headed off down the hall. After a few steps, Brandon turned around. "This ain't over," he said to Viktor and then, "and you ... one of these days you're gonna get caught without your precious phone."

"Oooh .. was that a threat caught live and broadcast across the Net?"

Brandon and his group stomped away.

The skinny kid approached Viktor. "Hi, I'm Jason, but most people call me Didge ... as in digital ... I'm kind of into tech ... anyway welcome to Mirror Point High."

"Are they always acting this way?" asked Viktor.

"Yeah, perennial school bullies."

"You have guts."

"Nah, you shine the light of day on them and they run like roaches. I always believe you have to do what's right, even if you're afraid. Hey, we're having a party in a couple of weeks, you wanna come?"

Viktor glanced at the calendar inside his locker door. "What day is it exactly?"

Didge brought up an app on his phone. "It's the 27th, Saturday at 6:00 PM."

Viktor hesitated. "That is night of the ... full moon."

"Yeah, exactly. It's going to be at Robbie's house. It's on top of the hill and there's a huge deck out back that looks over the whole town ... We're going to have a werewolf watch!"

Viktor paled. "A what?"

"You know that urban legend about the kid who turns into a werewolf? Well, he doesn't want to hurt anyone, so he locks himself in a covered steel cage in his back yard so he can't get out. But everyone can hear the howling. We're going to sit out on the deck and listen."

Viktor glanced around the hallway nervously. "But ... you don't really believe this, do you?"

"No, probably not here in Mirror Point, but the legend says before anyone ever finds the cage, his family moves on to a different town ... so you never know. Anyway, it's just for Halloween, you know, a chance to get the girls all scared ... wanting protection and all that. So are you in?"

"Um ... Okay, I will think about it." Viktor closed his locker and shouldered his backpack.

"Wow, we're going to be late for algebra, come on."

Brandon hung back and watched as Viktor strode down the hill from the high school with the sun shining warmly on his back. He had left Viktor alone for almost a week and it seemed Viktor was getting a feel for the school. Well, Brandon had to admit, he had roughed Viktor up a couple more times, but that was really going easy on him.

At school, there were the usual groups, the jocks, headed up by Brandon, and there were the cheerleaders. There were a large number of science nerds who loosely centered around Didge and Robbie Robinson. Then there was the cowboy bunch, and a few goth types, and then all the rest who didn't fit into, or want to be, in a classification. Brandon was relieved that Viktor had not fallen in with any of those groups. He did seem to be leaning a bit toward the science nerds and that had Brandon worried. That and a certain rumor that was circulating around the school.

It was a fine crystal blue October afternoon, leaves were just starting to turn and the warmth of Indian summer lingered in the air. Brandon sprinted down an alley to the next block and watched from the shadows as Viktor passed by. Once Viktor passed, he followed furtively at a safe distance. When Viktor had entered the front door of his house, Brandon slipped around the side of the garage and into the back yard.

The lot was overgrown with trees, branches hung low, so Brandon had plenty of cover. Patio furniture, a grill, an assortment of boxes and bicycles haphazardly filled the yard, signifying that unpacking from the recent move was still in progress. Brandon skirted the debris field and looked around. There in the back corner, almost hidden, was what he might be looking for. It was a large square object covered by canvas tarps. He approached cautiously. He lifted the canvas to reveal strong galvanized steel bars and industrial grade chain link. It was a cage alright, and not just any cage, you could hold a grizzly bear in this one. Scratches on the inside seemed to say that it recently had. A heavy frame door with a very large lock graced the front side. Brandon grinned and backed away.

After football practice that evening Brandon collected his crew. "Hey guys, huddle up." Brandon lowered his voice. "You know about that party the nerdy bunch is having this Saturday? The *dweeby werewolf* watch. The one nobody on the team was invited to?" Heads nodded in agreement.

"Well, we're going to crash that party and get those nerds out of our hair once and for all."

Brandon quickly explained about the cage in Viktor's back yard and how he suspected that the urban legend about the werewolf was true. "I've got a plan. Don't wash your gym clothes this week and bring your dirty gym bags to my house next Saturday."

The rank smell of old gym socks filled the car as Brandon pulled up and parked in front of Viktor's house. The sun hung low in the western sky. "Okay guys, bring those gym bags along." The four doors opened and 900 pounds of low IQ muscle stepped out onto to street. "Follow me."

Brandon headed across the street and up the hill away from Viktor's house. The gang followed after. "So why are we going this way?" asked one of his chums. "I thought this was about that new kid."

"Oh, it is," replied Brandon with a grin. "We're going up to the Robinson's house where the dweeb party is gonna be."

"What for?"

Brandon held up his gym bag. "We're leaving a scent trail."

The crew gave him a vacant look. Brandon rolled his eyes. "Okay, listen up, we leave a trail to the nerd party, and then come back and make sure the werewolf cage is unlocked. Once the werewolf is out, it follows the trail and then no more nerds. Get it?" His crew grinned in turn and followed Brandon up the street.

It was several blocks up the hill before they arrived at the Robinson's front door. Brandon took a sweat-stained T-shirt out of his bag and began rubbing it on the door. The others followed suit. "Okay, our work here is done." Brandon smirked and then pressed the doorbell hard before setting off down the hill at a run.

He and his gang retraced their steps to end up back at the car in front of Viktor's house. The sun had gone down by then and Brandon checked his watch. "Moon rise is in ten minutes. Let's do this." The gang followed him into Viktor's back yard. They worked their way around to the cage and lifted the canvas. Sure enough, there sat Viktor huddled in the cage.

"Well, lookie what we have here," said Brandon.

Viktor looked up blinking. "What are you doing here?"

"We came to see you turn into a wolf!" taunted Brandon.

"You should not be here … this is trespassing!"

"So sue me!" Brandon laughed. "Oh, look at this big bad lock. Afraid you're going to get out and hurt someone?" Brandon pulled some bolt cutters out of his bag. "We can't have that now can we?"

"No, don't do that," yelled Viktor. "You don't know what you are messing with!"

Brandon proceeded to cut the lock off the door. "Well, maybe I'm not afraid of dogs! Are you gonna come out and bite me?"

"No … put it back!" wailed Viktor.

"Do you grow a tail like a dog? Do you sniff butts like a dog?" Brandon taunted. "Hey, I've got something for you to sniff. How about my week old jockstrap?" Brandon pulled it out of his bag and threw it at Viktor through the bars. His gang laughed and did the same.

"You will regret that," Viktor's voice deepened to a growl. His eyes blazed fiercely, his face growing slightly elongated.

Brandon looked over his shoulder at the rising moon. "Okay, boys, time to go." The group jogged back out to the street and piled into Brandon's car. "Okay, everyone, windows up, we want him to follow the trail we left, not the car. Then we can watch all the fun from the park." His crew cranked their windows up and then Brandon calmly started the motor and slowly drove away.

Back in the cage the transformation was nearly complete. Viktor pulled the hoodie off over his wolfish head revealing a torso covered by silver grey hair, bristling along the spine. He howled, circled the cage, and then burst out through the door on all fours, sniffing along the ground for Brandon and his chums.

The Robinson house was filled with lively voices. Mr. and Mrs. Robinson, both teachers at Mirror Point High, were in the kitchen preparing snacks. Didge and Robbie were on the deck under the deepening sky. The first few stars shown out and a glow on the eastern horizon across the lake foretold of the rising moon. Didge scanned the town below through a pair of binoculars. "Wow Robbie, you can see everything from up here!"

From the kitchen Mrs. Robinson's voice rang out, "Kids, come inside! We have a little announcement to make." When all were gathered she continued, "I suppose you all know a little about werewolves."

Graycen spoke up, "It's a curse that turns people into vicious, murdering beasts on the full moon."

"Yes," replied Mrs. Robinson, "at least that is the legend. However, like most legends it's highly exaggerated. You have to understand that at the time of the legend's origin, people treated each other quite badly. Those were the days of inquisitions, torture, and witch burning. This tended to bring out the worst in both people and werewolves."

Chloe rolled her eyes. "I didn't come here, you know, expecting a lecture," she muttered toward Graycen under her breath. Graycen gave Chloe an elbow in the ribs.

"Did you have a question, Chloe?"

"Yeah, um, I mean, nobody, like, really believes that, right?"

"Actually, Chloe, as most legends do, this one has a basis in fact. Werewolves were, and are real, and persist to this day. However, becoming a vicious, murderous beast is only the most extreme, and rare, of outcomes."

"And you know this, like, how?"

"Well, I'm glad you asked." Mrs. Robinson gathered her husband and son Robbie next to her. "As you know, we've lived here in Mirror Point for many years, and you, gathered here tonight, are our closest friends. Tonight, we are going to let you in on a family secret, but you have to swear not to tell a soul." Mrs. Robinson raised her right hand.

The group all raised their hands and followed Mrs. Robinson in a short but carefully worded oath. "Well then," she looked at her husband and son, "let's do this."

"Now, I want to emphasize that none of you are in the least bit of danger, so don't freak out." With that, Mrs. Robinson stepped into the light of the rising moon. The transformation happened quickly. Her face elongated into a snout, her nose turning up. Her ears grew pointed and shifted upward on her head. Strong sharp claws sprung from her fingertips, her teeth grew into fangs, and fine white fur covered her body.

The little crowd took it fairly well, with only a few gasps. Didge had to be told to keep his camera turned off. In the end, Mrs. Robinson stood before them in werewolf form, still wearing her little round glasses, chef's hat and apron, a thick white fluffy tail wagging behind her. "So, does anyone have any questions?"

Chloe raised her hand.

"Yes Chloe?"

"Um, is, you know, that fur, like, real?"

"Yes it is. Would you like to feel it?"

"Yeah, okay, sure." Chloe reached out to pet Mrs. Robinson's hand-like paw. "Wow, it's soft."

"I use conditioner." Mrs. Robinson motioned to Robbie and he came to stand next to her. In a few moments he had transformed into something like a teenage Rottweiler. Next it was Mr. Robinson's turn, who came out looking a bit scarier, much more wolfish, with large drooling jaws, a hunched back, bulging shoulders with rippling muscles, and long claws.

Mrs. Robinson stepped forward. "Now, as you can see, the type of werewolf depends entirely on the type of person you start out as ...." She was interrupted by the sound of the front door bursting open. Loud growling and snuffling noises came quickly up the stairs, and suddenly, Viktor's werewolf form filled the kitchen doorway. His eyes blazed. The fur of his neck bristled. His teeth and claws were out, ready to kill.

Viktor paused and glanced around, taking in the presence of three other werewolves. Mrs. Robinson stepped forward. "Viktor? Is that you?"

Viktor's eyes widened, his bristles and ears drooped, his claws retracted and his tail tucked between his legs. He appeared about half the size of a moment ago. "Mrs. Robinson?"

"It is you! I'm so glad you could make it." Mrs. Robinson motioned him into the kitchen. "Come on in and have a snack."

Viktor slunk over to the table. Robbie came over to join him and they sniffed each other. Mrs. Robinson regarded the pair. "Viktor, it seems you've had a hard time recently. Can you tell us what happened?"

Speaking with jowls and fangs wasn't easy, especially while munching on meaty snacks, but Viktor eventually got the story about Brandon and his gang across to the group. Didge, for one, was outraged. "He's gone way beyond bullying this time! This is attempted murder!"

"I agree," added Mrs. Robinson, laying her hat, apron, and glasses on the table. "Something must be done."

"Well, if I know Brandon," said Didge, "he's out there somewhere watching for his little scheme to unfold." Didge picked up the binoculars and approached the glass doors to the deck. After a short time scanning, he ducked back. "Yeah, I saw them down at the park, standing around his car. They were looking up here toward the house."

"Okay," said Mrs. Robinson, "I have a plan." She went into the kitchen and returned with a cookie timer. She twisted the dial and said, "All the werewolves with me, the rest of you, when that timer rings, start screaming your heads off."

Brandon lowered his binoculars. "What the fuck is taking him so long?"

"Um, maybe he isn't really a werewolf?"

Brandon turned on his chum. "Idiot, you saw him … He was changing right in front of us."

"Oh yeah. Maybe he's just slow."

"I better hear some nerd screams soon!" Brandon paced the ground in front of his car. He strained his ears. At last, a chorus of distant screams wavered in the air. Brandon and his gang moved away from the car to get a better look. He raised the binoculars and laughed. "Yeah, something's happening up there. I see stuff flying around through the window."

A loud growl erupted from the bushes behind them and Viktor leapt out onto the trunk of Brandon's car. He crawled menacingly forward over the roof. "Found you!" he snarled.

The gang of four bunched together and edged away from the car. Just as they were ready to bolt to the right, a short brown and black werewolf emerged from the brush on that side. As the group turned to the left, a large white werewolf appeared to block that path as well. "I bring some of my friends to play," Viktor snarled.

With nowhere left to go, Brandon and his crew ran into the gathering darkness of the open play field. The werewolves kept pace easily, herding them toward the far side. Just as it appeared that escape might be possible, a very large werewolf sprang up to seal them in. Brandon and his friends huddled together under the light of the full moon as the four werewolves circled and closed in.

Brandon fell to his knees. "Pease don't kill me …. pleeeaaassee!" He fell to his hands and knees along with the rest of the group. Blubbering, Brandon choked out, "I don't want to die!" The wolves circled closer. "Here … you can have these guys," he offered, "just don't kill me!"

"Not cool, Brandon!" said one of the crew.

Brandon inched forward on his knees, tears rolling down his face, crying like a baby. "Please, please, Viktor, I'm sorry … I'll do anything."

"Anything?" growled Viktor.

Encouraged, Brandon shuffled forward, still sobbing. "Yes! I'll do anything … I won't tell anyone about you!"

"And your friends?"

"They won't either!" Brandon glanced around. "Right, guys?"

"Yeah, yeah we won't say nothin'," they chimed in.

The white werewolf spoke. "You can't trust them … I'm thirsty for their blood!" The other werewolves growled.

"It would be simpler just to kill them!" said the largest werewolf. Viktor nodded in agreement.

A wet stain spread around Brandon's crotch and he fell back against his gang members, wailing. "Please don't kill us! Please don't kill us!" and trailed off, bawling like an infant.

A small figure moved into view, silhouetted by the light of the eastern moon. As it drew nearer it could be seen taking video with a smart phone. "I think I've got some great footage here. This night camera mode works great!" said Didge.

Brandon looked up, shocked, and then instinctively lunged at Didge. He was instantly pinned to the ground by the lightning-fast forepaw of the large werewolf. "Don't even think about it," it snarled.

"You little shit!" Brandon yelled. "You better not be streaming this!"

"Oh, I'm not," replied Didge, "but it is going to the cloud, where it will stay, waiting for the right moment to go out over the Net."

The white werewolf moved in, drooling jaws inches from Brandon's face. "This one learns slow."

Brandon cowered. "I'll change! I promise! No more bullying!"

"Do you swear?" asked the white werewolf.

"I swear!"

"On your life?"

"Yes! I swear on my life!" wailed Brandon.

The white wolf put its snout to Brandon's ear. "I'll hold you to that … I look forward to the day you go back on your word!"

Brandon quailed and buried his face in the grass, his bowels emptied. The night around him went deathly still and when he looked up, he and his friends were alone in the moonlight on an empty field, sitting, trembling, as the stink of shit and piss filled the night air.

In the middle of the next week, Didge was surprised to find Brandon blocking his path in the hallway at school. This time however, Brandon was alone and seemed a bit hesitant. "We need to talk, Nerd!"

Didge looked him up and down. "I suppose we do."

"You better not release that video you took!"

"That," replied Didge, "is entirely up to you."

Viktor moved up behind Didge and he and Brandon exchanged glances.

"Why don't you try something new?" asked Didge.

"Like what?"

"Like maybe making friends." Didge extended a hand.

Reluctantly, Brandon took it, and offered up a weak smile. "Friends?"

"See … that's how it works," explained Didge. "In time, you might even grow to like it."

Viktor moved around beside Brandon and nodded toward the gymnasium. "Why don't you tell me about this *football* team? My parents gave me okay to have after school activities."

Deadman's Curve Claims Teen Victim

MIRROR POINT ECHO –
SATURDAY, FEBRUARY 16, 2019

Late last evening Mirror Point High School senior, Tavin Hellman, died when his yellow Hyundai Genesis veered off the deadly curve on Madd Falls Road. Friends say the teen had been drinking in the parking lot at a school dance just prior to the accident. This stretch of road is no stranger to accidents. The Echo has five reports of deadly accidents in its archives. The first one in 1923 when a horse and wagon owned by a Spokane farmer overturned. The previous one was seventeen years ago when another local teen's white Mazda drove off the exact same location on Madd Falls Road into Spirit Lake. Services will be held next weekend. Flowers may be sent to the family via Hellman's Garage.

... there was no one around to hear him.

Beware Animal Attack!
by Kristi Radford

Excerpt from the Mirror Point Echo:

As most of you are aware, Mr. Jonathan Phillip Moreland III passed away recently, leaving the entirety of his estate to the Mirror Point Animal Sanctuary, a no-kill animal shelter founded by Mr. Moreland. Johnny, as most knew him, believed strongly in animal rights. He was devoted to his pet cat and spent the majority of his time and money building the sanctuary.

Johnny's devotion to animals began out of a tragic accident. In 2002 while Mr. Moreland was away on business, his wife and two children were killed in a house fire. Only the family cat survived. It was determined that the fire was caused when the cat accidentally knocked over a candle. The cat was badly burned but made a full recovery thanks to the animal clinic.

"C'mon, Jack, keep up!" A boy yelled from the bike ahead.

Jack peddled faster, but Ryan's longer legs pushed him further and faster than Jack's ever could. He stood and peddled with all his might.

Ryan disappeared around a bend in the road.

Jack sat and groaned. Everything with Ryan was a race.

Tires screeched and a tirade of swearing filled the air.

Jack laughed. Ryan's mom would wash his mouth out with soap if she heard him utter the slightest curse. Even 'dam' used inappropriately earned a severe scolding. When Jack rounded the bend he saw Ryan's bike lying in the middle of the road. Ryan was on the shoulder gathering rocks. Jack skidded to a stop.

Ryan stood and threw one of the rocks towards the tree line. Jack looked and saw nothing.

"Fucking thing made me crash. It darted out in front of me." Ryan cursed. Blood ran down Ryan's leg from a deep gash that was coated with sand and grit from the road.

"Did you see where the mother-effer went?" Ryan yelled holding a good-sized rock in his hand.

Jack shook his head. He hoped whatever made Ryan crash was long gone. Even though Ryan was the meanest kid Jack knew, he was also Jack's best friend. Ryan was the best pitcher the Mirror Point Junior High baseball team had ever seen. The boys spent most weekends together playing catch. Jack only going home when Ryan's arm gave out or he hit him with a stray fastball.

"Nope." Jack bent over and lifted Ryan's bike. "C'mon, man I gotta get back in time to do chores before my mom gets home."

Ryan wound up and pitched the rock down the road. It sailed fifty yards, then bounced another fifty. Ryan took the bike from Jack and said, "Race you to old man Moreland's place."

Jack followed but didn't try to keep up. Old man Moreland's place was said to be haunted and Jack didn't like ghosts.

A cloud passed in front of the sun and a strong gust scattered dry leaves across the road. Jack shivered despite the warm afternoon. He peddled faster, knowing Ryan would give him hell if he had to wait too long.

The Moreland Estate was not really an estate. Yes there was a house and a fair amount of acreage. But the house was run down and pretty ramshackle. Not where you would expect a millionaire to live. There were shingles missing from the roof, and the porch sagged. A few of the upstairs windows were boarded over. According to local urban legend the house was haunted by Mr. Moreland's dead wife and kids. Jack didn't believe that. He knew this was the house Johnny grew up in, not the house his family died in. If it was haunted by anything it was Johnny's mother. He'd tried to tell Ryan it was a different house, but once Ryan made up his mind it was impossible to change.

Jack parked his bike next to Ryan's. This time it was upright leaning on the kickstand. Ryan was halfway to the house, a softball-size rock in his hand.

"Did you see him?" Ryan yelled excitedly.

"See what?"

"That fucking thing was standing on the railing." Ryan waved his arm for Jack to follow.

"I didn't see anything." Jack got off his bike, taking extra time to make sure the kickstand would hold before he followed.

The ground was patchy. Tall clumps of dried brown grass stuck up here and there. The wind rustled through the tree's making leaves cascade to the ground.

"There he is!" Ryan yelled, making Jack jump.

An orange blur disappeared under the bushes surrounding the porch.

"Jack, get me some rocks." Ryan took aim and threw a rock where the animal had disappeared.

Jack shook his head.

Ryan kicked at the bushes. "I swear if I catch you, I'm going to tie you up and throw you in the lake."

Jack checked his watch. "Leave it alone. I gotta go."

"What? No, help me find it first."

"If I don't get the chores done, I'm grounded and that means I can't catch for you."

"Fine. Go, but I'm staying."

Jack waved and headed to his bike. "See you tomorrow."

Excerpt from the Mirror Point Echo:

Lost Cat. Mr. Moreland made special stipulations in his will for the care of his beloved pet. When found Mr. Norris will be cared for at the sanctuary for the remainder of his days. He was last seen at the Moreland's estate on West Amity Road. He is a large orange cat with emerald green eyes. His fur is uneven and ragged from the burns he sustained as a kitten. Please help us locate this elderly cat. Contact the Mirror Point Animal Sanctuary at (425) Kil-lno1 with information.

"Where did you go, you mangy monster?" Ryan knelt and reached blindly into the bushes.

There was a hiss and the bushes moved.

Ryan laid down on his belly and inched his way under the bushes. The leaves parted. He could make out the animal's shape in the waning afternoon light. Ryan reached out and grabbed the tail. The animal yowled and slashed with its razor sharp claws.

Ryan's eye was punctured. Blood and tears coursed down his cheek. He grabbed his eye and tried to stand up but the bushes kept pushing him back down. He screamed and forced his way through while the bushes pushed, tugged and stabbed into his body.

Through his tear-filled good eye he saw the porch a few steps away. He lurched forward but tripped and impaled himself head first onto a nail. The nail entered the center of his forehead. He whimpered and sagged against the steps. He pushed against the steps but only pulled himself off the nail a fraction of an inch.

The animal emerged from the bushes. It jumped onto the back of his legs and slowly walked up to his back. He thrashed and kicked trying to knock the animal off, but the animal dug it's sharp claws into his flesh. The creature stopped at the base of his back.

He prayed it would go away. But it didn't. It jumped from Ryan's back onto his head, impaling him back down on the nail. Ryan screamed, but there was no one around to hear him. Blood coursed from his wounds. He cursed and flailed, finally knocking the animal off.

They were eye to eye.

The animal lapped at the blood running down his cheek. He grabbed the blood sucking beast around its belly and squeezed. It slashed at Ryan again, this time it sliced his carotid artery.

Adrenaline propelled him off the nail. Standing made the blood squirt from his neck. He gripped the wound and spun around trying to find help. But there was none.

He saw his bike. It was his only chance at survival. He lurched forward but stumbled over a clump of dried grass. He landed on the ground near the bushes. Blood sprayed with every beat of his heart. He struggled to his knees but the loss of blood was making him dizzy. He clawed and crawled his way toward his bike while his life force slowly drained from his body.

Excerpt from the Mirror Point Echo:

Tragedy strikes. The body of an unidentified young male was found this morning. The sheriff is baffled by what appears to be an animal attack. However, what kind of animal has yet to be determined.

"Sweetie, wake up. I have to ask you some questions."

"What?" he mumbled with his face still buried in his pillow.

"It's about Ryan." She patted his back.

"What about him?" Jack rolled over to look at his mom.

"His mom called. He never came home last night."

Jack scowled.

"Do you know where he could be?"

"We were out riding our bikes, but it got late and I left him."

"Where did you leave him?"

"The Moreland Estate."

"Sweetie, get dressed. I'm going to call Mrs. Stewart, then we are heading out to look for him."

Ten minutes later Jack and his mom were standing outside the Moreland Estate staring at the yellow sheriff tape surrounding the yard.

Jack frowned, confused by the tape. His hands shook and fear pricked his soul.

His mom spoke with a man wearing a uniform.

Jack looked toward the bushes where he'd last seen Ryan. There was a smear of blood on the ground. It wasn't much but dread filled him. "He killed it." Jack dropped to the ground. A tear slipped down his cheek. Ryan had a mean streak, but was he really mean enough to kill an animal?

"Jack, can you come over here please?" the deputy called.

Jack got to his feet and swiped at his eyes. He looked at the ground as he walked. He didn't want to see the blood again.

"Jack, can you tell me what happened yesterday?" The deputy took out a small notebook and pencil from his pocket. He licked the tip of his pencil and held it over the notebook.

"Well, sir, Ryan and I were riding our bikes. He was ahead of me and he crashed. When I caught up he said something made him crash. But I don't know what it was. He wanted to race to old Man Moreland's place, but he's too fast. I couldn't keep up. When I got here he said it was standing on the railing. I only saw an orange blur disappear under there." Jack pointed to the bushes. "I don't know how it could have beat us to the house. He said he was going to try to catch it. He wanted me to help, but I left. Do you know where Ryan is?"

"Thank you, young man. You can wait for your mom in the car." The deputy motioned for Jack's mom to follow him. They took a few steps away. Jack heard the deputy say they'd found a young man's body and asked for Ryan's parent's information.

Jack felt the world tilt. He swayed and sank to the ground, his back against the car.

Excerpt from the Mirror Point Echo:

The body of Ryan Stewart was discovered yesterday. He suffered from multiple lacerations from an unknown weapon. A grief counselor will be on hand at the Mirror Point Junior High to help students through this difficult time. A tip line has been set up for anyone with information on the case.

A week after Ryan's body was found he was laid to rest. Jack stood watching Ryan's mom cry. His throat ached and his eyes burned. When the service and the hugging was over Jack took his bike and rode back to the estate. The police tape was fluttering in the breeze, but the blood stain was gone thanks to a heavy fall rain that had lasted for three days. Three days of mourning his best friend while the sky cried for him.

Jack ducked under the tape and headed for the porch. The steps were crooked. When Jack sat he was careful not to sit on the nail that stuck up a half inch. The sky was dark with heavy clouds. The world compressed around him and a howl suddenly erupted from his throat. He cried long and hard. He cried until all that could be heard was a low keening moan.

Something soft nudged his hand and he instinctively pulled it to his chest. He held it tightly, taking comfort from its warmth. A mangy orange cat purred and nuzzled Jack's neck.

The End ... Or is it the beginning?

Deadly Drowning by DUI

WAY'S END OBSERVER
FRIDAY, APRIL 13, 2018

Early this morning the blue truck from Reliable Construction was pulled from Spirit Lake. Abel Shipley, the ferry captain, found the vehicle before his first run at 5am. All five members of the construction crew that had been working on the renovations at Thornton Lodge were killed. It is believed that they had been drinking in celebration of finishing the month-long job at the lodge. Sheriff Ramírez pronounced Driving Under the Influence as the cause of the accident. The vehicle and bodies were transported to Mirror Point on a special ferry run. The bodies will be held at the mortuary until they are formally identified and next of kin are notified. A candlelight vigil will be held at 8pm. this evening at Way's End Church. Five pints of beer will be filled and left un-drunk on the bar this evening at Smokey's Tavern in remembrance.

The Wedding Guest

by Sonya Rhen

The sword sliced through the air narrowly missing Charles' head. The echo of metal on stone rung in the hall.

Charles swung his mace catching his opponent on the side. He grunted with the effort. His body drenched in sweat; he could taste his victory.

"Ahhh!" came the battle cry as the sword once again flew through the air. This time the blade was wide off the mark. He countered with the mace and heard the gratifying clatter as the sword fell to the floor.

He stepped in close to his opponent, locked legs as they grappled to the floor. His body contorted with the effort of pinning the struggling figure beneath him.

Charles looked into the flashing brown eyes, gnashed his teeth and planted a fierce kiss on the lips below his. He felt a bite on his lower lip and the faint tang of blood mixed with the sweet taste of the mouth he explored.

"Ow!"

Angelica laughed. With a surge of strength she flipped him to his back. "I win."

He kissed her again. "Maybe we both win."

An hour later they were showered and dressed. Angelica had a cup of coffee on the marble kitchen counter where she sat swiping through screens on her tablet.

"Nothing like starting the day with a good workout," Charles said as he took out fresh squeezed orange juice from the state-of-the-art refrigerator. The screen on the door showing the juice sloshing on the shelf as it settled. "I like the feel of that new mace."

"I didn't." Angelica rubbed her sore side. "Where did you say it was from?"

"Mikel acquired it in Russia. It's from the 18th century," he said. "Did you need more padding?"

"No, I'll live."

"What are your plans today?"

Angelica looked up from the tablet. "I'm teaching zumba at The Sweat Box. Then Trina and I are discussing wedding plans after class. She wants to use the dungeon."

"Excellent."

Megan had only been working at the library for a few months. Before that she lived in Seattle. After her parents died there had been bills and she just couldn't afford to stay there anymore. Besides, she had nothing to stay there for.

She scanned the stack of books before her and placed them on the cart. She enjoyed the quiet of Way's End. She hadn't made a lot of good decisions in her life, but she felt this was one.

"Ms. Pipet?" Dave Williams appeared at the checkout desk. The half-Asian linebacker for the Way's End High School football team was a frequent visitor to the school's library. "Can you help me again?"

She sighed inwardly. She hated the stereotype of dumb football players, but outwardly Dave Williams was that personified, despite his Asian looks — another stereotype. He wasn't dumb. Only no one had ever given him any kind of encouragement to learn. It was as if teachers expected him to be innately smart. She hoped that working at the Way's End High School library would give her the opportunity to help kids like Dave. "Of course. What do you need?"

"I have this report due tomorrow ..."

Trina Quay brought the black compressed charcoal to the paper and scribbled heavy dark lines along the top. "Press firmly and as you go down ease off the paper, pressing a little softer. See how you can make a gradation from black to a light grey."

She put the charcoal down. "Now you can use your finger to blend the charcoal."

This was her last class of the day. After this she would head to the library, then her zumba class at The Sweat Box. She was ecstatic when Angelica suggested that she use Thornton Lodge for the wedding ceremony. It would be the perfect setting for her and Jake. The black, red and white decorations would blend well with all the stone masonry.

She walked around the room watching as students' pages grew black and smudged. Index fingers were completely black and some kids even had charcoal on their clothes and faces.

Good. They were really getting into their work. "*Magnifique!*"

After, she washed her hands well. Mrs. Small wouldn't allow her to even enter the Way Arcane and Rare Books Library with charcoal-covered fingers.

She loved the whole vibe at Way's End High School. The historic red brick building was designed to look like a castle and she felt at home the minute she stepped inside its doors. It was a shame the original hotel never opened to guests, but luckily the town got a deal on it for the high school.

The building was quiet with most of the students gone. The hard square heels of her shoes clattered on the worn marble stairs and echoed off the walls as she made her way to the ground floor library. She thought of the sacrifice, moving to this small town with Jake and all the changes she had made. No wonder weddings were considered one of life's more stressful events. But she was good at organizing and had no doubt she could pull it off smoothly.

She pushed open the heavy wooden double doors to the library and scanned for Mrs. Small, the head librarian.

"Excuse me." Dave Williams squeezed past her and out the doors, his arms laden with books.

At the desk stood the new librarian assistant. What was her name? Martha something. Something beginning with a "B".

"Hello, Martha? Uh, Mrs…" Trina began.

"Megan, Megan Pipet," Megan answered "and it's Ms."

"Ms. Pipet," Trina said distractedly as she glanced around. "Have you seen Mrs. Small?"

"I think she's over in the biographies." Megan pointed, then continued to check in books.

"Thanks, I..." Trina suddenly swung her head back to Megan. "So..., you're not married?"

Megan blushed, looked down at her naked ring finger. She shook her head and said quietly, "No."

Trina brought both hands down on the desk and peered at the mousy woman before her with renewed interest.

"And your parents, they live around here?"

"No, they died."

"Oh, so sorry." A hand with only the faintest traces of charcoal patted the paler one.

"Thank you."

"And the rest of your family? Brothers, sisters, cousins?"

"No, it's just me."

"So you just moved here?"

Megan nodded. "Seattle is getting too crowded and too expensive."

Trina smiled broadly. "I am so thrilled you've moved to Way's End!" She gave the hand another pat, then turned to find Mrs. Small. "I'll be seeing you around."

The tall figure of Mrs. Small lead the way down the creaky wood stairs to the basement. The bulb lighting the way flickered and buzzed.

"I think I found a book you'll like, but I'll keep looking if that doesn't work."

She walked past several tall wood shelves, pulled out a black leather-bound book.

Trina caressed the old worn cover as she placed it on the wood book stand. She opened the pages carefully. It was hand illustrated with beautiful colored drawings. She ran a finger over the words on the page. It felt good. It hummed, but it didn't feel perfect. She pulled the checkout card from the front pocket and glanced down at the names. "Can you keep looking for me?"

"Certainly," Mrs. Small said.

Trina eyed the books behind the glass case at the back of the room.

Mrs. Small followed her gaze. "You'll need to wear gloves if you want to look at those."

"May I?" Trina asked.

The librarian took the key ring from her pocket and unlocked the case. She handed over a clean pair of white gloves.

"I may be a while," Trina said.

Megan took the ten-minute ferry ride to Mirror Point. It had been several months, but now that she felt a little settled, she thought she would explore the neighboring town. Way's End was nice but quiet and isolated. Tourist season was over, so there was not much to see or do there.

She walked around the shops. She was impressed with the town's library, its picture window, and the huge mirror clock that reflected back the lake. Mirror Point was not a large town, but it was big enough to keep her busy for the entire day.

After having a slice of famous apple pie at The Piehole: Pies and More Café, she thought she could rest her feet a bit at the Mirror Point Grand Cinema. Besides it looked like rain, but she wasn't quite ready to head back yet.

The theater was nearly full when she entered. There were spots in the back and a few up front. She didn't like to sit in the very front, so she slid into the second seat in the third row. The plush red velvet seat with its wood armrests were a warm comfort in the quaint historic building.

The people sitting next to her gave her an odd look. Was her hair sticking up? Maybe everyone in Mirror Point knew each other and could tell she wasn't from here? Or maybe she was just being self-conscious.

She was enjoying the movie when the soft patter of rain began. Before long she could hear the louder beating of heavy rain. A cold drop hit the back of her neck. She looked behind her at the man staring intently at the screen. Beside him two teenagers were laughing.

She turned back to the movie. Another drop assaulted her. She wiped her neck and tried to ignore it. After the next drop, she looked around. She thought she heard tittering from the back of the theater. Another drop hit her and she looked up.

A drop fell from the ceiling and hit her squarely in the eye. *What? Seriously! How did the only movie theater in town have a leaky ceiling?*

The front row had an empty seat. She squeezed past knees in the tightly packed theater and made her way to the empty seat — only to find an empty chair back and a hinge with no seat bottom attached to it.

Now there was no mistaking the laughter from the back of the theater. She glanced up the rows, but there were no other empty seats. Her face felt hot with embarrassment as she made her way back to the leaky chair.

She pulled her collar up and finished the movie. Every few minutes feeling the splash of cold seeping into her clothing.

Wet and miserable, she walked past the statue of Julian Brioc, the town's founder, and to the ferry. She was just in time to see the ferry pulling away from the docks.

Megan let out a sigh as she took shelter in the small tourist shop at the ferry terminal. She bought a Mirror Point Centennial T-shirt and changed out of her wet one in the small bathroom stall. Then she waited an hour for the next ferry departure. *So much for a nice day out.*

The holidays had passed and Megan still felt as if she hardly knew anyone in town, except for maybe Dave Williams who came in when he needed homework help. She thought the art teacher might have been potential friend material, but she had seemed oddly distant after their first meeting in the library.

So it was surprising to her when she found the red envelop with her name in black calligraphy sitting in her box in the school's workroom. She took it to the teacher's lounge and opened it. Thick red paper with black embossed lettering read:

You are cordially invited to attend the wedding of
Katrina Quay to Master Jake Molinar

followed by the date and the address. It wasn't the local church, but some place called Thornton Lodge on The Bluffs. Megan had been in Way's End long enough to know that the town's wealthiest and most influential people lived on The Bluffs. She was surprised, but pleased that she had been invited. She felt she was finally beginning to be accepted by the town she had decided to make her home.

Jake Molinar came into the lounge. He was wearing his standard tweed suit and bow tie. On him, it was ironically hip. The dark-haired English teacher was well liked by the students, especially the female associated student body. He quoted Lord Byron and Poe at the drop of a hat. Megan appreciated his literary knowledge.

"I see you've received your invitation," he said. "I hope you'll join us in the celebration."

"Yes." Megan held up the envelop. "Thanks for inviting me. Are you and Trina… um… registered anywhere? You know ... like … for gifts?"

He smiled warmly at her. "Your attendance at our ceremony will be gift enough. After all, 'What is worth living for and what is worth dying for? The answer to each is the same. Only love.'"

She watched him fill his mug with coffee and leave. Such a nice man, and it didn't hurt that he was handsome as well. She smiled and tucked the invitation in her bag. The library was waiting.

That night Megan walked on the train tracks. It was dormant in the off season and a good path from her apartment to the main part of town. She walked past the sheriff's office where she could still see the faint outline of the words "Buster Brown" on the wall and the logo of the boy and dog peeking around the sign for the Way's End Sheriff's Office.

A few doors down The Sweat Box Studio was brightly lit. A well-toned woman was leading the group in a very energetic type of dance. The long black braids that hung past her waist bounced rhythmically to music Megan couldn't hear.

From the side view she could see Trina in with the group of women. The woman in front held up her left hand and, as one, the group turned. They seemed to be starring out the window at her, Trina front and center.

Megan felt her heart racing, startled. She recovered and waved at Trina. There was no acknowledgment as the group continued their counterclockwise circle until they were once again facing their leader. Probably they hadn't seen her in the dark.

She drew up her coat and continued down the tracks. Maybe she would get a membership to The Sweat Box Studio. She could ask Trina next time she saw her at school.

Megan could hear the old church bell tolling in town. It was the day of the wedding. She still wasn't dressed and the gift wasn't wrapped. She had one hour to do that and drive up the hill to The Bluffs.

She had a purple dress that billowed around her like a cloud when she walked. It was the nicest thing she owned. If she didn't wear it to Jake and Trina's wedding, she didn't know where she would ever wear it.

She pulled up in front of the old hunting lodge. A red jacketed valet relieved her of the keys. He drove her beater old green Datsun up the gravel path and out of sight behind the trees.

She walked up the stone steps. The log cabin style building loomed monstrously before her. The honey colored logs gleamed with varnish and sat on masonry of large round stones. She'd never seen a three-story log cabin before and hadn't expected anything the size of a hotel. Probably, they were members of the lodge.

A pair of crossed axes hung over the door, and above them an impressive pair of antlers. The double doors were opened for her by two more red jacketed men.

Her heels clicked on the stone floor as she took in all the guests elegantly dressed. On the far wall a roaring fire was lit in the stone fireplace that was big enough for her to walk into if it hadn't been burning. The head of a mountain goat looked at her from above the flames. On either side of the fireplace were shelves lined with books.

To her right was a staircase going up to an open balcony and below it a staircase going down. Both were lined with a log banister in a similar honey color. Angling up the stairs were heads of various other animals native to Washington. On the balcony Jake and Trina watched over the guests. The railing cut off her view, showing only their heads. In the triangle of wall over the couple was a grizzly bear skin. Megan looked away. It was silly; she knew they were dead, but she had always been afraid of taxidermy animals.

Above her head the ceiling was two stories tall. Hanging from the center was a chandelier forged from swords and daggers of all shapes and sizes. The light from them glinted off the blades.

To her left were floor-to-ceiling windows revealing tops of trees and the town far below. The tinted windows kept the sun's glare at bay.

"Your coat?" a delicate voice asked.

Megan handed it to a girl in a long black dress and red jacket. She held up her small present wrapped in white paper with shiny silver doves on it.

"Where do I put this?"

"Presents are there," the girl said. She pointed to a long table set up in the corner by the window.

Megan felt uncomfortable as she set her small gift on the table next to large boxes wrapped in beautiful red, black and silver paper with huge ornate bows. She hid her box in the back behind the others.

She did not belong here. This was not what she expected from a wedding for two teachers. She was wearing the nicest thing she owned and the wait staff was better dressed.

She thought about leaving, but she didn't even know where her car was, let alone the keys for it. It was easier to stay, so she did.

Megan didn't know any of the other wedding guests. Apparently, there were *hors d'oeuvres* before the ceremony. She made her way to the table, selecting some cheese to nibble on. There was the woman she had seen leading the exercise class at The Sweat Box Studio. She was wearing a white sleeveless gown which showed off her toned arms. Silver bangles adorned each wrist and a diamond choker encircled her slender neck.

Megan was fascinated with her and, without realizing it, had drawn near. She could hear the woman's rich voice which carried a slight Caribbean accent.

"So glad we could take care of your little problem." The woman had her hand on the arm of a man in an expensive looking charcoal grey suit.

"I'm so grateful," the man said. "Kids these days are so irresponsible. You have to look out for your own."

"We always do, Mr. TerVeer." A man with a goatee and elegant white tux joined them. He leaned down and kissed the woman on her clavicle. "Angelica is queen of delegation. Aren't you, my dear?"

She tossed her long braids over her shoulder and removed her hand from Mr. TerVeer, ran it down the face of the man in white and drew him into a kiss. "Yes, Dear. It worked out perfectly."

Megan blushed at the openly affectionate couple, but she couldn't seem to look away.

The woman caught her stare. "Ah, hello," she said. "This is your first time to our home. I don't believe we've met before."

She felt the woman's hand in hers and nodded before she could even begin to process the information.

"I'm Angelica Lula and this is my husband, Charles Thornton. Hal

TerVeer, here, is our neighbor just down the way." Her grip was firm and Megan roused herself to return the shake.

"Megan Pipet."

"Friend of Trina's?" Mr. TerVeer asked.

"I'm the new assistant librarian at Way's End High School." She released Angelica's hand to find it now grasped by Hal. "We work together." She couldn't exactly say they were friends.

"Hal TerVeer. Nice to meet you," he said with a wink.

Her hand passed along to Charles. He captured it with both of his in an oddly over-enthusiastic greeting. "Charles Thornton, Thornton Securities. So glad you could join us for the celebration."

A gong sounded and people followed its echo down the stairs. She felt Charles' hand briefly on her back, guiding her toward the stairwell.

The walls on the lower part of the house were stone, similar to the outside of the lodge. Megan decended past wood and metal shields hanging on the wall beside the stairs. A look out the picture windows on the opposite wall let her know this was ground level. Red fabric-draped chairs with black ribbons and bows were lined in rows on either side of a red runner. Another fireplace was lit in this room and book shelves lined the walls going around the fireplace with a gap for the window.

Megan took a seat near the back. Jake was handsomely dressed in a modern styled black tux. He stood at the front with a high table and a podium. The trees beyond, covered in a light dusting of snow, were a backdrop to the ceremony.

On the table a large white candle flickered. A highly polished silver bowl was filled with sand and two lumps attached to black cords were visible.

Music began playing and it was not the traditional Wedding March or Cannon in D that she was expecting. Chanting was piped in over hidden speakers. Gregorian chant? She didn't know. Trina appeared in the back of the room, even though Megan had not seen or heard her come down the stairs.

She was resplendent in a red lace wedding gown with a black satin pill box hat resting on her French Twist. A black half-veil reveled only red lips on her face. She walked down the aisle grasping a bouquet of red roses tied with black ribbon.

Charles and Angelica appeared at the front dressed in crimson robes. She could see the sleeves of his white jacket poking out from under the red fabric. He held an old green book in his hands. *So Charles Thornton of Thornton Securities was also some sort of minister.* Megan hadn't understood most of the ceremony. Apparently, it was in Latin or some other language. She pulled out a tissue, dabbed at her eyes and blew her nose when Jake and Trina professed their undying love in vows they had written themselves. She hardly knew them, but weddings always made her cry.

The couple turned to face them and Megan expected the kiss and the end of the ceremony. Her breath stopped when Charles stepped to the middle of the table. He picked up a small dagger that she hadn't seen hidden behind the silver bowl. A large ruby was on one end of the handle and a sharp looking silver blade gleamed on the other.

Charles recited more foreign words and handed the dagger to Jake. Trina held her left hand out, palm up, as she gazed lovingly at Jake. The dagger sliced her palm as she spoke, "My blood in your blood. Bind us till the end of days." She made a fist and squeezed a few drops of blood on each lump in the sand.

Then Jake held out his left hand and the blade slashed a red line across his palm. Trina stabbed the knife into the sand as Jake dripped blood, repeating the same pattern. "My blood in your blood. Bind us till the end of days."

Megan felt faint at the sight of all the blood.

Charles took their hands and placed them cut to cut. "Blood bind you till the end of days," he said as he wrapped their joined hands with a wide white ribbon.

That can't be sanitary, Megan thought as she saw red starting to seep through the ribbon.

Angelica reached into the bowl and extracted the lumps, revealing heart shaped vials with red swirling in the clear liquid. The vials were tied at the neck with a loop of black cording. She put a cork in each and held them up.

Charles placed a red sealing wax candle in the bound hands of Jake and Trina. They used the burning candle to light it, then dripped the melting red wax over the cork on each vial. Angelica placed one vial around each of their necks as she spoke. "You carry the power of heart's blood united from this day forward."

This was a bit weird for her, but she appreciated the sentiment. Even this brought a tear to Megan's eyes. The rest of the ceremony was more traditional. The kiss was more passionate than she was used to, but the couple was happy and smiling as they walked down the aisle together.

Megan turned to watch them, assuming they would go back up the stairs. She was surprised to see the book shelves sliding open on hidden gears. She could see the ceiling of the room beyond. A wrought iron chandelier hung with dozens of burning candles. Their light flickering eerie shadows on the stone walls where a medieval armory hung reflecting back the glow.

The couple descended into the semi-darkness. Charles and Angelica stood at either side of the opening like two red pillars.

"No celebration is complete without a feast," Charles said. "Let us eat and drink together for the beginning of Jake and Trina's newest journey in life."

People rose and began filing down the stairs. Meagan wondered how rude it would be if she left now. The sea of wedding guests swept her toward the stairs and she didn't have the courage or strength to fight it. She would be polite, congratulate the couple and leave when everyone was settled.

A hand at her elbow startled her. Charles smiled. "Allow me to escort you."

"Um… okay," Megan uttered. She felt the power in his guiding hand, though he didn't squeeze her arm. She wanted to shake it off, but he wasn't doing anything wrong.

As he led her down the stone stairs she could see that the swords and club things were decorated with red, black and white silk flowers and ribbons. *Those couldn't be manacles on the walls?* The chains were also laced with ribbons and flowers, so it was hard to tell what they were.

Jake and Trina shook hands and hugged guests at the base of the stairs. Charles stayed with her as she greeted the couple. The heady smell of candles and spices assaulted her. The room was set for a feast. Heavy wood chairs were arranged around old wooden tables laden with food. Candelabras lit each table.

On the far wall was a raised stone area like a stage. Four large throne-like chairs sat against a wall. In front of them was a stone table with intricately carved patterns on it. The room had no windows and she didn't see any electric lighting down here. It was almost as if they had a secret dungeon in their house.

Charles was guiding her to a chair closest to the front. She resisted.

"Oh, here is fine," Megan said, touching a chair at the back of the room.

"You're new in town; first time to our home," he said. "You should be our special guest. Sit in front where you can see better."

It was rude to refuse, so she sat at the front in a chair facing the stone table.

Charles let go of her elbow as Angelica joined him. She handed him the green book from the ceremony. She seemed to bow as she stepped back. He placed the book in the center of the stone table, then walked around it and took the largest chair in the middle.

I guess I know who's king in this house, Megan thought.

Jake soon joined him. She didn't understand why Trina wasn't sitting next to him. As she wondered this, Angelica and Trina set silver platters of food and silver goblets at either end of the stone table. Angelica took a bunch of grapes, plucked them one by one and began feeding Charles. A cheer went up from the guests, and Megan sat back in her chair in disbelief. Angelica continued by taking the goblet and holding it to his lips for him to drink. He sipped, then took the goblet from her.

He held it up and said, "To Jake and Trina! May this night's ceremony join them in blood and body till the end of days!" Charles drank and everyone took this as a sign, reaching for goblets of wine in front of them and drinking.

Megan sat frozen. She really should get up and leave. She did not belong here.

She felt an elbow from the man next to her. When she turned to look he winked, held up his goblet and made a show of toasting the couple and drinking heartily. She took a tentative sip. It was good wine, though she didn't drink much. The man smiled, and laughing, took another drink.

She watched as Trina joined Angelica in feeding the men, who occasionally reciprocated. Other guests began eating or feeding their partners. Between the servers and guests, her plate was now covered in food. People began to mingle and there was a photographer snapping shots of the couple with various guests and the host and hostess.

The food was good and she was hungry, but this place and these people were making her uncomfortable. She could tell without asking that their clothes were expensive. They seemed friendly but distant.

She wanted to fit in here in Way's End. Even though it was a small town, these people seemed above her, apart from her. She hoped that here would be different from Seattle. Despite their odd behavior, there was a cool confidence they each carried that she lacked. She didn't think she could ever be a part of it.

Wait staff dressed in all black took away empty plates and brought in full ones. Old bottles of wine were uncorked and lined the stone table. Guests talked to the four holding court as they poured themselves more wine.

Megan felt she could leave soon, but she wanted just a half cup more wine or even water. She needed something to wash down all the food. No water was in sight. She walked to the table where wine was flowing like water over the Madd Falls. A goblet tipped and wine flowed out along the table, into the crevices, flowing toward the green book. Megan's librarian instinct kicked in, and she snatched the book up before the wine could touch it.

Wait staff stepped in with towels to sop up the mess. "Excuse me, Miss."

She stepped back, still holding the book. It was old with faded green leather binding. No words were on the cover. She assumed it was some old Latin or Hebrew bible and she couldn't resist peeking inside.

Not a bible.

The pages were filled with brightly colored hand drawn pictures. The pictures had faded, but she could still make out the images. The smile froze on her face when she realized the tiny people in all the pictures were being eaten or tortured by demons and monsters. The few words written in the book were in a language she didn't recognize.

What was this book?

"It was a birthday present for Charles," Angelica said as she took the book from her hands. Charles stood on her other side and poured wine into her empty cup.

"The rarest book I own," he said. Close on her left Trina was standing with two women she recognized from The Sweat Box the other night.

A hand nudged her shoulder. "Scoot in. Trina, let's get a nice picture with your friends," the photographer said.

"She's not my friend." Trina waved dismissively and continued smiling with the other two women.

Megan stepped back and took a big gulp of wine. Trina was not her friend. She did not belong here. She needed to leave.

Another gulp drained the goblet.

She backed up to her seat and placed the goblet on the table. As she groped for her purse a hand held out another full goblet of wine.

"No, thanks." She looked up to find Jake holding it out for her.

"You can't leave yet. Have more wine."

"Congratulations, I'm happy for you, but I have to…" she started.

"Stay. Stay. There's no school tomorrow," he said. "It would mean a lot to us… to me."

She could sense his sincerity as he placed the goblet in her hands. "I'm driving."

"Transportation can be arranged for you." He smiled.

"Just this one."

The room grew warm. She didn't think she had that much to drink. Hal TerVeer and others greeted her. Somehow seeming friendlier than before. Perhaps she could fit in here.

Hands touched her back and stroked the sleeve of her purple dress.

She undid the top button of her collar. It was hot in here.

Voices and music swelled, filling the room. It seemed brighter and she closed her eyes for a second.

Her hands felt numb and heavy. There was a metallic taste in her mouth.

The room had grown quite dark, but she could sense people all around her, make out a few faces at odd angles.

Fingers, she thought vaguely.

She couldn't touch them. She looked down at her hands.

She blinked in confusion at the white gown covering her chest and arms. Her wrists were bound with silver cords. She twisted her hands but could not bring them up.

"Awake is better," Charles' voice above her head.

"The time is come." Angelica at her feet.

Jake and Trina stand on either side of her. The heart-shaped vials dangle over her. She sees the swirls of red, dancing, pulsing. They join hands across the stone table she knows she's on: where the wine had filled the grooves in rivers of red.

A third hand — *Charles?* — passes the ruby dagger to the waiting ones.

Megan's brain screams.

But not fast enough.

The dagger plunges faster than escaping sound.

"You made sure there were no pictures of her at the wedding?"

"Yes. It's a shame; she was sweet." Angelica poured water on the stone. She dipped her finger in the crimson liquid as it overflowed and swirled down the drain in the floor.

Charles grabbed her hand and sucked her finger. "Yes."

"Putting in the drain was a good idea."

"Worth the extra expense."

Morty, the mortician in Mirror Point, swept the ashes into an urn. He knew better than to ask about the special delivery that had come by ferry from Way's End. You had to have a good head for business to make your way in the world.

He chuckled. He had a keen sense of humor. He clicked the side of his mouth and shook his head. "Tavin, poor devil, you just gained four pounds."

Trina and Jake sat at their breakfast table sipping coffee from their new matching mugs: the smallest of their wedding gifts.

"'Come! let the burial rite be read–the funeral song be sung!—An anthem for the queenliest dead that ever died so young—A dirge for her the doubly dead in that she died so young,'" Jake quoted Poe. He held up the mug in tribute, took a sip and set it on the table.

Trina slid her mug next to Jake's. The odd shaped cups nestled together so the two red apples disappeared and formed a perfect heart. The card had read, "Two apples for two great teachers! Best wishes for a happy life together!"

"Tacky," Jake said.

Trina giggled. "That's what makes them *très chic!*" She sipped her coffee.

Jake winked at her and laughed. "I think you mean *tra—gique!*"

It was Friday and Dave had a report due on Monday. He had waited until the last minute again. He stood at the desk looking around.

Mrs. Small, the head librarian, came over to help him. She sometimes gave him that look, like she was annoyed.

"What happened to that other librarian?" he asked.

"You must be mistaken," Mrs. Small said in her authoritarian voice that he knew better than to argue with. "I've been the *only* librarian here for thirty-eight years!"

*A piercing **crack**, like clear-sky lightning, and ...*

Knotty Kitty

by Roland Trenary

So, yeah. My next-door (on the left) neighbor died. But she was old and, you know, old people die. All the time.

Don't get me wrong though. I'm going to miss her. I already do and we're, what, two weeks into August? Seems like months ago, and then the next minute sometimes I feel like it was yesterday. And I particularly hate when it's *like yesterday* because I still get a little teary. I try not to let anyone see, but my 'girlfriend' noticed.

"Jakey, got something in your eye? What's up, my Little Big Man?" she teased.

"Nothing. And leave that 'Little Man' stuff alone, won't you?"

"Aw, come on. Tell Nurse O'Houlihan. What's with the moisture-eyes?"

See, Mary-Alice-Darlene Eberhardt had graduated Mirror Point High School a whole year ago (and me just this June) and since she now worked a part-time job at The Pretty Thrifty Nifty Store she acted the 'grown-up.' Even though we'd been next-doorsies (on the right) practically forever and I'd *liked* her since tenth grade.

And to tell the truth, although we'd sat next to each other watching a lot of movies, I never kissed her even once yet. And I'm pretty sure she didn't suspect I'd want to. People can be dense.

"Maddy, it's just that ... that I'm never going to get oatmeal-cocoa-chip bars again in my life. Because, you know ... Miss Barney." I told her a truth.

I loved those bars.

"You could make your own," she said. "Or maybe I'll make you some," she whispered as she leaned over the counter. She glanced over her shoulder to see if her boss, Mrs. Brow, had heard.

Ten feet away the quiet Mrs. Brow turned and nonchalantly headed towards the rear of the store. Mary-Alice swung her gaze back to mine and I swear I saw twinkling there, in the corners of her eyes. She sniffed once also. We stood awkwardly for what seemed like two minutes, or maybe three.

Out of nowhere Mrs. Brow popped up right next to us. "Here's something you should have, Jake. I think you might need this ... now."

It was the cat thing. The cat picture that was like a large doily or something. Yellowed string or thread, looped and I don't know, tied into a flat cat shape in the middle of a lacy square of a thousand knots. Framed behind glass and probably old as all get-out. It hung up against the wrinkly wallpaper over Miss Barney's dining table. Well, *had* hung there, but now Mrs. Brow was holding it out to me in The Nifty.

"How the ...heck ...?" I stammered. It threw me, seeing it again and out of context. I cleared my throat.

She continued matter-of-factly, "Your late neighbor's niece brought it in, with a few books and old pieces of jewelry and so forth. I don't suspect you'd want or need necklaces or cookbooks. But this? I just felt maybe .... It's only a dollar, priced for you. A remembrance thing, if you like. It's a quite delicate piece, but as long as you keep it in the frame ..."

I muttered "Yes, thanks, but I don't have a dollar on me ..."

"I'll loan you," piped Mary-Alice. "Pay me back later, okay?" She winked.

My face flushed and began getting damp again so I choked out another quick "thanks," grabbed the thing, and rushed out the door as the little bell thunked against the jamb without ringing. I ducked down the alleyway to home. I didn't sleep, I think, all night.

Next afternoon I still lay in bed, blue comforter pulled to my chin, staring at that cat. No hooks on my walls, so the thing was propped on top of my dresser, leaning slightly backward. It was like I'd never looked at it before. The glass was a little wavy and reflect-y. I was trying to figure out again what the heck the cat was doing. It sat on its haunches with one front paw reaching for a ball. Its pupils weren't quite right though. Bulgy. Too round? Something ...? I alternated looking with just one eye at a time, blinking left-right-left-right, making it stutter-hop. *Cat-dancing* ...

A creaking noise pulled my attention away. Outside, next door. Then a loud thump! I whipped out of bed into my jeans and slipped the plaid shirt, still buttoned from yesterday, over my head. Jamming bare feet into my Keds I raced downstairs and almost flew across our porch to the side-walk.

"Hey, young fella," said an unfamiliar voice.

I skidded to a stop at the bottom of the next-door steps. A tallish man was standing above me where it seems that maybe the wind had caught Miss Barney's screen door and smashed it against the clapboards. That must have been the slam that had got me out of bed. The guy looked down at me, hitching his suitcoat open to hook his right thumb in his shiny leather belt. Scratching his ear with his other thumb, he said, "Come up here for a minute, would you? It's starting to sprinkle. Getting gusty too."

I took the five wooden steps up and got shelter under the eaves but didn't want to get too close to him. We stared. He stopped scratching and stuck out his hand.

"Doctor Hilly here. And you? You are ...?"

That couldn't be his real name, could it? Plus, he was sticking out his left hand to shake. Who does that? I jammed my hands in my pockets.

"I'm Jake and I live right there. I heard a slam from my bedroom." I risked my right hand, taking it out long enough to point towards our second floor, then found myself slipping into interrogator mode. "What's up? Don't you know nobody's home here? That I'm keeping an eye on things? Did you say 'Billy'?"

"No, I said 'Hilly'. Doctor William Hilly. From the hospital. I also moonlight as Mirror Point Coroner. Narrowly elected last November. But you're too young to have voted ..."

"Oh, no, and I remember now. I did vote, but it was for the other one, the woman coroner. Sorry." That was mostly all true.

He kept staring at me, frowning a little.

"Sure, okay. Anyway ..." he pretended to accept my statement and changed the subject. "In the case of your neighbor here, I'm consider-ing switching her death to 'unusual circumstances' status. So naturally I thought I'd poke around a bit in the house. Not sure what I'd be looking for, but still … you never know. Care to join me? The niece gave me a key before she left town." I must have frowned. He continued, "Come on. Maybe you can help, give things some context, assuming you don't get too freaked out by being in a dead person's house."

I was reasonably sure the house wouldn't bother me, but this guy was already fairly annoying. I thought I'd better keep an eye on him.

"Sure. Let's do it. You first."

It was silent in there once we'd closed the door behind us. Standing in her foyer for a minute I began to notice the rain drops hitting the windows. The wind rattled the door just a little, too. Like a mouse scuttling on linoleum. Dr. Hilly took a couple long-legged strides into the living room.

All Miss Barney's furniture was gone: old velvet couch, platform rocker, carved-leg coffee table and matching end tables. Even her faded, thin, ratty oriental rug. All gone. That felt weird. How could her home be here, but with no guts? Like, just a house now?

We followed the hallway to the back bedroom. Hers, I guessed. Also empty, but since I'd never been in there before it didn't register as so unusual. Hilly made his way around the perimeter, letting his hand trail behind him, touching the walls, as he glanced from ceiling to baseboard. He stuck his head into the closet, felt along the shelf over the clothes rod, quietly closed the door.

I decided not to go into the bathroom. I let him alone to poke around by himself, but I imagined that all the old misshapen soap bars, little glass bottles of lavender water and half-empty hotel toothpaste tubes had been trashed by the niece too.

He came out, humming something unrecognizable, and gave me another blankish look with a taut upper lip that seemed to be toying with the idea of a mustache. *Good luck, mister.* Then into the kitchen.

The immaculate harvest gold gas range and ancient white Kelvinator were standing guard. The fridge's droning compressor competed with Dr. Hilly's humming. He stopped. The chrome-Formica dinette set against the front wall was gone, along with even the ponderous plaid curtains from the windows. That whole dining area looked bright and buoyant now, like the metal appliances were scarcely heavy enough to keep the room from floating away.

I remembered that, back when I used to sit eating oatmeal-cocoa-chip bars at that table, I'd sometimes tried to look into the too-round eyes of that goofy woven cat, hanging there on the wall across from me.

And it was *still* there!

Whole house bare, and krazy-cat was in his old spot! I blinked a couple times. Still there, staring back at me! I squeezed my eyes so tight they started to burn.

"No No No No. Not here! It's not!" I mumbled through clenched teeth.

"Not what? What's not here?" His sharp tone bounced off the bare walls and ceilings like a spilled drawer of knives.

I turned towards his voice and ventured a peek, frantically hoping for a hint or a glimmer of understanding in his grey eyes.

"It's in my room! Not here! That cat ..." as I turned, pointing to the wall which was ... bare!

By the time we'd driven through the rain to his hospital office I'd calmed down, which was good because my heart had tried to escape through my ribs. My chest still hurt. He stethoscoped and pulsed me, shined a light in my eyes and assured himself of whatever, then squeakily rolled his own chair over to face mine, and sat, and leaned forward.

He managed to sound moderately concerned. "All right, Jake. You're okay now, but what brought all that panic on? What happened to you in that kitchen?"

"Weirdness. That's what!"

"And?" He drew the word out into five syllables at least. I told him about the cat thing: the *there* and *not there*, and *in my room too*. I really couldn't put my finger on why I had so totally freaked, because I told it relatively calmly now. He raised one eyebrow.

"That's it? A painting? A painting that wasn't there?"

"Look," I said, frustrated, "It's a ... it's not a ... never mind. I don't understand either. Maybe being in her house, all creepy, creaky and empty ... I got confused. Right? Shook up. I liked her as a neighbor chatting in the kitchen and eating bars. When she died so suddenly it .... I was shocked and sad and I got sent to stay with my uncle at Way's End Campground. He's the manager. That time up there helped, I think, like it was supposed to. I caught the ferry back a week ago… but now I'm wondering if I shouldn't have stayed longer."

I was tired of talking about me. I asked, "Doctor, what did you expect to find in an empty house? Why wait six weeks?"

He didn't answer immediately. Then, "Miss Barney's heart apparently just stopped, true. Yet there might have been something else too. Heart attacks aren't unusual in older folks like her but the family wanted further details, requesting an autopsy follow-up. Well, I wasn't quite expecting what I'd first found, and I've been waiting for some newer lab results from the resubmitted samples. I'm not sure why I'm telling you this. I shouldn't. Yet ..." he trailed off.

"Yet ...?"

"Well ... never mind. I've got to make sure, you know, before I actually share anything ... negative, or make any public announcement." Frowning, he got himself up out of his chair, glanced at the window and added, "It's later than I thought, but I see it's stopped raining. Can you get yourself home and I'll call you tomorrow, or in a couple days?"

I didn't expect him to drive me. And anyway, I needed the walk and fresh air to replace the bleachy hospitalness lodged in my nose. Besides, I still didn't trust him.

I pushed my way out the glass main door, already determined to cut straight across Restless Cemetery (named after Hyman Restless, the first to be buried there, way way back). The newer graves were up the grassy rise, in the rear, near a stunted Catalpa tree. I found Miss Barney. Six weeks since her burial, but still… no grass grew on her plot. Not *totally* surprising, as there were at least eight other plots scattered around that never greened up either, even after decades. Dry dirt splotches. Some folks thought it was kind of a local item of interest: 'Intermittent bad soil' they'd always said, whoever 'they' were and whatever 'they' meant. Certainly not a tourist attraction that I'd ever travel to see.

I paused, staring at her temporary marker. I'd heard that it took about two months to get a proper carved granite stone, which would have made everything seem even more permanent. *Permanent death ... but what else is there?*

I didn't move. I almost started smelling those oven-warm bars, which was ridiculous. But it made me flashback to my cat-kitchen freakout and I took off running for home.

The shortest distance between two points might be a straight line, but that's not how they designed this town. I had to cut a few corners, cross several back yards, and jump Jiminy Creek twice (because it meandered) to beat the world's record, and I did. Up my porch steps, in the door, up the staircase two steps at a time, and into my room.

And, it wasn't there! The frigging cat was gone from *here* too!

"This is nuts! This is total nuts! What the hell? Where's the *cat? My cat!*" No one was home to hear me. I went out and around the corner next door and peered in Miss Barney's window. Bare wall, no cat. I crossed the front yard, leaped the picket fence and tore the two blocks to Thrifty Nifty hoping to get there before they closed.

The bell thunked again as I burst in the front door.

A startled Mary-Alice-Darlene blurted, "Little Big Man, what the heck're you doing?"

"Maddy! My cat's gone!"

"You don't have a ... wait! The knit one? Miss Barney's? The one I, we, gave you yesterday?"

"I owe you a buck, I know! But yes, that one. The Coroner and I ..."

"Coroner?"

"Yeah. Long story. Anyway ... it's gone! Not in my room, not in Miss Barney's either after I thought I saw it there earlier today."

"Jakey, I'm confused." Her lips pursed and her perfect face scrunched a little before her eyes opened very wide. "But ... I just found *this* a little while ago, in the back room." She displayed a small book she'd apparently been reading at the counter when I busted in. "We, you and I, need to go through this, because, wow, it's ..." and she held it out to me, open, at the end of her reach, "Miss Barney's!"

"Come on then," I said.

We walked as fast as we could (while hoping not to draw attention) down Main Street and across the bridge to the beach. It was dusk and the place was deserted. We went straight to the old cedar picnic table under the park's one security light and plunked down next to each other, breathless and shivering a little. Just the cool night air? Maddy's shoulder was warm against mine as we huddled over the book.

The title, *The Scribble-In Book*, was embossed on the front. As she flipped back the cover I could see that it had been manufactured with blank pages, like a diary maybe, or journal. The first few pages were crowded with pencil and pen sketches of dorky birds and flowers, but on the seventh page the handwriting began:

> *I will forever cherish this book from Auntie Agnes. The wonderful pictures here are hers. Such a talented person! I am so sad, however, because she died a week ago. So suddenly and with not a hint of warning. All the town is heartbroken. But I am so lucky to be the recipient of this, her little sketchbook. Also, the lovely framed portrait of her late cat, Bub. Those two creatures had had a special bond, and that is for certain. I will always think of Bub and Dear Auntie Agnes whenever I gaze upon her intricately crafted feline 'yarn' rendering. I promise to hang it in a prominent spot in the hallway and look upon it every day until I die.*

I turned my face to meet Maddy's gaze. I whispered, "So Miss Barney had an Aunt Agnes?"

"Not even! Look a couple pages further. This part was written by an Ethyl Gasman, not Miss Barney. Check out her signature. Dated 1909. This was way before Miss Barney." She was right. Too long ago. Ancient almost.

Maddy gently placed her palm on my forearm. Then I felt urgency in her grip.

"Keep reading, Jakey," she quietly implored. I did.

There was a lot of writing in that little book, I'll tell you. We were glued to the bench as we took turns reading aloud, looking for answers or even just clues. One hour passed, then another. In the book, a kind of vague pattern emerged. One handwriting style jumped to another and another as the book made its way from one owner to the next. First Ethyl to a Bernice to a Janice to a Fred Orfmine who barely wrote anything yet had possession of the book for at least seventeen years. Followed by his daughter who wrote a lot of dull daily details of her uninteresting career in the Mirror

Point Utilities office. And an old man with shaky penmanship had created about fifty "witty" limericks over the course of an otherwise unremarkable 1948 summer. Two more women authors interspersed their thoughts-of-the-day with epigrams, recipes, and prayers clipped from Sunday newspapers and glued in.

The handwriting ended with Miss Barney, of course. Her last entry:

Jake is probably ready to take on the responsibility. Let it be his.

I gulped. "Now *me*? It's *my* book?"

Maddy nodded, "And your cat, too!"

Yeah. Was it only a coincidence that each author at some point wove the woven cat into their entries? No. In fact, each one had apparently, in turn, owned the framed feline themselves!

Of course, its current location was still a mystery to me. But ragged pools of thought flowed into each other until they flash-flooded my brain and spilled out.

"Maddy ... wait a minute! There were nine *The Scribble-In Book* authors, nine previous cat owners, and ... Miss Barney makes nine grassless graves in Restless Cemetery."

Yikes.

Mary-Alice-Darlene locked eyes with me. Her response was measured, and for half a minute she looked like she was thinking hard. Soon she smiled, exhaled a breathless "Oh yeah ..." then angled her head towards me. Her lips, so close to mine, opened wider.

The yellow high-pressure sodium bulb over our heads began to buzz angrily, unamused by its too-short, planned obsolescence.

A piercing *crack*, like clear-sky lightning, and the black arms of Night embraced us.

Tonight is the anniversary ...

The Boys

by Toni Kief

Andrew Jackson Hammer, Ya-Hoh County Sheriff

How ironic that tonight of all nights would be a new moon and Sheriff Andrew Jackson Hammer's retirement. He served Ya-Hoh county for 41 years, yet it feels he hasn't paid the debt from day one.

Tick-Tock.

The obsession has taken his youth, family, and still to this day he has no tangible answers. Tonight is the anniversary of when he saw the boy standing next to the mailbox. The memory feels as if no time has passed; tonight he waits for the sun to dip behind the horizon and he will make things right.

Jack Hammer's memory ticks off what seemed like a brief history and yet, an eternity. He parks on the side of the road and his mind goes back to the last weeks before being discharged from the Army military police. Jack and Bruce had a night of many beers and high spirits. They had become friends as soon as they met in basic training.

Tick-Tock.

Here it was the end of the military and the beginning of a new life. They started with a roll of stamps, lists of addresses for law enforcement agencies, a tablet, some mimeograph copies of resumes, and a box of envelopes. As the evening wore on, and with each beer they consumed things became more inappropriate. Bruce sent an application to the KGB, and Jack filed to run for sheriff of a town only some old guy at the end of the bar knew about. It was a joke, but on December 14, 1957, Jack received a certified letter informing him he had won by seven votes, and he owed $78 for a filing fee. Much later he learned that he was the only candidate on the ballot and that there were a total of eight votes. The one he lost was a write-in for Brett Maverick.

The timing was close as Jack had to muster out of the army, and he had to pack everything he owned and strip his savings account to get to Way's End before January 1st. It took two days to drive to this town not found on any of the gas station road maps. He had a sketched map from a library and then after multiple stops asking directions, and more hours of driving through the overgrown forest on a raggedy two-lane road, he was there.

Finding a room was easy; Jack was the only guest at the Motel 4 Tourist Cabins. He unpacked and hurried to meet with the outgoing sheriff, Ed Bullock. Ed had retired, sold his house, and was moving to Boca Raton. His decision to leave was the reason for the timing of the election. There would only be two hours to meet before the old man caught the ferry and left Way's End for good. Trying to remember the address, Jack searched and noticed most of the buildings were unnumbered, and only four streets had name signs. Jack turned on a third unnamed street when his headlights washed across a child.

Tick-Tock.

The boy appeared from nowhere; a frail, dirty kid of about five looked directly into Jack's eyes and his soul. Jack slowed and scanned the area. Not noticing any cause for concern, he drove on. A quick check of his rearview mirror, Jack felt his hair stand on end as the boy stared; his eyes anchored on Jack's pick-up truck as he drove away.

The outgoing sheriff, Ed Bullock stood waving in the front yard as Jack arrived. Sheriff Ed handed Jack a crumpled map of the county and a box of uniforms, cuffs, and a gun. After loading the box into Jack's truck, they walked into the nearly empty house. Jack remembers hearing chatter in the kitchen area, and this was when he was introduced to Sheriff Ed's wife, Nadine, and Darlene Fresno.

Tick-Tock.

Jack learned the stunning woman was a newlywed and a night student at the Mirror Point Community College. Mrs. Bullock had trained her in clerical duties, to handle the phones, and to keep the office neat. Initially, he was taken by her beauty, but within minutes her inner strength filled the room. It was immediately clear she wouldn't take any guff, and Jack had a good feeling that they would build a strong team of two for Ya-Hoh county.

Sheriff Bullock pinned a gold badge on Jack's blue jacket and handed over the keys to the 1954 Ford Black and White with *Sheriff* stenciled on the doors. Then Ed shooed Jack out into the night. Not sure what to do next, Jack drove to the ferry dock and worked his way back through all of the open businesses for a quick introduction and a gallant attempt to re-member names. Luckily this was the smallest town he had ever seen, and Jack had time to patrol into the county roads seeing the forest differently than the ride into town. He drove past the Best Way Inn Bed and Breakfast three times that night, checking on the boy. Only one dim light on the up-per floor was visible, the same as tonight. Jack planned to stop the next day and ask about the child.

That first night ended at nearly 3 a.m. when Jack settled into the mo-tel bed in cabin number four. Tonight, in this, his last meditation, Jack remembered the feel of the clock as he set the alarm for 9 a.m. He was to meet Darlene Fresno at ten in the coffee shop next to the motel.

Tick-Tock.

Sheriff Bullock had explained he worked from home since the original office was destroyed in the flood of 1956. Jack planned to take Mrs. Fresno around to find some office possibilities. She knew the town and should be the one to make the final decision. At exactly ten, Jack walked in with a rough list of possibilities in hand. Mrs. Fresno was waiting with a crusty old man; little did Jack know she had negotiated a lease of the old Buster Brown Shoe Store. The price was right, and there was plenty of room. He was overwhelmed as she raved about the luxury of two bathrooms and three pairs of size seven shoes in the storage room.

Jack's original plans were quashed as he signed a twenty-year lease with Mr. Tanner. He paid for their coffees and, once handed the key, Jack and Mrs. Fresno left for the new location. Respecting the obvious balance of power, Jack carried a typewriter and rotary calculator into the abandoned store. She had an old wood desk near the front door, and he left the office equipment there. Darlene waved Jack over to the side wall. There was a three-legged folding table with a note pad, a jar of pens, and a file cabinet that held up the missing corner of his makeshift desk.

Jack looked about. It was clear Mrs. Fresno had a plan; the place was perfect.

Tick-Tock.

He continued to unload her car and follow her instructions as best he could. She confirmed that the phone would be installed later that day. This was not what Jack had anticipated, but he knew he would adapt. There was a lawn chair against the side wall. He unfolded it and sat down. This was when Mrs. Fresno plopped a box of open cases on his lap. He was about to open the top folder when a panel truck pulled in with supplies and Darlene's husband, James Fresno, stepped out.

Fresno was a large, loud man and the only contractor in Way's End. He bragged that the majority of his work was across the lake in Mirror Point, and he had to stay there if his jobs extended until after dark. (Jack would learn about the lake later.) It was clear that he was doing this remodel as a favor to his bride and handed Jack the sketch for the office set up. Two unidentified helpers unloaded three steel-reinforced doors and a load of iron bars to build cells on the left side of the store. Jack crept away, to try to leave in all of the hubbub. She didn't miss his move. He admitted he had planned to walk to Sheriff Ed's house to recover his pickup truck from the driveway. Mrs. Fresno made it clear: Jack was to call her Darlene, because Mrs. Fresno was her mother-in-law.

Tick-Tock.

All these years later, he watches the sun creep towards the horizon, and Jack continues to reminisce about the feeling of hope he had when he drove to the motel to prepare for his second-night patrol. This night, Jack looks down at his lap. With a chuckle, he thinks of the oversized uniforms that were given to him by the old sheriff. They were too large then, and now they fit perfectly, especially around his middle.

Tick-Tock.

Jack spent this entire last week awash in memories, and he knew today would be the culmination of the surprised lifetime in Way's End. Maybe the world's longest joke. Darlene was always the base of his reflections. He would miss her face (when she greeted him), her vicious humor, and her official cop-voice on the phones. He wondered if she would miss him as desperately as he missed her already. Darlene staffed the office from eight to four the entire time of his tenure. He had been right; they were the perfect yin and yang of small-town law enforcement.

It had been his second week as sheriff, while sorting through the pile of open cases, when Jack noticed a disturbing recurrence. Spirit Lake had regurgitated an odd variety of feet onto the banks of Hangman's Island. None ever matched and they all wore a variety of footwear. It was puzzling to him that Sheriff Ed hadn't mentioned this anomaly when they met. Jack noticed that they were to leave all of the investigations to prison wardens. He read and sorted before he called to Darlene. She shared the legends and confirmed the first was discovered in 1889, nearly seventy years ago. Many of Jack's days off were then spent in Mirror Point at the police station and the library in a search for help and answers. He discovered that the Presbyterian church on First Street had a corner in the cemetery where the feet were buried with just one unmarked headstone. If there was ever a true investigation, Jack hoped for the rest of the remains.

It wasn't long into his tenure that Jack had noticed Smokey's Tavern didn't close at night. Smokey Jr. simply turned off the lights and quieted the music. In all the years of his nightly patrols, the parking lot was never empty on the weekends. He smiled. It wasn't long before he knew everyone in town, and they recognized that Sheriff Hammer was a soft touch and good for a ride. It was Darlene that was the strong arm of the law. If someone drank too much on the weekend, they would wait for Sheriff Jack to patrol past the bus bench, and with a wave, they could get a ride home. It always tickled him that Way's End had a bus stop and no bus. Jack knew this practice of drunk delivery was a major prevention of injuries, property damage, and the dreaded paperwork.

Even though it was still a small town, the demands expanded with the growth of the community. Jack had frequent meetings with the Ya-Hoh County board in the hope of expansion. After months of arguing both money and necessity, they finally agreed to hire part-time students. The community college Criminal Justice students readily filled the extra hours for a minimum wage and letters of recommendation. As the clocked ticked off the years, he was grateful that they had helped drag Jack into technological compliance.

Tick-Tock.

Jack checked the time on his phone and reminisced when his CB radio was replaced with a variety of cell phones, each one smaller and more complex. It had become a simple task for the evening office assistant to forward the calls to the new sheriff and deputy as they left the office. If it weren't for Darlene, they would still be on the CB radio, but she had forced him into every phone update. Since 1990 she had programmed MC Hammer's song "U Can't Touch This" as his ring tone. She never stopped finding it funny.

Jack discovered he had a particular skill the town considered a gift, and he felt it a curse. He could see, and on a rare occasion talk to, the haunts that inhabited the village. The first and most frequent calls were to the Best Way Inn. There were several rotating entities, the boy, a couple of women, and a loud, aggressive old man. Jack was shocked by the third call in a week reporting someone wailing at the guests, and knocking on doors. When Jack arrived he walked through the halls and finally, in the darkest of corners he confronted the shadow.

Not sure what to do, Jack spoke as he followed the image through the halls, "I'm honored to meet you, Mr. Way." It was a hopeful guess on who the spirit might be. The shadow slowed and seemed to turn. "You have birthed a fine town. We honor you and your memory. Mr. and Mrs. Hartness have opened your home to share your story with visitors."

Tick-Tock.

The shadow stopped, and Jack could feel the attention shift. "I just moved to town, and I'm the new Sheriff. My name is Andrew Jackson Hammer." He continued to talk about his short history, and about the fearful calls he had received. The shadow started to shift away, so Jack hurried. "I know it isn't your intent to frighten people and I'm not going to ask you to leave." The shadow stopped and turned back. "Could you please keep your visits away from the bedrooms? It would be greatly appreciated."

The tourists would visit for the mysteries and possible contact with the lost souls. From that day on Mr. Way kept his moaning patrols to the first-floor living area and the attic. Never did he screech in the sleeping areas again.

It was Darlene who was able to get *Unsolved Mysteries* to help with the feet that kicked out of the lake every few years. The investigator they sent was a pompous ass, but he did bring in the best forensics. Darlene went with them to the island; Jack was relieved that he could stay in the background. They interviewed the warden and a particular guard. But they would not allow any conversations with inmates. Jack recalled being over-whelmed with moans and calls from a garbage dump on the toe of the island as they were escorted to the boat.

Tick-Tock.

Convinced on that day there were murders, Jack vowed he would be back if another foot, body or even a little information appeared. The pro-ducer told Jack they came away with nothing and the show never aired.

That same night, Jack couldn't help but wonder if the old legends had any value, and in a whisper, he asked for answers from the other side of liv-ing. As a positive, he was able to give a few families in Mirror Point some peace with two victim identifications. Jack's career was filled with ongoing hauntings, unmatched feet, and Sasquatch sightings.

He swore not to let the warden keep the local authorities out of any discoveries. It would only be the new inhabitants and tourists that com-plained of sightings of The Captain and Tennille on the road to Thornton's Lodge. This small Sasquatch family were the original inhabitants of Way's End, and they allowed the town to exist. Jack wondered if their small fam-ily was included in the census.

There was one memory he could not erase. Jack couldn't stop as it re-played as he watched the sun drift lower on the horizon. He closed his eyes and he was back to that extra-long night of drunks and bar fights. Jack had returned to the office and was finishing up when exhaustion overtook him. Even now, 19 years later, he felt the ache in his low back and the comfort of his head melting into the pillow. Jack had slipped into a rare deep sleep he only seemed to get in the front cell nearest the phone. He woke slightly when headlights illuminated the small window of the rear metal door. He started to doze back off when his bed shifted. It was Darlene. She snuggled closely, and he could feel her silent sobs. After twenty-two years her hus-band, James, had left. Jack held her, wishing to delay the morning light. He didn't want to illuminate her still beautiful face and have this moment end. Four weeks later James returned home. Neither ever spoke of that night. Jack stored it away as a private memory of a singular man who silently loved a woman from first sight.

Tick-Tock.

Darlene's son James Junior was born *prematurely* at eight pounds, seven ounces. Jack wasn't the only one in town wondering how big that boy would have been if he was full term. With a sigh, Jack compares the boy's face to his own one more time. It had been an unspoken contract never to question and never ask.

The image of the smiling Buster Brown and his dog, Tige, continued to peek around the Sheriff's Department sign. Over the decades Jack's patrols continued from the late afternoon into the night. The population of Way's End doubled, and then doubled again, and then a third time. Jack liked to think he was part of the growth. He promised on this night he could resolve one of the many mysteries in the settlement at the end of all roads.

As the days, weeks and years passed Sheriff Hammer issued tickets, drove drunks home before daylight, intervened on the marital disputes (mostly at the Gunther house), and investigated weekly reports of what Darlene called UBHs, unidentified break and haunts. With all of the demands, Jack never expected his life was to be this village.

Tick-Tock.

It wasn't the feet or the people that kept him in Way's End. It was the community, everyday happenings, and the brown eyes of the boy by the mailbox that held him. As the years, full moons, and all-nighters raced past there were more hauntings than crime and more questions than answers. He was 28 years in office before the county expanded policing to fund a deputy. This year, Jack supported a new guy for sheriff, and Jack's retirement began at the luncheon the last day of the year. The Twentieth century, Y2K didn't include Jack Hammer.

Tonight, the week of Jack's last new moon. As he left the retirement party, he gave the same gold badge to his replacement. He was honored by most of the town showing up for the goodbye at Smokey's Tavern. They laughed, told stories and shared a few tears. It was inevitable his mind had to travel back to the brown-eyed boy by the mailbox. All of these years Jack only had the stories he had made up about the boy with sketchy whys and hows. This time alone was the first he could think out loud about the plan that Jack kept private for decades.

Tonight, is the culmination of an accidental career and the year 1999. The talk on the news forecasted the probability this could be the last night before the world crashed.

Tick.

Parked on the side of the road, the exact location he first saw the boy in front of the Bed and Breakfast. As the sun sets Jack vows aloud to wait at the mailbox as long as it takes. This time it isn't to gather clues or ask questions, but to look into a small dirty face with love. The boxes of research and interviews were burned this morning in the wood stove in the back of the seldom-used cells at the Sheriff's Office. He left the key on the same wooden desk that was there from the first day. Jack is confident that there is only one thing he could do as he left a note. He accepted that some stories have no beginning and others no end. Tonight's duty is that Andrew Jackson Hammer will take the hand of one small child and with his Colt Police .38, that he had never fired, will accompany the boy to the Light.

TOCK!

... she didn't want to humiliate him.

First Do No Harm
by Robin Ridenour

Vera's throat tightened. Should she tell him?

She gazed at Arthur working diligently at the dining room table. The morning sun slanted across the paper and made the silver strands in his hair shine. He'd have forgotten that today was their anniversary. *Thirteen years.* But if she mentioned it, he'd feel awful.

She'd found love late in life, held back by her skeptical nature and acerbic sense of humor. Those traits had served her well growing up with alcoholic parents and as an investigative reporter but had sent men running for the hills.

Not Arthur, though. Erudite and intelligent, the new editor at the Seattle Times gave as good as he got. They were married within the year, the bride thirty-seven, the groom almost fifty.

So handsome, Clint Eastwood with a geeky flair, in his faded chambray shirt. Through the window behind him, the crimson maple leaves were brilliant, beautiful – and dying.

Arthur slapped down his pencil and rubbed his hand across his face with a sigh. "What's a six-letter word for 'zebra relative'?"

Vera hesitated. He was still sharp enough to know if she sandbagged, but she didn't want to humiliate him. "Quagga." Her chest constricted. He'd always been the one to help her with vocabulary. Since the diagnosis, he doggedly completed one crossword a day to try to keep from losing ground. He took vitamins and exercised. He also read incessantly and had joined a bridge group, even though he detested the game. Learning Mandarin had proved too difficult, his struggle heartbreaking to see.

It was a blessing that his gung-ho, optimistic nature hadn't changed. And that he was physically strong – less likely to die of bedsores or pneumonia if things worsened. *But more likely to linger for years.* Her lips pressed together. How cavalier that sounded, as if she didn't care, as if the diagnosis hadn't crushed her, but she'd always coped best by being rational and prepared.

Vera glanced at the clock. She served as his timer now. Not only to keep them on schedule but because otherwise he'd continue with a hopeless task for hours, until tears of shame and frustration welled in his eyes. This particular crossword made her uneasy anyway, during her quick glance before she brought in the paper. The other words included "passenger pigeon," "mastodon," and "spotted owl" – all species that were extinct or threatened. "Sweetheart, we've got to leave in fifteen minutes."

He looked at her, his brow furrowed.

"The new doctor, remember?"

Arthur had been the one who found the clinical trial online, eager to try something promising, motivated to help others even if it might prove a failure for him. *Always such a good guy.*

"Oh, that's right." He stood. His hopeful smile took Vera's breath away. "It's a beautiful day for a drive."

"It's a long ways to Mirror Point, so I thought I'd drive." She patted his hand to take the sting out. "But if we stop at Vince's for lunch, you can take us home." He still drove sometimes when she was with him, only to places that he knew well. Like Vince's. They'd gone to the quaint Italian place for their first date and it remained his favorite restaurant.

They laughed about their early clashes at the newspaper as she drove to Dr. Maxwell's office and parked in the bright sunshine. They crossed the parking lot, dried leaves scudding across their path, to the outreach clinic at Brioc Memorial Hospital.

Outside, a woman with long black hair sat on a bench, tears streaming down her face, as she rocked back and forth. A distraught family member? Vera slowed, but the lady didn't make eye contact, and they walked past to arrive at the bright, sparsely furnished waiting room with ten minutes to spare.

A woman at the desk greeted them. While she checked Arthur in, the receptionist leaned in and dropped her voice. "Dr. Maxwell even does all his own evaluations for the trial. That level of dedication is almost unheard of."

Arthur turned to Vera, beaming. She returned his smile and repressed the misgivings that edged into the back of her mind. She'd once helped bring down a doctor who covered his falsified research by doing his own data entry, although her cursory investigation of Maxwell had revealed no red flags, just a recent grad from Vanderbilt. Too soon to expect any publications. Strange that he'd choose to practice way out here.

"Arthur." A sturdy-looking young man in a white coat approached with a smile, extending his hand. Vera dismissed her irritation at the casual use of Arthur's first name. *It's not disrespect, just a tool they use to put us at ease and establish rapport.*

Dr. Maxwell had a firm handshake and a boyish face. Vera studied the young doctor. Mid-thirties. He'd be at the peak of his enthusiasm and that would be a good thing. He spoke passionately about his research and showed them old photographs of his father, also an MD, and his grandfather, both of whom had developed early dementia. The family resemblance was uncanny.

Vera's hand tightened on Arthur's as Maxwell described the decline of his loved ones. It seemed to inspire Arthur, though.

"I like that it's personal to him," he said in a low voice, as they followed Dr. Maxwell for a tour.

"These are the new patients about to start." Dr. Maxwell opened the door of the lockdown unit. "It's closed – we can't have them wander off. We take them in cohorts of seven at a time – there's a statistical reason but I like to think that it's a lucky number. Their intake evaluation consists of five days of outpatient testing. Residential treatment lasts for up to four weeks, initially. The results are so good that many no longer continue treatment after that."

Vera frowned. *Nope. That's too good to be true.* "How can that –" They rounded the corner and she stopped, her hand rising to her mouth.

In seven chairs scattered around the large room, people hunched drooling or staring vacantly at uncompleted puzzles. A young woman in scrubs moved quietly through the room, tending them like so many potted plants. She wiped the chin of a thin man slumped in a wheelchair, then turned to right a frail-looking woman sporting food stains, who was sliding off a couch in slow motion.

Vera couldn't breathe. This could be Arthur in a few years.

The doctor's pager beeped. "Excuse me." He stepped out of the room.

Vera backed away, heart pounding. She bumped into a woman seated behind her, bright spots of rouge brightening pale cheeks, like a marionette. A paper cup of water tumbled to the floor. "Oh, I'm sorry!" Vera reached for the fallen cup as the patient did. A red band hung from the woman's brittle wrist. 'Violet Stevens, cohort 11-15-18.' *Two months ago? That can't be right.* Vera frowned at the aide scurrying over. "I thought this was the new group." Vera gestured to the wristband.

The young woman's eyes widened. "Oh, dear. Someone's put on the wrong band. This isn't even Violet."

The patient turned dull eyes to the aide but remained mute.

The aide snipped off the plastic strip. "Isn't that right, Pearl?"

Pearl stared across the room, a shiny trickle at the corner of her mouth.

What if Vera hadn't drawn attention to it? When Dr. Maxwell returned, she said, "The bracelet on one lady was dated two months ago, but you said those were pre-treament patients. The aide said the bracelet was wrong."

The doctor's eyebrows drew together. "That's unfortunate. I'll personally take care of it. I take a breach like that very seriously." His grim expression gave way to his customary smile. "Let's go see the treated group."

Six vivacious seniors stood chatting in pairs, like a cocktail party. Engaged. Fully alert. Snippets of lively conversation reached Vera.

"—heading to Europe for three weeks after this—"

"—in the service for twenty years—"

"—just arrived today from Austin—"

"—with the current housing market—"

Wait, what? Vera's head snapped around. She must have misheard; they were all talking at once. Dr. Maxwell walked them back to his office.

"Well, what do you think?" he said. "We only have one spot left for this cohort. The next one won't start for another twelve weeks."

"Let's go for it," said Arthur, with some of his old confidence. "The last group looked great."

Vera caught her husband's eye. "Arthur, don't you want to think about it for a few days?"

"Of course," said Dr. Maxwell. "The last spot should fill today but we'll have another cohort in a few months. The best results are in patients who haven't had a significant decline, though, and Arthur here looks like the best candidate I've seen in some time." He smiled. "It's unlikely he'll worsen much in that short time."

Vera's eyes narrowed.

But that was all it took. Arthur painstakingly signed all the forms despite her suggestion that he hold off, and once they arrived at Vince's, his appetite was good enough to lessen Vera's apprehension. "I can't wait to start on Monday." Arthur cheerfully forked up bowtie pasta. "Don't worry, honey." He dragged bread through olive oil. "You always worry too much. It'll be fine."

His teasing and unfettered optimism felt like old times, but a tendril of unease took root inside her, and he remained unwilling to reconsider.

"Arthur, I'll bring around the car." She headed for the parking lot and called her old private investigator contact. "James? It's Vera. Fine, fine. Listen, I need a favor. I need some information on a Dr. Stewart Maxwell, a dementia researcher in Mirror Point." She glared at the building. "His father was an MD, and his father and grandfather were dementia patients. Got his degree from Vanderbilt." She paused, listening. "I don't know, something doesn't seem right. I'm wondering if his research is legitimate. Can you also check disciplinary actions, things like that? Thanks, James – I owe you."

Monday morning, Arthur finished his puzzle with lightning speed, only needing her help with "quotidian," then they made the long trip to Mirror Point. On the ferry, Arthur bounced on the seat like a child. "I think this is going to work." His hopeful smile brought a lump to her throat.

Please, please let it help him. Her tears blurred the billboards as she drove out of the ferry terminal.

They arrived with a few minutes to spare, and Arthur went over to the fish tank. "Look at this one. It's … that kind with feelers."

A nurse took them to the testing room, then politely ushered Vera out. "It's best for him to have no distractions." But each time they led her back to observe through a glass window, Arthur was working at a computer, Dr. Maxwell's hand on his shoulder.

"Isn't that distracting?" she asked the lady. *What was he doing glued to her husband?*

"Oh, no," said the nurse, "the initial evaluation for the trial is so intense that it reassures patients."

Vera suppressed her annoyance at hearing her husband referred to as a "patient."

An aide wheeled past a frail woman in a wheelchair, long black hair hanging in limp strands.

Vera frowned – the lady looked familiar – then shook her head. *Nothing else I can do here anyway.* She spent the rest of the time in the waiting room, wrestling with insurance, paying bills, and transferring funds. Finances had been one of Arthur's many strengths, but she could unburden him now. She'd been lucky that he'd bowed out of the more demanding responsibilities with such good grace.

Each day of the intake left Arthur more and more worn out. Initially sunny in the mornings, he trudged out of the facility subdued, even irritable. On Thursday, the fourth day of his testing, she buckled him into the passenger seat. "So, how did it go today?"

"Fine. It was fine. Stop giving me the third degree." His tone was harsh, alien.

Vera blinked, and they drove back in silence. She couldn't eat anything at Vince's, but Arthur seemed to have forgotten his outburst.

Friday morning, he asked, "What's a six-letter geometric shape starting with 'C'?"

Her mouth fell open. "Circle."

"Okay." He filled in the squares, humming. Not embarrassed at his deficits at all.

Vera bit her lip. "Arthur, I'm worried that this testing is too stressful for you." She kept her voice even. "Maybe after you finish today, you could take next week off. That would still be within Dr. Maxwell's window to start."

His head snapped up. "Why? It's all set up. I want to start treatment as soon as I can." He scowled, face flushing. "You don't want me to get better. You want to take over everything. Is that it?" He leaped up, veins bulging in his forehead, and took a step toward her, hands clenched.

Vera recoiled with a sharp intake of breath. He'd never been paranoid, let alone violent. He knew she was on his side. He had to know. She stared at him, trembling.

Arthur blinked then covered his face with his hands. "I'm so sorry, Vera. I don't know what's the matter with me. I guess it must be the stress. You're right. And I trust you. I do. If you think I should wait another week, then I'll wait."

Oh, thank God.

She squeezed his hand. The evaluation had been so hard on him. A week would help him recover. *And give James more time to dig into Maxwell.* But maybe she was getting paranoid from stress, too. What could James really find on such a new doc?

Once they arrived at the facility for the last day of the intake, she relinquished Arthur to Dr. Maxwell. A vague resentment knotted inside at the sight of him, so tall and strong, with his hand steadying her husband, frail and hunched by comparison. Dr. Maxwell raised no objection when she informed him they'd decided to wait another week.

Monday dawned bright and cold. She left Arthur at home with the crossword, while she did the grocery shopping and errands. *I'm so glad he agreed to take this week to recover.* He was uncharacteristically quiet today, but it was good to see his concentration back, and he'd even put on a nice shirt and slacks. Toward the end of last week, he'd started to doodle instead of finishing the crossword, and changed into sweats the second he got home.

Vera was in the checkout line when James called.

"Vera, there's no disciplinary action, but he's moved around a lot. A new office every two years or so for the past twenty-two years."

Vera's heart jolted. *Twenty-two years?* Maxwell was too young to have practiced that long.

James went on. "No interviews or publications about his research, either. You said his father and grandfather had dementia?"

"Yes," Vera whispered, clutching the phone.

"Yeah, well, his grandfather died in World War I at age twenty-three, and his father in a car accident at twenty-nine."

Vera's blood chilled. "What?" *Oh, God – Arthur was dressed up ....* "Thanks – I've got to go." She stumbled from the store, leaving her full grocery cart behind. She hit speed dial but it went to Arthur's voice mail. Oh, God.

Vera rushed home, dashed up the front steps and found a note on the kitchen table. She struggled to read his scrawl:

I changed my mind. Took a cab to Maxwell's. Wait until you see me. I know the transformation will be incredible. Love, Arthur

No, no. Oh, God. Vera dialed with a shaky finger.

"Dr. Maxwell's office."

"This is Vera Dudley. Is my husband Arthur there? I'd like to speak with him."

"I'm sorry, Mrs. Dudley, he's starting therapy and can't be interrupted."

Shit! "He decided to wait. You get him right now. I demand that you stop his treatment."

"I'm sorry, ma'am, but he asked to start today. His testing shows he's a competent adult so there's nothing –"

Vera hung up and headed for Mirror Point like a cruise missile. Instead of waiting an hour for the ferry, she rented a car and tore along the bumpy, winding lake road like an off-road rally driver. She burst into the office, heart pounding with dread. "Where is he?"

The aide darted a glance at a door, and Vera rushed it. "You can't go in there –"

Dr. Maxwell stood leaning across the table, his back to her, shuddering, drawing gasping breaths.

Vera faltered and drew back, her face flushed. She had the wrong room. *Is he ...?*

Dr. Maxwell turned, face glowing, eyes brilliant. His hand dropped from her husband's shoulder, slumped across from him.

Vera rushed to her husband's side and shook him. "Arthur!"

Arthur stared vacantly, a thin line of saliva dribbling onto his shirt.

"Arthur!" Her cry echoed throughout the room.

Dr. Maxwell stretched. Snapping with vitality, he strode to the door, then turned with a wide smile. "I'm sorry, Vera. It doesn't always work out well – for the patients." He winked. "Hard on families sometimes, too."

He locked the door behind him, leaving her with the empty husk that had been Arthur.

Centennial Sausage Fest

MIRROR POINT ECHO
COMMUNITY PAGE
FRIDAY, SEPTEMBER 13, 2019

Advance tickets are now available for the Sausage Fest. Get yours now to avoid the rush! Enjoy prize-winning delicious sausage, pies, and cold beer in the big tent. The city council gratefully acknowledges the generosity of our donors: Reba Hailey, The Piehole, and the Goodman family.

... he had tried desperately, uselessly, to save them.

Jojerry
by Susan Brown

The sun's slanted rays leaked through the worn fabric of the sleeping bag. Lee squeezed his eyes closed, trying to force himself back into sleep. The nightmares were so much better than the night.

There was perhaps an hour until sunset. For a few minutes Lee watched a little girl shrieking as she slid down a slide into her father's arms. He tried so hard to imagine what it would be like to live again in a family, to be happy.

It was no use. Night would fall, silence would ooze across the deserted roads of the town, and Jojerry would come. It had been more than two weeks since it last fed. Lee knew Jojerry would hunt tonight.

Slowly Lee gathered the bag around himself and sat up. How many years had he been sleeping on this or that bench in the Founders Park in the center of town? The police didn't bother to roust him any more. He didn't shoplift or beg, didn't create a nuisance of himself, just watched the people of the town and waited to see who next Jojerry would devour – body, soul, existence. At one time he had tried desperately, uselessly, to save them. Now he simply watched without hope.

"So, Lee Eagle Eyes, who's going to disappear tonight?" The officer sipped on his coffee, eyes glimmering in amusement.

"Don't know yet, Chuck," Lee muttered. He squinted at the setting sun. "Too early ..."

"Better not be me. I'm going over to Seattle for the weekend." He laughed and strode away. "When you do know who's gone missing, buddy, you let me know."

Lee watched almost without emotion. The ridicule, the general acceptance that he was several cans short of a six pack no longer bothered him. He was too weary, right down to his soul. He'd seen the monster suck the breath out, and then gnosh on the warm bodies, of too many people. Maybe he was insane ... probably insane ... but not the way they all thought.

He had parted from sanity when he was eleven years old.

Sixteen summers ago. The big camping trip by the foothills. He'd begged to go along, and his brother, Joe, had shrugged, given him a friendly punch in the shoulder, and said okay he could come along with him and Jerry, his best friend. The boys had pitched their tent, laid out the sleeping bags, and then gotten to the serious business of building a fire and eating. Lee remembered how his marshmallow stick had caught fire and the marshmallow had flamed down into the grass. They had all laughed and laughed ...

"Yeow! Who farted?" Jerry yelled.

"It was you!" Joe shouted and they started laughing again, so hard they nearly fell over. But the stench worsened.

"What's that?" Lee demanded. He waved his glowing stick at a lump of ground, kind of the shape (and definitely the smell) of a giant turd. "Wow! It's moving! Gross!"

He turned to his brother, but Joe was just standing, hands hanging loose, his toasting stick jammed with seven marshmallows dipping into the weeds.

"Joe?" Lee's voice quivered. "Jerry? We need to get out of here!"

But neither of them moved. Didn't seem to hear him.

Lee whimpered and danced back into the shadows. The air stunk bad enough to make him want to throw up. Sweet. Putrid. The thing smeared over the ground, oozed close and closer.

"Joe!" Lee screamed.

His brother just stood there. Just stood as the formless monster rose up, and with a gloppily formed mouth, sucked out Joe's choking breath ... his soul. Mewling sounds bubbled from Lee's throat. His knees gave out. He screamed and screamed again ... but there was no sound. The thing chewed into Joe's belly, slurping and sucking on the slithering entrails. The spewing blood finally slowed but the thing lapped up every drop, sucked in every scrap of gristle, bone, and the mat of curly hair that a few minutes before had rippled above Joe's forehead.

When all that had been Joe had been devoured, the monster had turned to Jerry, who all through the horror stood motionless, smiling witlessly. Lee fainted when the thing gnawed a hole through Jerry's yellow t-shirt and his red blood and glistening guts fell out.

The sun was shining over Lee's face when he finally crawled back to consciousness. Even before he opened his eyes he convulsed into scream after scream.

The sound of a car engine ... his dad had come.

"So how was your night in the wilds?" his dad called.

Lee threw up, retched again, and as his dad rushed to him, wept. "Joe ..." he sobbed. "That thing ate Joe ...."

"Who?" his dad asked. "Who's Joe? That must have been some nightmare, Lee. I knew letting you camp out here by yourself was a mistake ...."

Sixteen years ago ... and in one nightmare, the world forgot that Joe and Jerry had ever existed. Overnight Lee became an only child, and his parents never remembered their firstborn son. No one but Lee had grieved for him.

It had been months before he could think about it. No one believed him. They sniggered or talked earnestly, but no one ever believed him. Lee took to creeping out his bedroom window at night. The monster only ate every couple of weeks. Once, Lee had trailed it back to a mud sink near the foot of the mountains. For some reason, the thing was as blind to Lee, as everyone else was oblivious to the rotting stench of the monster.

How old was the thing? How many souls had that monster devoured? How many living, loving, breathing people were obliterated from all memories, from existence? But Lee would not forget. The nameless monster had a name in his mind – Jojerry. Lee's brother and his brother's best friend. Devoured and forgotten.

Lee slowly rolled up his old sleeping bag and watched the retreating figure of the officer. No one remembered the lost ones except him. No one saw the monster, except him. No one spent every night hunting the thing, trying uselessly to save its victims.

No one else was sane enough to be as crazy as he was.

Lee padded down the road to the diner and ordered the special. He didn't care about eating, but without food he would have no strength. Welfare checks kept him alive. When the thing devoured his parents, he had been too exhausted to try and claim the estate. Their house stood empty, supposedly abandoned. No one remembered them; legends and stories had been substituted instead. His own story was reconfigured in the mind of the town – a wanderer from somewhere else.

As he spooned up some soup, Lee considered what part of town to patrol. The stench carried a mile or so, but he never knew where Jojerry would ooze to, or even if it was hunting tonight. Lately the thing had sucked up children more often than the old who had outworn their place in society.

Lee briefly wondered if it had any intelligence but decided no. It was just a sludge of evil – no plan, no purpose – just the purity of evil. Maybe an evil that had existed since the beginning of time.

A desperate plan had been hovering in his mind. If the thing was utterly evil, then maybe goodness or innocence could oppose it. Lee carefully avoided any hint of crime. Jojerry could ooze through any aperture large or small, so even in jail, no one was safe. And besides, there was no one else to bear witness to the victims.

Slouching out of the diner, he walked purposefully toward the church. Nothing he had ever tried – weapons, water, fire – nothing had done more than occasionally turn the thing aside. But with leisurely indifference, it had simply reached another victim. And another and another. Never ending.

And then the stench drifted into Lee's nose.

Tears rolled down his cheeks as Lee turned toward the smell, steps slowing despite his determination. Sometimes he wished the thing would make an end of him, in mercy release him from this hell. But it never did.

There. Lights shone in the elementary school. Dimly Lee remembered the parent conferences of his childhood. The slug thing oozed toward the lights, stretching upward and through an open window. Lee shouted, then watched helplessly as the thing devoured a smiling man and woman. Always the same ... except ...

Screaming.

Shrieking and howling rattling the windows. Lee pressed against the pane. The teacher, dark-haired and plump, screamed and swung books at the thing. As always, the missiles simply fell off the gelatinous, heaving form. But she kept throwing. And screaming.

Lee faded back. The thing had eaten. There would be no more victims tonight. Probably none for a couple of weeks. Wearily he wondered what children would become orphans with no memory of ever having parents.

For a moment he pressed his hands over his ears, wishing the teacher would just shut up. And then he dropped his arms and turned back abruptly.

She had seen.

He wasn't alone in the horror. Someone else had witnessed the evil.

Hope and joy surging through him, Lee blundered into the school, into the classroom where a small crowd had gathered in response to the teacher's shrieks.

"Please, everyone," the principal took control. "Ms. Renee is unwell. I'm taking her to a clinic and we'll reschedule. Thank you ..."

Lee faded back into the shadows. He knew what would happen. They would do their best to convince her she had imagined it, that the people the thing had devoured had never existed, that a few pills would set her right. He knew he should feel sorry for her, but the euphoria of knowing someone would at last believe him flooded out every other emotion.

When he saw the police officer approaching, he laughed aloud. "You'll see!" he yelled. The man ignored him.

Lee retreated into the night, rapidly calculating how long he should wait before approaching Miss Renee.

She was sitting almost motionless in the park. Only her twisting fingers showed her agitation. Lee approached from an angle, eyeing her measuringly. With belated sympathy he imagined what she had been through. School was in session but she was not in her classroom, perhaps would never be allowed in a classroom again. He had never been offered an adult career and in the enormity of being the lone witness to evil, had never thought about it. Now he wondered briefly what path he would have taken if Jojerry did not hunt their town. He shrugged. That life was gone from him. But now, he wasn't alone.

"Miss Renee?" he said softly.

She raised her eyes slowly, as though normal response was something she barely remembered.

"I saw it too," Lee told her.

Her face contorted and she made a motion to strike him away. "No," she snapped. "No ... don't mock me."

"I'm not." He squatted on the grass in front of her, not too close. "When I was eleven that thing murdered my brother, Joe, and his friend, Jerry. No one saw it but me. No one sees it but me. And everyone ..." He swallowed convulsively. "Everyone forgets them."

"I saw it," Miss Renee whispered. "I remember."

"Yeah." Once again, the unutterable joy of not being alone washed over Lee. "No one else sees it."

"But you know it's true." Her voice was stronger. "We'll tell them together ..."

Already Lee was shaking his head. "They won't believe us. We can't prove it and no one remembers." In spite of himself his voice caught. "No one remembers ...."

"There must be records!" the woman insisted. "Births, marriages ... deaths. Just not deaths."

Lee stared at the grass. "We can see them. No one else sees the documents or the printed records even if we set the papers down in front of them. Like we live in one world and they're in another."

"No," she wailed, "it can't be true ...." She sank back on the bench, twisting her fingers again. "Who are you?" she asked abruptly. "I'm Mary Renee. I'm ... I was the second grade teacher over there." She gestured at the school building just visible through the trees.

"I'm Lee. Good to meet you, Mary."

She stared at him as if he was mad. Of course, he was mad. Lee laughed.

For the next two weeks, Lee was almost happy. Mary pumped him for information. He told her everything, so pathetically grateful to have anyone believe him, listen to him. He was so pleased she wasn't going mad. That because he knew, she didn't have to be broken by the evil.

Until the next time Jojerry hunted. She stood beside him whimpering and screaming as the thing devoured three of the children who had been in her class. Awkwardly, he patted her shoulder and clamped his mouth shut so that he wouldn't utter the incredibly stupid jokes that kept galloping through his mind. Someone believed him. The endless loneliness, the humanity that Jojerry stole from him was broken because Mary witnessed too.

"We have to do something," Mary hissed. She had sat on the bench, sobbing all night. Her face was swollen, almost distorted by grief.

"What?" Lee held his hands apart in hopelessness. "I've tried weapons, fire, water ... even holy water. Nothing made any difference." He bowed his head. "I bear witness. My curse ... now yours."

"No!" Mary stood upright, hands clenched. "It is evil. Pure evil and nothing can overcome evil but goodness and purity."

Lee snorted. "So, where are you going to get that?"

"Me," Mary stared off toward the sun, squinting her eyes a little. "I can't live like this. I can't just sit by and watch that ... that thing take the life of the children."

In spite of himself, Lee was a little impressed. A little shamed.

"Show me the place where this evil hides."

"Mary, I don't see what good ..." he argued.

"No," she snapped. "You haven't seen good."

She strode down the road, not looking back. Lee followed, forlornly, feeling like a chastised dog. They passed beyond the edge of town and panted as they crossed the rough land between the buildings and the foothills.

The stench as they neared the sinkhole made Lee want to throw up. Mary said nothing, but she pressed a crumpled tissue over her nose.

"Where?" she demanded.

Wordlessly he pointed. The putrid mud roiled slowly, occasionally belching fumes into the air. Nothing grew within yards of Jojerry's slime.

Mary stood, teeth clenched, eyes closed. She pulled a golden cross out from beneath her shirt and clutched it tightly. Lee heard her whispering a long prayer, begging God to protect and help her.

"I will sacrifice myself," she whispered hoarsely. "I offer myself, to cleanse this evil."

"No, Mary," Lee cried. "Please!"

She ignored him. Step by step she moved closer and closer to the sucking mud. It seemed to Lee that the roiling sludge burbled more rapidly.

"Mary! Don't leave me."

She never looked back, but stepped boldly into the muck. At first she seemed to sink slowly, but then she began to thrash, to scream, to beg. Lee stumbled over the stinking mud, lay in it to reach for her, but she was sucked down.

Gone.

Lee waited for hours, sitting frozen in the fetid slime. But Mary did not reappear. The mud did not stop boiling.

Three days later, Jojerry hunted a child. The little girl who Lee had watched playing in the park. The next day, no one remembered the little girl, just as no one remembered Mary Renee.

Lee sat in the park, rocking back and forth, back and forth on the bench.

"Anyone disappeared lately?" the officer jibed and laughed.

"Just me," Lee whispered. "Just me."

It gave that purr again, this time louder ...

The Fight
by Deron Sedy

They say when prey meets predator, it's fight-or-flight. Not entirely accurate. The biological response is more correctly labeled fight, flight, or FREEZE.

When the creature's head swiveled, and its amber eyes met mine ... yeah, I froze.

All my fool mind could do was consider whether it was sentient. As if that mattered.

Six-inch canines. Probably double my body mass. Snarl at having met a potential threat. Those mattered.

How far had Lindsay gotten? She, with my unborn child inside. Those mattered.

For what it was worth, the creature was equally indecisive, still as a boulder. After that first baring of teeth, a nostril flare and a tense, purr-like oscillation were the only hints as to its evaluation of me.

I chided myself for the wasted moments spent in inaction. I had "good in a crisis" on my resume. I'd spent my spare time over the past year building up a social media presence as a survivalist, hoping to launch my own line of outdoor gear – my way out of the desk job. I completed four week-long survival skills workshops this year alone. *Snap out of it. Survey the situation. Seconds matter. Survive.*

My first thought had been black bear, only because they live in the area, and they sometimes walk on hind feet. But this was far too big. Theoretically, a grizzly might wander this far south, but the creature in front of me would be anomalously large even for that. Might it have been a species of bear I'd never heard of? No. There are eight; I knew this. If this was a bear, it was a ninth, undiscovered type. And anyway, its face, its bipedal dexterity—they were too ape-like. Too human-like.

Which led my untethered mind to wilder explanations ....

Sasquatch?

I've seen studies on soldiers and first responders. Supposedly, in moments of extreme stress, the young ones, the fit ones, they experience transcendent mental clarity. Some report feeling that time itself has slowed. I think that had happened to me once in an overtime high school soccer game. Malcolm Gladwell mentions it in one of his books. Not the famous one. *Whatever. Focus.*

Either I was experiencing the phenomenon now – my existence expanding to fit more thoughts and moments than natural – or the creature was waiting for me to make the first move.

Regardless, knee-deep in Cascade Foothills snow, adrenaline tightening my thighs, I needed a plan. Last night's snow flurries brought another eight inches of fresh accumulation. Enough to slow me, but likely not enough to affect something as big as the creature. Great. My rifle was back at camp, and my adversary blocked my path. If getting a gun was my move, first I would have to dash past the creature. Fresh snow made the terrain appear deceptively even. It was a recipe for a busted ankle.

The creature chuffed, forcing two twirls of vapor to rise lazily into the alpine air. I felt like the beast somehow knew I'd considered outperforming it athletically and had scoffed at the thought.

In the moments before I had seen the creature, my mind strayed to that morning's argument with Lindsay. That's how I'd gotten myself trapped. I wasn't paying attention to the trail in front of me, which runs against everything I've been taught. Now, those powerful legs would only need to cover ten yards to reach me.

It gave that purr again, this time louder and more strained. It lifted its nose to get a better smell of me, still considering. Friend? Foe? Food?

Then a trail of drool left its mouth via one of those dagger fangs. *Not good.*

The creature was uphill. No matter my choice, gravity was to his advantage. Her advantage? *Who cares?* To my right was a cliff face of impassible rock. Even if I reached the wall before the creature, even if I could kick myself up off the lower rocks to grasp the first handhold, I'd not likely pull my weight up before the creature could yank me back down. My remaining options were to my left and – what direction was that? – south, behind me. The first was steep and the latter was steeper.

A morbid conclusion locked into place. My mind accepted, less than willingly, a hitherto never-experienced awareness of my position on the food chain. Left, right, north, south … there was no way out, and I was futilely outmatched.

I would die here.

The realization sent the blood from my face. I would never hold my son. I would never embarrass him in front of his school friends. I would never teach him to play soccer.

All around me the distributed hiss of the morning's snowburst continued. Thick flakes clung to eyelashes I dared not blink. Time must not have slowed so much after all.

Okay, I thought, *if every choice is a losing one, can I at least optimize the outcome?* Could I buy Lindsay's escape? Might she slip back to civilization, if given the amount of time it would take for the monster to consume me? Was I enough meat to make this thing a meal?

Lead the creature as far as possible from Lindsay. But I didn't know where she'd gone. She'd huffed out of the tent saying she needed air. I stayed to relight a fire and have breakfast ready as an apology when she returned. Then she didn't. We'd left tracks everywhere the day before, gathering wood. So by the time I went after her, my near-hour of cooking had made any new tracks look much the same as the old ones. At this point, Lindsay might be behind me on the trail, or she might have gone north into the woods past our camp. *Or – oh, I hadn't thought of that. Please not that.*

Without warning, the standstill ended. The creature dropped to all fours and charged. It crossed the snow between us in a breath. I had only enough warning to lurch in my chosen direction – west. Off-trail would have been Lindsay's least likely choice, so that's where I should steer this thing.

An instant later I toppled. Skull met snow-covered stone. A blinding flash overtook my field of vision. Involuntarily I sucked for breath, but my lungs refused me. How had I lost my footing so abruptly? My vision cleared just in time to witness the ghastly reason for my imbalance. The creature had my ankle between those imposing fangs. I hated myself for being impressed. Evolution had gifted the creature many times over. Its lower jaw slid back and forth like an overtall hacksaw, the action efficiently slicing my Achilles tendon. A sickening pop emitted and echoed from the snowy mountainside. It was pain like nothing I'd ever experienced.

I spun supine, pivoting on my trapped ankle, denying myself acknowledgment of what damage the motion might have caused. With my other foot, I kicked at the beast's mouth. *Dislodge yourself. Maybe bruise a tender nostril. Knock out a tooth.* Could I make myself more trouble than a meal was worth?

And in the next moment, I chastised myself for allowing hope. I was David against Goliath, slingless. The creature's reflexes were so impressively beyond mine. In one deft action, it dropped my first leg and snatched the other, mid-kick. The sliding jaw worked its terrible effect again, now on my other ankle. This creature might or might not be sentient, but one thing was certain: it had a strategy. First it would maim its prey.

Another rush of intense pain, but this time a dizzy dissociation accompanied it. *I can't go into shock. Resist.*

I kicked and jerked with both legs. It was enough to make the creature let go. I had a vague sense that maybe the second ankle wasn't as damaged as the first, but I also feared that both would be useless if asked to bear weight. Momentum sent my knees back toward my forehead, like a poorly executed tuck on the way to a reverse somersault.

The motion caused a rock to jab the small of my back. No, not a rock ... *Idiot! How? HOW had I forgotten?*

My argument with Lindsay was how. We'd awoken to cold morning temperatures, too cold to fall back to sleep. I hadn't felt like getting up to re-light a fire, so we just huddled in the sleeping bag. Shared body heat led to kissing, which in turn led to some healthy morning sex. When it was over, warm, we opened one of the slanted tent's triangular windows to see fresh snow the night had unexpectedly brought.

Lindsay had quickly realized the slower terrain would make it near impossible for us to trek back in time for the Mirror Point ferry. She would miss her friend's gallery opening. It was my fault. She hadn't wanted to come anyway. *She doesn't like hunting. How can you kill animals anyway?*

Amid the squabble, I'd unthinkingly pulled my pants back on so that I could pursue Lindsay out of the tent. I hadn't equipped anything, per se.

A few items I'd been carrying the day before were suddenly at my waist again, is all. My mind wasn't on any of that as we entered chapter twenty-six of the same fight we'd been having for two years.

And that's how my KNIFE – attached at the small of my back in a horizontal belt sheath – didn't make my earlier appraisal of advantages. So much for my theory of an expanded consciousness during moments of stress. Might I have killed this beast, had I come on this trip alone? *Too late. What difference does it make? Focus. You have a weapon.*

The creature pawed at my shoulders to keep me from rolling away, placing its bulk above me. *Find something soft.* I passed my knife to my offhand and swung it up in a wide arc. I missed my intended target: its eye.

Instead, my blade found a home in the creature's neck. *That works.* I tried to pull forward or twist. Anything to maximize the damage I inflicted in what might be my one shot.

But the creature roared at the injury and reared back, pulling the knife from my hand as it did so. The brute rose up to its full height – easily twelve feet – and sneered animalistically down at me.

I had angered it.

Now the creature dove at me from its full height and sank its teeth into my chest. Agony drove a scream out of me. This was different than the earlier attacks, too. This time, the monster didn't seek to incapacitate. Perhaps almost as a punishment, it was ready to consume.

I desperately scrambled backward, my neck screwed around and away, to keep my shoulder as far back from the thing as possible. But that meant my eyes were inches from its maw as it snuffed its teeth forward to regain purchase, then tear flesh from my pectoralis. The creature rose to chew quickly, twice, smacking before it swallowed.

I couldn't help noticing it had spared me the mercy of a killing blow. The creature might have just as easily crushed my windpipe or torn out my jugular.

No. I was to be eaten alive.

Then something surprised both the creature and me. A scream rang through the crisp morning air. Lindsay? It was from the direction of the camp, maybe. The creature turned full attention in her direction, smelling the breeze and appraising her as it had done with me before.

I wanted her away, somewhere safe, true. The only consolation prize I might still realize was her escape, one life sacrificed to save two. But part of me also wanted to spare her the grisly aspects of what was about to happen. My city girl – my VEGAN city girl – truly shouldn't have come with me. I'd insisted. *Focus!*

I can't. Everything's fuzzy. Why is everything fuzzy?

She'd suggested every manner of alternative weekend logistics, but I'd won by saying I needed someone to take photos for my Instagram feed. Hadn't she been telling me I needed to take my wilderness supplies business more seriously?

Oh! I'm dizzy because I'm losing blood. Makes sense. Too much blood gone.

My oxygen-deprived brain offered me the twisted logic that if someone with Lindsay's sensibilities had to watch the carnality of me being eaten, she'd never want to be with me.

"Lindsay, RUN!" I shouted, the words slurred. Am I missing teeth?

Where had the knife fallen? Even if I knew, there was no getting it. Again, seemingly anticipating my thoughts, the creature pressed one of those skillet-sized feet onto my chest, pinning me easily in place so it could contemplate Lindsay with its full attention. It made the decision to charge after her.

Oh, no you don't.

I would strike at the creature with what I had left: fists.

Agony shot from both ankles. I used my legs as best I could to lunge at the creature. I grabbed a fistful of neck hair with my left and pulled on it for leverage to deliver a haymaker with my right. This was my last effort, I understood as I executed it. Best make it count.

The strangest smug satisfaction filled me, to hear a whimper of pain escape the creature, bizarrely like the whine of a kicked dog. I'd at least landed a blow, and this monster wasn't used to that. But my trifling scoreboard moment ended as the creature whipped its head back around to me, then snagged my forearm in those jaws. It lifted me off the ground with an effortless jerk of its neck and tossed me aside, as one does a jacket onto a chair at the end of a long day.

I came down against a tree, shoulder-first.

An outraged roar. Galloping footfalls. Back towards me. I'd re-earned its attention.

Ha. I win, Creature.

I struggled through a mental fog, willing my thoughts to organize themselves around any last move that might prolong my existence the few more seconds that might make or break Lindsay's escape. I took inventory.

My heart was pumping overly hard.

Everything hurt, but my nervous system seemed most interested in letting me know about a problem near my left lung. Alas, we were well past the usefulness of pain as a mechanism of preservation. I was vaguely aware of the creature standing over me, proclaiming its dominance with an elk-like, high-pitched roar.

A rock? A stick? Where's the knife?

I wasn't sure I could manage to grasp anything if I tried. Breathing was difficult. The metallic taste of blood filled my mouth. There was no more holding on to consciousness. One final sensory perception, just before the darkness overtook me: a gunshot.

"Seventy-five cents."

Huh?

"Do you want to spin again?"

I woke to the sound of *The Price is Right* on television. It took a few minutes to clear the cobwebs and understand where I was. In a shared hospital room, my compatriot whiled the day away with Drew Carey. The absurdity of existence revealed its face to me. Your daybreak might include mortal combat with an unknown man-beast, but that won't stop CBS's morning game show line-up. Heavy medication was battling to spare me any more suffering – at least for today. Still, several ribs protested when I chuckled.

"You're awake!" Lindsay sprang from the cushioned bench by my bed-side. "Nurse!"

"Linds –" My hand reached to her belly.

"We're fine. They checked me out a couple days ago."

"Park rangers? Did – ?" Words didn't flow right. I entertained a quick, prayerful thought. *Please let that be temporary.*

"– they save your ass? Umm, NO." Lindsay pointed a finger back to herself, her mouth widening into her best faux-insulted expression. "Rifles aren't as hard to work as boys pretend."

"Babe. Are we famous?" I wondered.

"I swear I hit it center in the chest. I saw blood spray out the other side. I couldn't have missed its heart, not by much."

Any thoughts I'd had of the ultimate hunting trophy – of a social media campaign propelling my survival gear business – melted as they formed.

"Took a couple days for them to send a team back. No one saw the point, didn't believe me, until I made the deputy come look at you. But by then the snow had melted, so no tracks, no blood patterns. Dogs followed a trail up the mountain, but it was too steep. We're not famous. We're crackpots."

We sat in silence for a good minute. I held Lindsay's hand.

"I'm so sorry," I murmured.

"I know," she said. "Me too."

"Will you marry me?"

Her face displayed so many emotions in that single moment. She actually laughed first, but then saw I meant it, grew solemn, then gave in to tears of joy. It was almost unnoticeable: her one, tiny, betraying glance down my body. Almost.

I looked down for the first time.

Both my feet were missing.

Oh.

At once I rued my proposal. Lindsay and I were defined by our shared love of hiking. Was hiking gone to us now? Was I condemning her to a life of pushing around my wheelchair? Am I stuck with my desk job? How do you fit a car for hand controls?

"Yes. Of course, yes," Lindsay bubbled.

"No, Linds, I –"

"Shut up. I said yes."

And shut up I did. A woman wounds Bigfoot for you then agrees to marriage ... well, you go with that.

The Fight © 2019 Deron Sedy

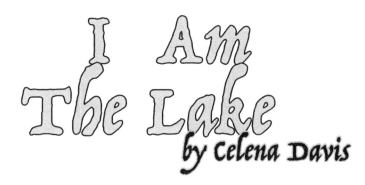

I Am The Lake
by Celena Davis

I am the lake. Those who honored and respected my kind, give me many names. I don't come out during the day because the sun weakens me, but at night I take over. The sun is too bright, but when the sun is in a solar eclipse it's safe. I know that the moon is just a reflection of the sun, but it is not as bright as the sun during the day. I don't know why I can't go out in the sun, I just know that it weakens my power. My being changes the chemistry of the water, and I produce a fast-acting parasitic fog. For centuries, I have been thought to be just a myth, and only a few know the truth about me. The island is my scepter in this never-ending lake. Even I haven't seen the bottom yet. I don't always need to be in the water, though I do for your sanity, if nothing else, though I don't have to.

The lake is my home, since before the natives came around. For centuries I have allowed people to cross over me, but there's always a toll to pay. Your prison has several prisoners who attempted to escape by water. I only let a few live, though not very often. Every life I take away, a foot here and there will wash up on the sandy shore.

And your bunkers make me laugh, trying to protect yourselves from dangers unknown. I go through them, and you try blocking me, so I let you win on some level … for now at least that is. I have no interest in your debris and goodies everywhere.

Recently, there have been more souls taken, all for a reason. I'm tired of all your disrespect: oil from boats or propellers that injure one of my many, many arms. So I'm gathering my strength for the time when the skies are dark for days and the moon is at its fullest. I am taking over. No holding back on my powers. I will unleash it all until I am treated like I once was … a higher being, with powers you can't even imagine. Go ahead, stock up on your food, or create weapons in an attempt to kill me. Your precious metals do nothing to me.

I know your weakness, and your patterns in thinking. I am unstoppable, no matter what you try. Nothing will stop me, no matter what you do. I am immortal to your materials and thrive on your souls. I love the work I do, but recently your kind has been making it hard with your boats and debris floating about. You know something strange has been happening lately, but don't know what it is or why. Well, let me tell you, it was I who make things disappear or die. I am like the grim reaper, but I don't wait till it's your time to go. You die whether you want to or not, old or young.

When I come out of the water my body is over twenty feet tall. Each of my eight arms are ten feet long. I can blend into my surroundings, making it hard for you to see me. I can shapeshift to look like your kind if I ever care to; you will never know who or where I am. I have been born with multiple powers. I have studied your kind since the beginning of time. I watched as you all took the courage to enter into my home, take some of my food source. Yes, I can eat the fish, but it isn't as satisfying as human bodies. You are rich in nutrients and minerals, not to mention your blood.

I love, thirst, long for your blood and organs. I don't care much for your feet, though, but others of my kind love to eat feet; they live in the ocean. Now about your beloved metal and materials, do you honestly think it can keep something like me from entering? I can melt metals and use them to help me become stronger. My organs and bones are made of metal, but my muscles and skin are made of godly materials that you haven't seen and can't comprehend.

If you cut off a limb, it makes another "me" and my limb grows back stronger. Every part of my being can replace itself; I am strong and immortal. My eyes, can see better than your night vision goggles; I see your heat signatures. Not to mention my super strong sense of smell and taste. I can always track your species down without any trouble. Nothing can stop me, not even the weather, or natural disasters. They only add more room for me to occupy. I can control your minds, speak through your kind, or rise from this water I live in and speak for myself. But for now I will wait a little longer, but be warned, once I attack, there's no going back. So prepare while you can, before it's too late, for ...

I

Am

The

Lake

I Am the Lake © 2019 Celena Davis

... the entire library was a product of death.

The Mirror Clock

by Linda Jordan

Let me tell you about the mirror clock in the library of Mirror Point. The mirror itself was crafted at a glass workshop in a small town in France, whose name has since been lost. The town, long abandoned and its inhabitants dead and gone. Forgotten.

That town survived the cruelty of the Inquisition, the horror of the Black Death and the despair of World War II.

Evil lurked in the shadows. Plague seeped from the stones and bitterness swam through the stream which flowed through the town.

The mirror was commissioned by Imogene Thompson. Her father, Burl Thompson, had been a schoolteacher in Mirror Point. Burl received a large fortune when his wealthy brother passed away. He designed a stunningly beautiful library for Mirror Point in the Art Deco style. Bought the land, then promptly died, leaving his daughter the fortune. Imogene made sure his plans were carried out.

So you see, the entire library was a product of death.

The pièce de résistance was the grand staircase of cream-colored marble which rose up through the center towards the back of the building. It ended in a landing, halfway between floors. From each end of the landing gracefully-curved stairs swooped upwards, leading to the top floor.

On the landing and visible from both floors, stood the massive mirror clock. An entire wall made of mirror, created in the old way, by affixing silver to the back of a huge glass plate. It faced the stairs. People's eyes were always drawn to it. On top of the mirror was mounted the numbers and hands of the clock.

What people didn't realize was that the mirror, having been created in that small town in France, bore all the evil of that place: concentrated within the mirror itself.

It wasn't until Gemma Peterson awoke the evil that it caught Mirror Point's attention.

Gemma walked down the empty street towards the library. It felt colder today. The trees were bare and rain threatened. The wind off the lake blasted her face. Why hadn't she worn a coat like Mom told her? She hated fall.

Several strands of long hair swirled across her eyes. She shoved them away. Her backpack grew heavier the longer she walked. School had been horrible today. She hated all of them.

Angry teachers because some asshole hadn't done their work. They took it out on all the students. They were also pissed because she hit Jeremy Thacker. The asshat. He'd been making fun of her for always wearing black.

What was that about anyway? Everyone wore black. Not as often as she did, but Jesus Christ.

The jocks had been assholes. The cool kids, snobby. The weirdos and geeks off on their own, hated by everyone else. Everyone had someone to hang with. Except her. She fit in nowhere.

She couldn't wait to get out of this shitty town. Just a few months, she'd graduate and be gone. Hitchhike to a big city.

She hated the 'Rents. They were the worst. Always ragging on her about everything. Nothing she ever did was right. The undone dishes. Her bad grades. Her clothes all over the floor. The messy room she shared with her little sister, Gwen. Who was one of the cool kids, the bitch.

Gemma clenched her fists as she stomped down the street. She wanted to punch somebody.

Everyone hated her and she hated them all right back. She wished they were all dead. The whole town. Every single one of them. Her worst nightmare would be to spend eternity with this bunch of assholes. She just wanted to be alone.

She was there. The only place she felt right in this shit town. The library.

She went inside the huge glass doors. The building was stupid rich. It made her feel like she was someplace other than Mirror Point.

She ran up the grand staircase, stopped on the wide landing and stared at her reflection in the mirror clock. The mirror looked weird. Old and distorted. It made her look taller than she was.

She wore her uniform. Black hoodie over black t-shirt and black jeans. With black Converse. Her brown hair was the only patch of color. She'd have dyed that black except the 'Rents would pitch a fit. They were so old-school about everything.

Gemma hated the way she looked. Her lips were too big and sexy. Her hair too stringy. And lately, her breasts too big. She didn't want that kind of attention. From anyone.

She touched the cold mirror where there was a dark distortion near her face. The darkness moved when her fingers made contact. As if there was someone stuck. Trapped inside the mirror.

She felt shivers up her spine. Not in a good way.

Gemma walked up to the second floor. She went to the far corner behind the shelves. There was a table no one ever used. It was the only place in this whole wide world she could be alone. Be herself.

The ceiling was lower up here, on this floor. It was darker in this corner, no windows on this side of the big room. It felt safe and enclosed. Best of all, hardly anyone ever came up on this floor.

She could see the stairs from here. And the mirror clock. The darkness in the mirror.

Gemma plonked her pack down on the table and sat on the hard wood chair. It had been a long day.

She'd packed a huge lunch today in order to eat here and skip dinner at home. Gwen, the bitch, was trying out for cheerleading about now. Gemma knew she couldn't face the dinner table tonight.

She texted Mom, *At library working on history paper home at 9.*

That should satisfy them.

Gemma got up and went to the woo woo section. She closed her eyes. *What do I want to read today?*

She touched a book and pulled it out. Opened her eyes and looked at the back first.

It was a worn black book made of real leather. An old, old book. Turning it over, she read the title written in fading gold letters. *Martin Black's Book of Spells, Incantations, Hexes, and Summoning Demons.*

The edges of the pages were done in gold, too. The paper thin and fine. She flipped through it. It had a lot of old illustrations, hand drawn by someone who could draw. The publication date in the front was in Roman numerals. She couldn't figure the date out. The book was old.

Gemma took it back to her table and sat down. She slouched in the chair with her feet up on the table, hidden by the bulk of her pack. Just in case a librarian came by. She'd only seen one up here once.

She looked for a table of contents, but there was none. Then began reading.

Within an hour, Gemma had learned hexes and spells to curse everyone she knew. All she needed was to call up a demon. That required a candle and a few other things, which she didn't have handy. She'd have to bring them tomorrow.

She devoured the book until nine, when the lights flashed. Closing time.

Gemma wasn't going to chance losing the book. She stashed it in her pack, not checking it out. Then headed for home.

The next day after school got out, Gemma went back to the library. She'd found all the supplies last night. Slipped them into her pack. Gwen hadn't even noticed. She'd been too busy prancing around their room.

"I'm a cheerleader!" she'd told Gemma excitedly, jumping up and down.

Jesus wept. Her sister was clueless.

Gemma ran up the first set of stairs, walked across the landing. The darkness in the mirror followed her. She stared at the mirror again. A gray face moved forward, as if trying to break out of the glass. Then retreated. Only to be replaced by another gray face. And another. Almost as if the mirror contained their tortured souls.

She touched the mirror, put her entire palm on it. Felt its coolness. Felt the agony and bitterness of those souls.

Gemma could actually feel their pain when she touched the mirror. It felt just like hers.

Could she summon those souls? Release them from the mirror? Maybe they would take care of her problems in this world. Or perhaps they would just be kindred spirits. Friends.

"I will try to find a way to release you," Gemma said.

One of the faces opened its eyes and looked at her with an agonized gaze.

She would do it. She would find a way.

Gemma ran up the other set of stairs and went to her table in the corner. One of the overhead lights nearby was burnt out. Which made everything darker than normal. Perfect.

On the floor, behind the table, she spread out a large black shawl nicked from Gwen. Last night while her sister was in the bathroom primping, Gemma had painted one of the symbols from the book onto the scarf. With her sister's blood-red nail polish. It even had time to dry before her sister came back from the bathroom.

In the center of the shawl, Gemma squatted and set the black candle she'd bought online a couple of months ago. It sat inside a tall metal container. She took the lid off and put it next to the candle. Trimming the wick, she hoped to keep the smoke down. It wouldn't be good if the library's sprinkler system went off.

At one end of the symbol she put a white skull of some creature on the scarf. Dog? Coyote? She'd found it years ago.

At the other end, a tiny jar of her own blood. She hoped crimson-tide blood would work. It should be more powerful than just regular blood. Being the start of an unborn baby and all.

To one side, she put a smooth piece of black obsidian. She hoped the volcanic glass would tie it to the mirror.

The last thing was a large raven's feather. She set that down on the other side of the symbol.

Then Gemma stood and looked at the book, quickly thumbing through the pages. There. That spell was for releasing beings. Or demons.

She memorized the words as best she could. The writer had said in the first chapter that in Magick, intention was more important than the actual words. The other worlds didn't necessarily speak our language, but they understood intention.

Lighting the candle, Gemma tossed the closed book of matches into her open pack. She stood at one end of the symbol, near her blood.

Then began to whisper the words.

Dark words, unspoken for centuries. Never before said in this town. Words of hatred and anger. She called for the release of those souls trapped in the mirror.

Gemma could see the mirror from where she stood. See all the wounded phantoms trying to get out.

She felt the power swirling around her. Black smoke roiled up, coiling around her body like a huge snake climbing up into the air.

Her skin tingled, shocked by small sparks.

She could smell a shift in the circulated air. A scent like the smoke from guns. Like when her dad once took her to a firing range as a kid. She could even taste the smell.

The surface of the mirror wobbled as if reaching out towards the spell. Pulling the smoke to it. The cloud of black obliged. It crossed the floor and flowed towards the mirror. Weakening the mirror's hold on those souls.

The mirror's surface opened. Melted.

Gemma saw black streams flowing from the mirror. Hundreds of souls.

Many surged up the stairs. Others went down.

She watched as they wildly rushed around the second floor. Free to move again. After being trapped for decades. Their energy felt chaotic and violent to her.

Then Gemma felt them touch her. Her skin crawled with the cold. Tore where they bit at her. She opened her mouth to scream and the dead souls went inside, filling the vacant holes of her own dying soul. Lodging where the hatred lay.

She clawed at her eyes and tore at her own skin.

"But I saved you. Go kill my enemies."

"You are also your enemy," they whispered.

She ran across the second floor, down both sets of stairs. The souls still ripping at her. Her eyes filled with red pain. She raced out the front door and across the street. Through the park, she screamed. She ran to the end of the pier on the lake.

And off it.

Gemma couldn't swim. Had never learned.

The souls ripped and bit at her all the way down. She gulped in the water. Felt it filling her lungs, even as her body longed for life.

All those souls would be bound to her forever. She could never be alone again. No matter what she did.

Gemma didn't flail. She just gave up. Lost herself. Slowly passing the shadows of the pier pilings, long tall shapes in the water. She sank to the bottom of the darkness, not kicking, not flailing. Just letting herself descend.

All she felt was pain.

Then nothing.

The town wasn't so lucky.

We hope you had fun on your tour of our sleepy little towns of Mirror Point and Way's End in

Tasting Evil
The Complete Collection

If you enjoyed Tasting Evil, please take the time to leave a review. Reviews help other readers find good books.

To find more stories from authors you loved here, keep reading this book: you will find links and bios for your favorite authors.

And discover even more great authors from the Writers Cooperative of the Pacific Northwest at our website:
http://writers-coop.com/

Joel Swetin
Arlington, WA

Joel Swetin, originally from Chicago, lived for a number of years on a Kibbutz in Israel and now resides on the banks of the Stillaguamish River. He is a semi-retired safety professional, dividing his time teaching safety classes and being partner-in-crime to his wife/author Susan Old.

E.G. Sergoyan
Pacific Northwest

E.G. Sergoyan writes non-fiction books including: The Gathering Place – a collection from the Armenian Social Club in Old Shanghai; Tales of Ohan – about Christians living in the Ottoman Empire; and ghost thrillers. He lives in the NW enjoying the mountains, underwater scenery, and knotting oriental rugs on a Tabriz loom.

Contact Author through http://writers-coop.com/

Sonya Rhen
Kirkland, WA

Sonya Rhen is the author of the humorous Space Tripping series. She lives on the "Eastside" with her husband, two children, two cats and a very anxious dog. When she's not writing you might find her dancing.

https://sonyarhen.wordpress.com/

Stephen Christiansen
Everett, WA

Stephen Christiansen is the author of the Dark Elf Orbbelgguren Series. He also dabbles in thrillers and sci-fi. He lives in Everett with his wife and daughter. When he's not writing he's working out in the garden.

https://www.facebook.com/stephen.christiansen.9

Kai Bertrand
Seattle, WA

Kai Bertrand loves the paranormal and her writing reflects it. She creates stories with quirky characters that display her sassy sense of humor. Kai lives with her family which includes two spoiled cats. Plotting the next great caper with friends is what she does when she's not writing.

www.kaibertrand.com

https://www.amazon.com/-/e/B07GZGXQRT

Deron Sedy

Lake Stevens, WA

Deron Sedy spends about 40% of his time working as a user experience designer, 15% following politics, 20% gardening, 65% being a dad, 4% fishing, and the remaining 82% writing.

https://writerDeron.com

Chloe Holiday

Pacific Northwest

Chloe writes contemporary romance with a fun, beach-read vibe. She lives in a small town east of Seattle with her husband and too many chickens.

http://www.chloeholiday.com/
Email: Chloeholiday@outlook.com

Celena Davis

Lake Stevens and Marysville, WA

Celena Davis is a very artistic 21 year old writer. Oldest of 4 children, has always been interested in the arts, she's been writing since she was in 5th grade, and she loves spending time with family. She is level 1 autistic but she's not letting that stop her at writing.

You can contact Celena through the Writers Cooperative of
the Pacific Northwest http://writers-coop.com/
celenadavis97@gmail.com

Toni Kief

Marysville, WA

Toni Kief, a Midwesterner from a family of high spirits. As an adult she moved to her maternal hometown, Marysville, Washington. Toni started writing at the age of sixty and defines her genre as OA – older adult/boomer fiction. The plan is to stay for the view, family, and friends.

www.tonikief.com

Toni is one of the founding directors of the Writers Cooperative of
the Pacific Northwest.

The Writers Co-op www.writers-coop.com

Yazz Ustaris

Lynnwood, WA

Yazz Ustaris grew up in Mountlake Terrace and currently lives in Lynnwood. Yazz has always possessed a passion for writing. She has published the first two books in her YA fiction series, The Suicide Project, and is currently at work on book three.

https://www.facebook.com/yazzustaris/
Thesuicideprojectseries@gmail.com

Susan Old

Arlington, WA

Susan Old is the author of Rare Blood, a caffeinated vampire romp. She is a Peace Corps alumnus, and retired addiction therapist. When not writing about nocturnal maniacs, she volunteers at an animal shelter and two museums. She lives on a river near Granite Falls with her hubby/editor and freeloading cats and dogs.

susanold.com
zairesue@gmail.com

Hugh Mannfield

Pacific Northwest

Hugh Mannfield helped design rocket boosters, jet aircraft, and the space station. He brings science experience to science fiction in the Stormbold Adventures and the Our Place in Space series, and cutting edge physics in Einstein and Aliens. He enjoys time outdoors on his mini ranch with his wife, daughters, and horse.

Contact at: hugh.mannfield@frontier.com or fluidspacetheory.com

Christine Gustavson-Udd

Bothell, WA

Christine is an artist/author, she has degrees in art and elementary education. When she isn't writing, she enjoys crocheting (while snuggled up with her calico cat) and walks with her husband and their Cockerchon. Her picture books and short stories are available on Amazon.

Find links at www.booknut.biz.

She can be contacted at booknut012@gmail.com

Matthew Buza

Monroe, WA

Matthew Buza is a part-time author and a stay-at-home dad. He's not afraid to list off his favorite 90 podcasts he's currently subscribed to, talk forever about storytelling, and argue about college football.

www.matthewbuza.com

Robin Ridenour

Pacific Northwest

After ten eventful years in the military, Robin doesn't follow orders but instead lives in the woods east of Seattle writing thrillers, aided by a support team of one human and three dogs.

Twitter: @ridenour_robin

Email: robinridenourwriter@gmail.com

Kristi Radford

Sultan, WA

Kristi Radford lives in the beautiful Pacific Northwest with her family and 9 chickens. When she is not taking care of the 'family' she can be found scribbling story ideas and taking pictures.

https://kristiradfordbooks.wixsite.com/kristiradfordbooks

Roland Trenary

Kingston, WA

Roland Trenary self-published illustrated magazines back in the 1970s (inspired by the works of Edgar Rice Burroughs and Mahlon Blaine); then came musical performance, Lindy Hop, and ballroom dance teaching; then music, fiction and non-fiction writing, and graphic design. Washington, Minnesota, and Arizona currently split his time.

Contact: roland@groundedoutlet.com

knottykitty@trenary.com

Susan Brown

Lake Stevens, WA

Susan Brown's books ripple with strong characters and fast action – whether in fantasy, teen adventure, or romances (written with Anne Stephenson as Stephanie Browning). Dragons, bullies, and falling in love, plus all the ins and outs of contemporary life, can be found in Susan Brown's novels!

www.Susanbrownwrites.com

https://www.facebook.com/StephanieBrowningRomance/

Susan is one of the founding directors of the Writers Cooperative of the Pacific Northwest.

The Writers Co-op www.writers-coop.com

Linda Jordan

Tulalip, WA

Linda Jordan writes complex magical stories with fascinating characters and unique worlds. Her most recent book is Rescue Mission, The Islands of Seattle, Book 1. She lives in the rainy wilds with her family, too many cats, a cluster of koi and a seemingly infinite number of slugs and snails.

She can be found online at: www.lindajordan.net

Made in the USA
Monee, IL
12 May 2021

67223734R00163